ECHOES FROM THE HOCKER HOUSE

ECHOES FROM THE HOCKER HOUSE

STORIES BY VIRGINIA WATTS

DEVIL'S PARTY PRESS | LOS ANGELES

ACKNOWLEDGMENTS

"Aerial View" originally appeared in *Streetlight Magazine*.
"Starscraper" originally appeared in *The Chaffin Journal*.
"Homecoming" originally appeared in *The Bookends Review*.
"August" originally appeared in *SPLASH!*.
"Queenie" originally appeared in *Two Thirds North*.
"Elias Wolf" originally appeared in *Broadkill Review*.

ECHOES FROM THE HOCKER HOUSE

ISBN: 978-1-957224-17-6

For my father, Ralph F. Watts,
whose belief in me was unfailing

CONTENTS

ECHOES FROM THE HOCKER HOUSE

Aerial View

Hannah Fisher closes the curtains in every room of the farmhouse night and day over windowsills she used to stuff with juice glasses that brimmed with seasonal wildflowers: delicate, snow-white Queen Anne's Lace, purple chicory, periwinkle cornflowers. Gone are the times she performed miracles with the monthly household budget and squeezed out extra cash to prepare elaborate, formal dinners on the weekends, recipes she downloaded from her laptop. If there was any spare change after that, she would drive fifty minutes to the Wal-Mart in Scutters Mill and return with cases of French vanilla and lavender-scented candles bungeed into their pickup truck's rusty, dusty bed.

Rex had played along with the dream that Hannah could imbue their rundown, nearly one-hundred-year-old homestead with some romantic ambiance. It was no secret neither of them was getting any younger. For Rex's thirty-fifth birthday over a year ago now, Hannah prepared one of his favorite meals. She thought she had done everything right, but the entree turned out tougher than shoe leather. Rex had been so sweet about it, responding with a quote from his favorite Quentin Tarantino movie: "Goddamn, that's a pretty fucking good chicken cordon bleu!"

Hannah misses when sexual banter kept company with the creaky, wooden floorboards under their bed. The silly phrases they used to say to each other: *Rex, I shaved my legs this morning. You'll never believe this, Hannah, but my jock itch cleared up overnight.* Back then, when Hannah finished stacking the evening dishes inside the drying rack and headed toward the bedroom, Rex would follow right behind her.

It has become impossible for her to remember the last time any bit of her skin was near any bit of Rex, the last time they celebrated

1

something or laughed together. Rex and Hannah used to make each other hoot and holler all the time. Humor eased the rigor of the daily chores of running a beef cattle farm. These days Hannah forgets what Rex's mouth looks like as a smile. She wonders if she will ever laugh like she used to, like *they* used to. *It's kind of true,* she thinks, *that your belly jumps up and down and giggles right along with you when you are genuinely joyful and cracked up about something.*

Hannah's stomach exists in a constant state of sour swish now. Whenever she lets something slip down her esophagus, the contents sizzle deep inside her like the Pop Rocks candy she used to love as a kid: little cherry crystals that crackled and popped, magical fireworks exploding on her tongue. They still sell the stuff at Wal-Mart. As soon as things start looking up, she'll treat herself to a packet.

This day Rex stomps into the kitchen like he's already got his heavy-treaded barn boots strapped on. He halts in front of the kitchen sink. Hannah bites her bottom lip. The curtains above the two stainless steel basins are closed tight as a puppet theatre curtain before a performance begins.

"Jesus," he spews.

He grabs and rips fabric from the window frame. The spring-mounted, metal curtain rod boomerangs over the top of Hannah's head. She doesn't flinch.

"Rex. For Christ's sake. Your grandmother embroidered those curtains by hand. That's her blood, sweat, and tears you just tore up to smithereens. You beheaded a little Amish boy and his pet lamb. I hope you're happy."

Rex twirls around, faces Hannah with a sneer followed by a blank look, as if he's never seen his wife before, a wife before, or anyone sitting at this Formica table inside the kitchen where he was born and raised. "Stop closing all the curtains in this house, Hannah. I got to be able to see out to the pastures. You know that. In fact, I am gonna rip down all the window hangings all over this house and burn 'em in the backyard right this minute. Solve this little problem once and for all. Fuck it!"

Hannah rests her forehead down on the cool table. The table smells like toast, raisin toast. It smells of happy kids, a pure, fresh-air life on a prosperous Hereford cattle farm.

Things begin to ping and crash in the living room. Rex will move to the master bedroom next, *two windows in there,* then on to the bathroom, *one window there.* So much for privacy, but no one visits the farm anymore, and the main road is a mile away. Rex's brother used to come for Sunday dinner every weekend, but Cash moved to Nashville.

Hannah lifts her head. It's no use crying. Maybe it's for the best. She's been closing the curtains for her own sanity. The whole situation on the farm commandeers her brain during the daytime and her subconscious at night. She used to be able to rest peacefully under sheets dried in sweet country air topped with a heavy quilt, but not anymore. It's gotten to the point where she can't eat or sleep, at least not like any Hannah she recognizes.

It is part Walt Disney and part Alfred Hitchcock who invade Hannah's dream state, images from their creative efforts on the silver screen all mixed up inside her head. When Lawrence the rooster sounds off before sunup because every farm has to have an annoying-ass rooster, Hannah pops her eyes open and tastes blood; the insides of her cheeks chewed into raw, hanging flaps she flicks up and down with her tongue: ticking off her daily chore list.

Hannah swivels her neck toward the open sky outside the kitchen window. She can't stop herself from looking out there, so how can she expect Rex to be doing any better? This morning's sky is not peppered with anything. It is empty. No entity, no hand of fate or toe of Satan stirring circular shapes around and around up there. No sickening, aerial whirlpool. Hannah gasps, accepts some air into her lungs. The sudden rush of oxygen expands her chest and leaves her dizzy.

She will feast upon a blessedly empty sky. A rare moment to savor. Why is the sky blue and not some other color? Maybe she was absent that day of middle school when the other kids got taught that one. But, really, there wouldn't be a better color choice. Nobody gets sick of blue. Imagine if the sky was always orange. Blue works best as a background for Earth's life. There are a few clouds, but clouds are okay. Clouds are supposed to be up in the sky.

Hannah glances down at cold, black coffee inside the chipped Scooby-Doo mug her father-in-law always used. Carly Simon said there were clouds in her coffee. Clouds don't belong in coffee. Things shouldn't appear where they don't belong. Carly Simon must have been having a rough time when she discovered clouds floating across the surface of her morning brew, fed up with life, and Warren Beatty's ego, and who knows what else.

Hannah pinches her eyes tight, wishes fervently for nothing else but shades of blue—azure, aquamarine, turquoise, a baby's blue, any kind of blue—and only clouds to appear in the atmosphere over the top of the farm. *Please, nothing but blue sky and clouds over these nine acres. Is that too much to ask? Maybe one or two stray hot air balloons per year when the Mifflin County Fair is running would be acceptable, but that's it, not anything else, ever.*

Rex marches back into the kitchen with a stack of torn-up curtains and the living room drapes in his arms, wheezing and grunting. His frame in the periphery is massive, a boulder of a man who ducks doorframes to enter and exit rooms in most structures except barns and the Grange Hall.

Hannah is not going to give Rex the satisfaction of the front of her face today. She turns her attention toward last year's calendar, pinned underneath plastic alphabet-letter refrigerator magnets. The magnets are a holdover from Rex's youth. Only the "Z" is missing. Steady-handed, she raises Scooby to her lips and sucks in some liquid. Rex heads to the backyard with a bang. *That should just about do it for the screen door. How long can anything hang on by hinges?*

She should warn Rex that burning fabric, especially those polyester living room drapes with thermal linings, will produce copious billows of noxious smoke. She should close the house windows too, but *The hell with it. It's the middle of August in the middle of Tennessee, and it's hot.* On the upside, maybe someone will think the barn, silo, house—the whole kit and caboodle—are burning down and come to their rescue. Then she could invite them to stay for tonight's featured dinner: canned pea soup and crackers. Hannah gags.

As the kitchen slowly fills with acrid smoke, Hannah considers the details of last night's dream. All her dreams are similar. They begin with the vultures from Disney's movie *The Jungle Book*: Buzzie, Flaps, Ziggy, and Dizzy, those adorable guys with their shaggy haircuts and Liverpudlian accents. Hannah suspects she giggles in her sleep as the dream gets underway and the feathered quartet exchange their famous banter: *Whatcha wanna do? I dunno. Okay, but whatcha wanna do?*

This is when Hitchcock enters belly first, and just like that, the mock Beatles birds have bloodred eyes, growl like wolves, sprout dripping talons, and hideous dagger beaks. Hannah shivers just thinking of them. In the dreams, she searches for and locates herself far below, standing in the middle of a cornfield row. She is shading her eyes, looking skyward toward the row of birds, her body no bigger than a black ant on a picnic table. When the birds screech and launch, spears sailing earthward, Hannah starts sprinting.

Hannah wakes up running in bed, sweating, her face wet with tears. Outside in the backyard, she spies the orange tip of Rex's cigarette. He stays like that, wide-awake, erect in a lawn chair all night, watching heaven, as if anyone can get their hands around heaven.

Last summer, it was Hannah who found the first calf, freshly born and freshly dead, in the south meadow. A baby girl, stone-still under the weeping willow tree all the heifers favor for birthing. They've been choosing that spot since Rex's grandparents were running the farm. It is easy to see why. The ground stays shady and cool. A nearby creek trickles. Soft, dense moss grows plentiful. The clover is plump. Hannah imagines the clover there must taste sweeter too.

As Hannah approached the south meadow early that morning, her heart filled with ice water. She knew something was terribly wrong. The mother cow was clearly agitated, pacing around her newborn, mooing mournfully, tossing her head. Hannah hit the brake on the tractor and leaped off, jarring her spine, not feeling any pain until later when the adrenalin wore off.

She took one look at the scene and lost her breakfast. Never saw anything like it. Calf's eyes pecked clean way. Only things left were two crimson pockets oozing pink, frothy puss. Something had plucked out the babe's tongue, leaving a hollow mouth hanging open. The hide meant to cover the backside was torn away. All the rump flesh eaten. Deep holes spreading across the calf's soft underbelly leaked crimson onto the green moss. The poor thing had surely suffered.

Hannah screamed for Rex, but he was too far away. When she was able to stand up, she stumbled to the tractor and went to find him.

Since then, the black vultures have killed six more newborn calves on the Fisher Hereford Farm, one not even all the way out of the birth canal. The birds devour the calves while they are still alive, gouge the eyes before moving on to other soft parts. Their kind of killing begins with a blinding. That's how you know it was them.

Rex began corralling as many pregnant heifers inside the barn as possible, but the barn is a small one. All of them don't fit at once. Beef cattle are large animals. If only they could afford to build a bigger barn, but they can't. It wouldn't save all of them anyway. Even on nearby farms with bigger barns, there are plenty of dead calves. You never know exactly when birth is coming, and cattle must eat and get fresh air sometimes.

Hannah has googled and read more than a person would ever want to know about the habits of black vultures. They are a unique species, not at all like the common turkey vultures that have always been around these parts. Turkey vultures consume the dead, not the living. When she learned that hanging up dead, black vultures might help keep the live ones away, Rex strapped body after body to fence posts, bright orange wire reflecting sunlight all over the farm, but the effigies only worked for a week or so. After that, the birds stopped caring about their dead comrades and returned with a vengeance.

No one really knows why black vultures arrived in Mifflin County or exactly where they came from. There are plenty of theories rolling over these pastures, spilling through the soft divides between private farmland, but answers to those questions won't change anything. No one knows what to do about them now that they are here. Not the veterinarians, the local government, the Department of Agriculture of the State of Tennessee, or God himself.

Coughing, choking, Hannah stumbles outside. Rex has left a smoldering mess in the backyard firepit. Thick gray smog fills the sky over the house chimney, barn roof, silver-topped silo. A strong locomotive of a wind has been chugging all morning, transporting the smoke cargo in the direction of the main road. If this force of nature keeps up, people stepping outside of the buildings along Main Street of Scutters Mill are bound to smell something incendiary in the air.

Rex's figure, straight-backed in the driver's seat of their biggest tractor, splits a sunny, green-coated horizon in half. He is barreling toward the south meadow. The sky out that way is in motion again, little black specks circling, circling—skydivers of death, killer raptors, merciless beasts—multiplying, burgeoning, growing stronger and more resolute with every passing day.

Hannah brings her hand to the base of her throat, grips it. She is powerless. She always is when she spots the vultures. Her mouth flies open. Even though there is no sense in crying, even though it won't change a thing, she wails.

Rex's howl comes back to Hannah's ears now, a noise from a body of Rex, but this isn't Rex's voice. Rex named this howl his "war cry," but the tone sounds more like the time Hannah's cousin Jem accidentally shot himself in his own foot. Hannah had been the only person with Jem that day. They were both nine years old, and they weren't supposed to be messing around with the hunting rifles, but they were. Neither of them knew how to handle a gun so what began with a blast ended with the two of them wailing.

Soon Rex's gunshots will echo across these fields where peaceful intentions are only a memory. Some migratory bird act limits how many black vultures a human being can blast out of the sky on any given day, but Rex has long forgotten about limits. Rex can shoot all day and all night if he wants to. Hannah could join him. Together, they could bring down twice as many, bury themselves in stiff, feathery shapes. It won't matter. That's like thinking you could bottle up the ocean temporarily and clean the sandy bottom. The birds are going to keep on coming and coming.

It's all killing around here now. There's nothing left.

Sometimes, in Hannah's dreams, she stops running and turns

around in that cornfield, opens her arms and her eyes as wide as she can, and surrenders. It feels good when the birds plunge their beaks into her eye sockets, and hot liquid, thicker than tears, streams down her cheeks.

Hannah grabs the newest firewood first, the pile most recently chopped and stacked for the woodstove, and throws it on top of the curtains to create an even more impressive, milky sky full of destruction. Green wood makes the densest smoke. Flames curl and leap. The roar muffles Rex's gunshots. She touches her fingertips to her forehead. Hot as ember. When a spark lands in her hair, searing her scalp, she crinkles her nose, grins, and reluctantly brushes it away.

Swirling red and blue lights pop up in the distance out by the windmill. Sheriff Trotter's olive-green sedan crests the top of the hill. *Of course the sheriff would drive out to make sure everything was okay.* She should have thought of this distress signal herself and sooner than today, but her heart's been stubborn, fighting the idea of stranding Rex, leaving him out here all alone. She kept stalling, giving everything more time, hoping for a change of luck, that packet of cherry Pop Rocks, the chance of life feeling sweet and tangy again.

Hannah ducks into the house, snatches her handbag and laptop from the coffee table. Her brain is racing through her list: Jem won't mind if she sleeps on the couch in his apartment. He could use some help with the rent. They're always looking for helpers at the nursing home in Scutters Mill, or maybe she can land a waitressing job at the new 24-hour truck stop. She'll call Cash and beg him to take a trip back to see his brother as soon as he can.

Clutching the only two things she wants to bring forward from this life, Hannah bursts through the front door and begins running barefoot on bare earth she can no longer call home.

The Bitterest Winter

Laurel is convinced they are the most asinine use of steel and beam she has ever seen. The city is literally teeming with them, thousands of itty-bitty landings suited for the hallux toes of passerines and nothing else. For a bird, sick of flapping wings grown heavy as leaden panels in a blizzard, they must represent countless sanctuaries in an urban sea. Balconies might be good for honeybees and other creatures that pollinate, but the flowerpots apartment dwellers jam into the corners of these cramped spaces are reminiscent of the garish blooms surrounding an open casket inside a funeral home. One thing is for sure: balconies aren't good for people.

Laurel had never thought about urban architecture before her husband Trent decided they were moving to Chicago when Laurel was six months pregnant. Now, vertical shapes engulf her. "Skyscrapers." Such an obvious name. "High-rises." *Well, no shit.* Man wouldn't need to erect anything that blocks the God-given sky, sun, and horizon if he didn't insist on trying to cram so many people into one parcel of the earth. The airborne, tacked-on bird rest stops only make matters worse. They look like zippers running penthouse to ground level, mimicking the people on the sidewalks below, arms glued down so bodies can't bump against others. *Atrocities up in the clouds and clothespin people below,* that's what Laurel thinks of Chicago.

"The firm found us a magnificent apartment with panoramic views of Lake Michigan from the living room and bedroom," Trent had announced cheerfully while they were packing boxes to leave their little hometown of Denton Falls in rural Pennsylvania and make the move to the infamous Windy City.

Laurel didn't respond. Leaving Denton Falls had never been the plan. The plan was that after Trent graduated from law school, they would build a life in Pennsylvania close to Denton Falls, if not right smack in the middle of it. Laurel would paint portraits of Main Street and the original stone buildings, the library, the bank and trust. Her watercolors would capture the beauty of the surrounding countryside: red brick barns, horses in pastures, gold-headed cornfields, streams with fishermen casting their lines. She would echo the Andrew Wyeth prints she began collecting in middle school, and she would paint the people she knew, the descendants of the original families.

Brenda, Laurel's older sister and best friend, lives in Denton Falls with her husband, Dean. Brenda and Dean purchased one of the red brick Victorians on Water Street that Laurel and Trent had always talked about buying: a home surrounded by gardens bursting with color, apricot-orange daylilies, white and dark purple lilac bushes, and two McCoy flowerpots of featherhead ferns flanking the original, stained-glass front door.

Brenda and Dean have a one-year-old son. Sam won't care about Uncle Trent and Aunt Laurel, who live in some faraway place called Chicago. A couple of days at Christmas doesn't stick with a child. The checkout lady at Weis Supermarket will be more familiar.

The problem is, Trent Hill is not one to give up. That day, as he was duck-taping U-Haul packing boxes with lightning speed and right-angled accuracy, he didn't skip one overly confident beat: "And that's not all. The best part is that we have a balcony. Isn't that fantastic?"

"Why is that fantastic?" Laurel felt her cheeks flare hot as a gas stove flame. "What *exactly* are we supposed to do out there on our balcony? You can't walk around on those things. Remember that one at the Westin in Boston when we went to your cousin's wedding? What are we going to do out there? Pirouette around in twin circles?"

Trent frowned deeply then, finally annoyed with the task of trying to convince his wife that starting a new kind of life living in a famous, historic Midwest City was going to be an unforgettable, expanding experience for them both.

Laurel felt pleased momentarily.

It wasn't that Laurel hadn't been happy about Trent's success during law school. Everything was fine until his favorite professors began brainwashing him. Once Trent bought into the idea that the best and brightest lawyers only practice law in the big cities like New York or Los Angeles or Chicago, there was no going back to the couple's original plans for their life together.

During the months leading up to their relocation, Trent had

lectured Laurel nonstop like any young, budding, white-collar criminal prosecutor fresh out of law school chomping at the bit to prove himself. They'd both spent too much time already in the same region, county, and state. The same little town, socializing with the same people in the same houses, patronizing the same local businesses. Eating the same food. Smelling manure on damp days. Driving through dusty cornfields to neighboring towns that looked exactly like Denton Falls. The open sky had become a suffocating monotony for him. It was time to "…break out of the country music, banjo-driven soundtrack and see the rest of what the world has to offer," is how he put it.

"You never read any of the books about Chicago I bought for you. Once you have the baby and he gets old enough, Chicago is packed full of parks and art galleries. There's a world-famous children's museum at the Navy Pier with a Ferris wheel. You love Ferris wheels! All you'll have to do is put on your shoes. Everything is right outside your doorstep. What do you think of that?"

What she thought was that she didn't want to argue with Trent too much. An unborn baby shouldn't hear discordant sounds. That might be damaging, and it didn't matter, anyhow, what she thought. Trent was determined to go. She'd miss out on finishing her final months of college, but then again, *She does have her whole life to finish a worthless bachelor's degree in fine arts.* Trent didn't say that, but she knew that's what he thought.

—

January, and the baby is nearly eight months old. Chicago is blanketed by four feet of weighty snowfall. Lake Michigan is granite gray, abandoned by boat life. It stands in the distance like a fallen mirror.

Laurel refuses to leave the apartment with her infant daughter until people stop toppling over with cases of influenza. She keeps the local television news running on silent to track the latest statistics citywide: a conveyor belt of red letters at the bottom of the screen. Many of the poor victims stand below her apartment windows, wrapped up, bus stop mummies, shoulders jumping up and down steady as the pistons under a truck hood, hacking, spreading disease, scarves of all colors sailing behind them at the same odd, sharp angle. The winds that whip in from the massive lake are wicked.

Cami was born in early June in Chicago, making her a native. What followed was one of the hottest summers on record. Laurel had kept her newborn safe inside the apartment then too. By early October, when the weather was finally pleasant enough to start taking the baby outside, Laurel had no interest in exploring Chicago. No one could deny that crime statistics often lead off evening news reports. Mother and daughter don't venture anywhere except the pediatrician's office and Whole Foods every Wednesday morning.

"It's just you and me, sweet pea," Laurel whispers to Cami several times a day.

Cami is a happy baby, full of smiles, her eyes a family heirloom shared by her mother, grandmother, great-grandmother, and Aunt Brenda: pale gray eyes, the shade of sky that brings a soft spring rain. Laurel hopes Cami gets Brenda's hair instead of her thin, wispy brown hair. Brenda's hair is wavy and thick, ebony as coal, one reason her sister made such a convincing witch at Halloween.

Today Laurel has some treats to look forward to for lunch. Yesterday morning, she begged Trent to stay home from work long enough for her to hurry through Whole Foods without the baby. The store, a mecca of manufactured wholesomeness, is a joke, but it's close to the apartment. The people shopping there have no idea what farm-to-table is. Laurel knows what beans and tomatoes and apples and strawberries taste like when they are homegrown and freshly picked. Laurel notices the young mothers like herself in Whole Foods. Hears them introducing themselves and their babies, bending toward opposite strollers, acting like they find a stranger's baby as adorable as their own, hatching up plans to meet for beet and pistachio salads, freshly roasted coffee, some mommy bonding time. *Fuck that.* Laurel isn't getting sucked into a phony life. Anyway, Trent will get this city thing out of his system eventually, and the two of them will be back home in Denton Falls before she knows it.

The Trent she fell in love with is still in there somewhere, whether he's in Chicago or on the moon. Soon he will start to miss their walks around Fuller Lake as much as she does, watching dark fish leaping from the surface. He will think about how they used to build a campfire every weekend. How he would reach for Laurel's hand. He will want to hear church bells tolling, faintly echoed by Mount Davis. He will be sorry he missed the first snowfall in Denton Falls, how quiet the world is there, how pretty the elm trees are along Main Street dusted white, how everyone comes outside with sleds and toboggans.

Cami is down for her first nap of the day. Trent will call at 11:45. Laurel will prepare her own lunch at 12:00. Cami will sleep until 1:00. It is now 11:30.

Laurel tiptoes into the bathroom and locks the door. Trent never returns during the day. He works a dependable twelve-hour day, six days of the week, but she locks the door anyway. When she locks that door, she could be anywhere. All bathrooms have the same essentials: a toilet, sink, shower, towel bar, vanity mirror. Laurel lights the candle she leaves on top of the toilet and turns to face her reflection inside a stark rectangle.

She is thin for the first time in her life, and she approves of what the body change is accomplishing with her face. Her cheekbones finally have definition. She has been coping with chubby cheeks all her life: *A solid, muscular squirrel, mouth stuffed with nuts,* that's how she thought of herself. The lack of direct sunlight has done wonders for her freckles too. They are disappearing. Maybe one of these days she won't look anything like the softball pitching, wisecracking, Bazooka-bubble-popping tomboy she once was.

Laurel performs for the bathroom mirror. Facial expressions. The features of the human visage have infinite stories to tell. She can whimper, sob, and weep on demand now. The trick is it takes a lot of practice. She's put in the time. When she's not locked in the bathroom, she mimics the one photograph of herself she likes, her gaze dream-filled, carefree, from the photograph of her and Trent on the day she started college and he began law school. She's got that expression down pat too.

A Mediterranean wrap with tzatziki cucumber sauce awaits her in the refrigerator, so Laurel tries smiling and giggling in anticipation. Brenda has an intense gag reflex when it comes to cucumbers. When they were growing up, Laurel would sneak cucumbers into the family dinner salad whenever she could just to see her sister's reaction. It wasn't nice of her, *but damn, was it funny.* You'd think Brenda had been served a heaping helping of rotted corpse. Laurel's giggle sounds genuine, but the smile isn't as convincing as it should be. She'll have to work on that.

She really should call Brenda today or tomorrow, or at least by next Friday. She hasn't been returning her sister's voice messages. It's so hard to hear Sam in the background, and she really doesn't want Brenda to go on and on about what happened during dinner at Mom's on Sunday, how the pork roast was tough as usual, how Dad still watches *Jeopardy* every night, gets every answer wrong except if the answer is, "Who was Mickey Mantle."

Laurel jams her nose upward with her pointer finger, transforms herself into the squinty-eyed piggy she used to be when she would hang over the side of the top bunk, poke her head into her sister's so-called personal space, and grunt. Laurel's pig imitation is impressive even here, all alone, with no audience. Some real laughter banks off the shower tiles and returns itself to Laurel, a sound that loosens her chest just a smidgen before her cell phone rings from the top of the kitchen counter.

"Shit!" Laurel hurries to the phone. Cami's sleep cannot end this early.

"Hi honey, how's your day?" Trent's customary greeting.

Laurel's stomach growls. She hesitates. Maybe she should blurt something about the little discovery she made this morning, the folder from a local realtor with the listings of brownstones for sale in Hyde Park she found buried under a stack of paper on Trent's desk, his handwritten comments in the margins, what he liked and didn't like, but inexplicably, Laurel feels like laughing instead so she swallows hard.

"Great!" Laurel says. "I am just about to leave and have lunch at that corner place with the gyros. You know the one we noticed on 55th Street near the organic dry cleaners?"

Laurel can hear Trent tapping his laptop keys rapid fire. He covers the phone and says something to someone, likely his personal assistant, Clare. Clare is Japanese. Glossy hair, flawless skin, no hips, concave stomach. Perfectly fitted pencil skirts. White silk blouses. Impeccable business attire enhanced by elegant black pearl drop earrings and just a whiff of expensive perfume. Laurel didn't know pearls could be black before she met Clare.

Laurel glances down at her yoga pants and one of Trent's discarded oxford button-downs.

"That's nice," Trent asks after a long pause filled with more muffled words to the beauty, Clare. "Alone?"

"No, with the mother and baby group," Laurel sings out sweetly. "I hope you won't be late tonight. I bought ingredients to make spaghetti sauce from scratch."

"Sorry, I would love that, my favorite, but I'm just about to deliver the closing arguments in this mammoth racketeering case. *The Tribune* might interview me later today. I'm waiting to hear. How cool is that? Don't expect me for dinner. I'm sorry. I'll make it up to you this weekend. I gotta fly, babe."

"That's…" Laurel begins, but the line drops dead.

Laurel steps back, sighs, surveys the living room. The apartment is not terrible as far as rentals go, a galley kitchen with new stainless steel appliances. There's nothing wrong with the simple lines of the Ikea furnishings in the living room. Some of Laurel's watercolors from college look decent on the walls, especially her parents' house, the roof a mosaic of bright autumn leaves shed from trees someone planted ridiculously close to the front porch over a hundred years ago. Trent isn't wrong. She doesn't need a completed degree to pick up brushes and palettes again. Back home, she painted nearly every day.

The balcony stares back at Laurel. Trent decorated it with two teak chairs and a table from Target as a surprise for Laurel when she returned home from the hospital with Cami. It was a lazy effort. He bought a half-priced Memorial Day display, but as Laurel's mom always says, "It's the thought that counts." On the other hand, when Brenda gave birth to Sam, Dean surprised her with a cameo ring she had admired while passing the window of Staub's Jewelry Store on Water Street.

These days, Trent seems to have forgotten the apartment has a balcony. If he isn't sleeping, he is in the second bedroom with his head buried in his laptop. Trent uses the second bedroom as a home office. Shares the space with diplomas and a polished, cherry wood desk.

The flowerpots of red and white impatiens Trent tucked into a corner of the balcony just shy of the rainwater line died a slow and thirsty death out there. Even so, the little American flag held on for dear life, snapping bravely through autumn's blustery days. It is hibernating now, insulated by a tiny camel hump of snow.

In the birthing suite of the University of Chicago Hospital, Laurel missed having Cami inside her belly as soon as she felt her slide out. She accepted the swaddled newborn from the midwife, tried to glow and grin, but she wanted to put the baby right back inside of her, where everything was taken care of, safe and under control.

Not long after Cami came home, Laurel began gathering feathers that escaped from bed pillows. Then, various types of paper, sleeves from takeout drink straws, worthless predictions from fortune cookies, paper airplanes she made and decorated with calligraphy messages in case anyone found them, mostly the first lines of literature she loves. Like first impressions of people and places, there must be something special about the first line of anything if you're going to stay with it and ride it out to the bitter end. From *Jane Eyre* by Charlotte Bronte: "There was no possibility of taking a walk that day." Dodie Smith's start for *I Capture the Castle*: "I write this sitting in my kitchen sink." The unforgettable beginning of Eudora Welty's short story *First Love*: "Whatever happened, it happened in extraordinary times, in a season of dreams, and in Natchez it was the bitterest winter of all."

Laurel would step out onto the balcony, walk to the edge, lean way over on her stomach until only the tips of her big toes had contact with solid ground, and toss. Gray feathers and strips of white flipped over and over, descended in artless patterns toward an oblivious world far below Laurel's bare feet.

Pocket change had been the next to go over the side of the balcony and into the gaping mouth of the city. Some pennies but mostly dimes because dimes are light and thin. If a falling dime should happen to find a head top, surely it wouldn't cause any actual pain or harm. Throughout October and November, Laurel flipped coins like they do at the beginning of football games to determine who kicks off and who receives. On nice days, sunshine caught the silver on fire for a brilliant bullet of a second before Laurel lost sight of the coin. Unfortunately, at sixteen floors above ground level, she can't hear when things ping sidewalk cement.

Tired of hurling money, Laura moved on to her paintbrushes. She had always felt guilty about owning such an extensive collection of Kolinsky sable brushes, the finest watercolor brushes in the world. She wasn't talented enough for the premier brushes, a gift from her parents, *...and just think of the poor, Siberian weasels when someone hacked off their tails to manufacture ridiculously thick, luxuriant brushes. Artists are silly. They have ridiculously high opinions of themselves, thinking they can recreate the beauty of the natural world on a flat canvas.* Laurel is done fooling herself.

Out went all the brushes, but just the tops of the rounds, flats, spotter, riggers, ovals, and mops. Laurel severed the brush hairs from their wooden handles on her kitchen cutting board. As always, she would lean over the balcony edge as far as she could go, up high on the tips of her two big toes. The brush tops didn't stay suspended and float away like the downy dandelion heads Brenda and Laurel blew into the breeze when they were kids, but they scattered apart and fell as gracefully as they could. Since her Arches watercolor paper had already flown away as airplanes, Laurel also got rid of her kneaded rubber erasers next. Ripped those to pieces.

During December, Laurel began smashing her palette trays into smithereens by dropping Trent's old bowling ball on top of them. She launched the plastic bits over the side of the balcony, one handful of dusty confetti at a time.

Yesterday, she parted with the last tube of watercolor paint, emptying its contents into the garbage disposal first. Laura had packed only tiny sample paints for the move to Chicago, smaller than the free toothpaste Trent brings home from international flights, no heavier than a dime. She will miss their exotic names. No more Purple Lake, Sap Green, or Pyrrole Scarlet, but it can't be helped.

Laurel lights the candles in silver candlesticks that belonged to her grandmother and chews her lunch seated at the kitchen island.

By 12:25, the food is finished, and there's no sign that anyone has eaten anything today.

The baby monitor on the windowsill in the living room is

completely unnecessary. Cami is sixteen steps at the end of the hallway, sleeping inside her crib in a corner of the master bedroom, but Laurel uses the monitor anyway, on high volume. Cami's sleep sounds, the way her blankets rustle, are good company.

Laurel worries that Cami doesn't get enough fresh air. Fresh air. One of her mother's and her grandmother's tried and true cures for everything: headache, sour stomach, sore tooth, stuffed sinuses, cheating boyfriend, flat tire, no sleep, zits for prom, wisdom teeth removal, feeling lonely, not feeling. "Keep your windows wide open at night for fresh air and you'll stay good and healthy and live long." "Get outside in the fresh air and you'll find a way to stop feeling sorry for yourself."

It doesn't seem too windy today. The treetops in the park along the river walk are at a standstill. It is cold, but the sun is bright. Maybe after Cami has her lunch, Laurel will carry her outside onto the balcony for a few measured minutes of air.

Laurel slices open one of the many boxes that have remained sealed since the move from Denton Falls: *Laurel - Childhood.*

It takes work to get through Trent's layers of thick, perfectly applied packing tape. This is one of the boxes Laurel didn't plan to open for many years, at least not until Cami was old enough to care about seeing the dolls her mother used to play with, but she opens it anyway.

The baby doll is smaller than Cami, but she'll have to do. Laurel brings the doll's belly to her nose and sniffs. Same sweet smell, reminiscent of her grandmother's rose lotions. Laurel never named the doll. She was just: "Baby." The doll has a lot of hair for a baby. Her crystal blue eyes fall closed as Laurel lies her down to zip her inside one of Cami's footed snowsuits.

Baby always looks so peaceful when she is asleep.

Slipping on her coat, Laurel puts her over her shoulder and steps outside onto the balcony.

The day is miraculously calm.

The sun feels like the sun.

The city sounds are muted by snow.

Laurel walks six steps to the left side, then six steps to the right, patting the baby's back so she won't squirm or fuss.

The fresh air isn't half bad today. It's not like Denton Falls, but at least there's an absence of exhaust.

Laurel glances over at the railing she has leaned over almost every day for months now. Pats the baby again. *There, there.* As long as Laurel stays far away from there, this new routine will be good for Cami.

Laurel adjusts the baby in her arms, kisses her cheek. Her skin doesn't feel too cold. Just a few more steps will be good for her.

The Echoes in Gleeva

Settled under the patchwork quilt, the one her grandmother Marie made, Gleeva closes her eyes, making the bedroom dark, and assesses the current pitch of the house. Tomorrow is her fortieth birthday.

As a child, her body rested horizontally here, but the floor has been gradually tipping Gleeva upright ever since. When Clifford was still alive, they talked into this darkness every night, a twig table with legs as graceful and vulnerable as a doe wedged between their twin beds. That table was the first piece of furniture Clifford crafted, so it was understandable the legs turned out spindly. Gleeva usually grew quiet first, lulled toward dreaming by her twin brother's voice.

"Which would you rather, Clifford? Would you rather slide down in the daytime sitting on the back porch with your favorite food in your lap or in night's light, like right now?"

"In the day, so I can see what's in the middle of the trees on the way down, but I have to finish the porch belt first. I only got to swipe one seatbelt from Samson's Junk Emporium, a nifty silver buckle from the front seat of a Grand Fury, but it's busted up, can't use it. Goliath started barking real mean, so I had to take off quick."

"That can't be a real car name: Grand Fury. That means a massive anger. What letters did you see? I think it would be a whole lot prettier to slide down at night, under a full moon, when everything outside looks like those yo-yos we had that glowed in the dark. Yours had Evil Knievel on it. Remember?"

"I remember," he said.

"And there's nothing in the middle of trees that is different from what is in the tops or the bottoms of them," Gleeva said.

19

"I guess I'll find out. People don't know what's in the middle of trees as big as skyscrapers, Gleev. It's not like you can step on an elevator, choose a floor, and ride up there."

"I still think I am meant to go too," Gleeva said.

"You are not meant to go, and it was a Grand Fury!" Clifford's scream escaped through the window that night, echoed in the deep gut of the valley, a wide mouth cradling a dense forest, a lumber mill on the bank of the Harpeth River, and the Village of Freys, Population: 577.

Every night the twins talked over the treetops swaying outside of their bedroom window, their words drifted toward the rust and gray rooftops of Freys that were no bigger than toy building blocks, their giggles joined the white smoke escaping the stacks of the chugging mill. On cloudless nights, under the biggest moons, their hopes and dreams sailed away on the currents of the Harpeth River, a liquid fissure burned into the horizon, a hairline crack spread over the surface of a hardboiled egg.

"It was a Grand Fury. Grand Coupe. Brougham two-door, 121.5-inch wheelbase. Manufactured in Kenosha, Wisconsin. Grand Fury!"

People never understood Clifford's screaming. He sounded angry. He frightened people, but Clifford didn't scream because he was angry. He screamed when he was sad, and he was only sad when he thought Gleeva or Marie or their Uncle Bernard or their friend Connie didn't believe something he believed. Gleeva would have understood if Clifford had screamed every single word he ever spoke into a world where the only people in the only town he would ever set foot in mocked him and called him "Cyclops."

Clifford began hyperventilating that night over the whole Grand Fury thing: something that happened when he forgot to take the deep breaths Dr. Bishop prescribed. Clifford's lungs were no bigger than a grown man's fists. Gleeva had to act quickly.

"Okay, Grand Fury it is. Hey, I might be heading into town tomorrow. Connie called earlier. What treat do you want this time? Tell me now in case you sleep late. Vienna sausages or a Slim Jim? We should only have one junkie thing each. I am getting a jar of Fluff," Gleeva sang this soothing information toward their ceiling.

"Vienna sausages this time," he answered.

It was a silly idea, questioning Clifford's knowledge about any vehicle. He was a dedicated scholar of cars and trucks. Marie had sparked this obsession. Every Christmas and birthday until she died and left the twins alone in the house, Marie gifted Clifford with a die-cast toy vehicle, a replica of real life. Doors and hoods that opened and closed. White fire truck ladders that rotated in complete circles.

Clifford complained about the ladders being plastic instead of metal. He liked things precise. The die-casts seemed a cruel gift for a boy born without an eye of any kind on one side of his head and an eye on the other side that was stuck looking to the left: a boy that would never learn to drive, but that's what Marie had given Clifford, and the gifts had delighted him.

Over the years, Gleeva loaded her school backpack with offerings from the county's mobile library for Clifford. Anything she could find on the shelves devoted to "Automobiles" under the title: "Common Hobbies." She purchased every new issue of Motor Trend and Car and Driver displayed at the IGA grocery checkout too.

And then there was Uncle Bernard's involvement in the whole thing. He operated a used car lot in Freys. The first morning of every new year, a car would exit the lot, a Ford or Pontiac that happened to have the most gas in its tank that morning. Uncle Bernard, Marie's older and only sibling, never missed his annual drive up the mountainside to his sister's mailbox before he opened the car lot for the day.

Gleeva and Clifford would be waiting for their uncle behind sheer living room curtains. When the car with the For Sale sign in a side window honked twice and pulled away, the twins ran outside for their holiday gifts: a stack of glossy car sales magazines and a marked-up copy of last year's Kelley's Blue Book for Clifford, and paperback books for Gleeva: *Nancy Drew*, *Anne of Green Gables*, *Jane Eyre*, and when she got older, works by Faulkner, Eudora Welty, and some Stephen King stuck in here and there just for some wicked fun.

Before Clifford gave up completely on school and reading things besides the trade-in values of used cars, Gleeva launched a valiant effort to help her brother learn to read. She made vocabulary flashcards with colorful sticker clues for difficult words. She stood to his left, holding books at the perfect height and angle, pointing over the top at each word as he went along, but there was nothing Clifford could do about the one eye he had. It didn't move far from side to side. He had to stop in the middle of every sentence and turn his head before he could mouth out the rest. After a few pages, the eye grew red and drippy.

Eventually everyone agreed that eight grades were plenty for Clifford. Better for him to stay away from Freys altogether. He'd had enough bloodied-up nostrils, and bruises where a right eye should have grown. The school bullies who decked him were slick. They materialized at the last minute from the basement of the rectory, from a car parked along the street. The only consolation was that hitting the empty side of Clifford's head was like slamming your knuckles into a granite slab: most people only did it once.

Clifford had been a standout in one school subject: geometry. Maybe his eye didn't take to the straight lines of letters, but shapes and angles, coordinates, degrees, those were different. The middle school math teacher, Mr. Clark, made a loose-leaf copy of the *Big Ideas Math* textbook for Clifford so he could hold one page up at a time to examine it. Clifford didn't have to study the examples of the related angles long before he could solve all the comprehension problems at the end of the chapter.

When Clifford died, Mr. Clark drove up the mountain, stepped onto the front porch of the house, and knocked. Gleeva almost opened the door. When she was sure he was gone, she unlocked the door and found a box of navel oranges at her ankles. She dropped the oranges one by one and kicked them across the grass yard, where they met the edge of the cliff and dropped away forever.

Her first year alone in the house without Clifford had been difficult. Whenever the moon was full, she tearfully dragged the shoebox from underneath his bed to keep Clifford's sky chart going like she'd promised. Twelve times that year, she positioned herself on his bed and held the sheet of tracing paper at arm's length, moving her left arm forward and back like a telescope lens until it was the same size as the window frame. She traced the outlines of the far mountains, the river line, the shapes of closer hills, the arms, elbows, and fingertips of the trees reaching up to her from the valley's floor below. In the morning, under the glare of the kitchen's fluorescent ceiling lights, her drawings never matched up to the quality of the ones Clifford left behind, but she did her best.

In the end, Gleeva couldn't find a good reason to continue measuring how quickly the bedroom window was losing sky, how fast the house was tipping. Gleeva had always witnessed what she called the house's "ticks and tocks" in her own way. She first noticed a tick and tock soaking in a hot bathtub following their fifth birthday dinner. She was underneath the soapy water, rinsing buttercream icing from her hair, when the red plastic boat above her head pecked its way steadily toward the cliff and collided with the side of the tub. There had been many things like that, countless tiny repetitions over the years. Her gold cross on the end of its braided chain swinging away from her bedpost on its own, the top layer of sugar grains inside a canister tumbling straight as fired arrows toward the open gut of the valley. Balls of yarn, tennis balls, anything round that got loose, would roll and line up along the back of the house where the house leaned into the cliff.

There had been a new tick and tock before she crawled into bed that night before her fortieth birthday, a tick and a tock in the float of the single mini marshmallow she dropped onto the surface of her hot chocolate. The tiny pillow traveled in rapid circles, a motion that reminded Gleeva of the way she and Clifford would spin their inner tubes in the creek across the road. That had been one of Clifford's favorite things, walking across the road and getting into the creek water with his tube. Gleeva would lead him around the tadpoles in the shallows. It wasn't possible for Clifford to bend his neck far enough to see his own feet and save the baby fish. Things like that worried him. Once they reached the deep water, he was fine on his own.

When Gleeva looked up from the steaming hot chocolate to her smile reflected in the kitchen windowpane framed by the mailbox at the driveway's end, her heart pinched painfully for her brother. Over the years, the twins often slipped things inside the box for Marie, a Valentine's Day card from a school art class, a fistful of white wildflowers, a perfect spelling test grade, a piece of fool's gold, a plastic whistle from a box of Cracker Jack so Marie could call them home from the creek. After Marie was gone, the twins took turns leaving surprises for each other. The last surprise Clifford left for Gleeva was a Ziploc baggy filled with cold, wet watercress. She liked to make lunch sandwiches with the tangy greens, spreading cream cheese on quartered slices of brown bread.

—

Gleeva is awake early on the morning of her forty-first birthday. There is nothing except tree trunks outside the bedroom now. No sun. No clouds. No leaves. Nothing green. Just thick, straight, gray spines. The house has been slipping faster than ever. Elegant twig furniture Clifford crafted to fill every room of the house has quickened its march. Gleeva drew white chalk circles around the feet of Clifford's furniture, and now those original footprints stand far away in shadows.

Gleeva begins her birthday by dusting the finely sanded surfaces and curved limbs of Clifford's furniture with an oiled chambray cloth. Marie's original Hoover upright vacuum still does a good job on the hand-knotted Persian rugs, one in every room, soft and deeply piled, dyed rich as gemstones, red for courage, brilliant yellow for joy, sapphire blue for hope, and emerald for honesty.

Next, Gleeva lifts and polishes Marie's collection of painted porcelain vases depicting wintery scenes: decorated wreaths on village shop doors, horse-drawn sleighs under snowfall. There are sixty-seven vases to handle each week, but Gleeva doesn't mind. This has always been her job, and Connie isn't known for being on time.

When Gleeva doesn't hear tires crunching into driveway gravel by eleven o'clock, she shrugs and begins polishing the dining room's sterling silver service. The dining room's corner cupboards are the densest and thickly hewn of Clifford's pieces. They were his last creations named for famous sumo wrestlers: Akebono and Kisenosato, but now, Gleeva can't remember which is which.

Clifford constructed his furniture from long, thin tree branches and twigs he gathered from the surrounding woods. He soaked what he gathered in hot cornflower oil so he could twist and braid the rods into table legs and chair arms, oval circles to hold mirror glass, woven tabletops, and sofa seats he sanded flat. He sealed the furniture with Bulls Eye Shellac, which turned the wood a shiny, reddish gold, the same color as alfalfa honey. Clifford's twig furniture is the one thing Gleeva hates to see fall over the cliff. She doesn't like picturing it busted, mangled, left to freeze underneath snow.

The phone rings. Connie will arrive shortly. Connie is the only neighbor up here in the clouds. She lives a mile away in a Winnebago her late husband bought in the village of Murfreesboro in the spring of 1971. Rodney steered the motorhome back to Freys as a surprise for Connie's birthday. Connie hopped inside, and the two reached the mountaintop just as the sun was setting. When Rodney switched the ignition off, his heart gave out right there in the driver's seat. A few months later, Connie moved into the Winnebago permanently. On the day she moved in, she removed the keys from the ignition where Rodney had left them and tossed them into the valley.

Although Marie and Clifford rarely left the mountain when they were alive, Gleeva did. She would accompany Connie on errands in Freys or a jaunt to another town. If not for Connie, Gleeva would have missed seeing the inside of a mall and a movie theater. She would never have fallen in love with the taste of a Big Mac or how a stomach drops when a Ferris wheel suddenly lurches downward.

Seven-year-old Gleeva wasn't afraid when the Ferris wheel got stuck at the Lion's Association Carnival and Auction. At the very top, she had swayed her dangling legs with abandon, waved, and smiled down at Connie. The deep dark that night made the lights of the rides and the game booths brilliant and bold. Clifford would have loved seeing colors like that. He would have loved hearing the bells ring, the whistles, the air guns firing at spinning target wheels, the sound of caramel popcorn popping, but at least he got to taste some of the corn when Gleeva brought some home for him.

When the last silver teaspoon is polished and gleaming, Gleeva drops her cleaning blouse into the hallway hamper and pads toward the bedroom closet. The metal bar squeaks as she slides the clothes back and forth on their hangers, searching for the pale blue sweater with the silver collar, the color of a tinkling Christmas bell, so perfect for the first day of December. Gleeva slips the sweater over her head and runs a brush through her thick, long, glossy black hair. She gifts the nape of her neck with a few pumps of perfume, applies mascara with careful strokes, taps her lips red, and heads to the den to wait for Connie.

Keeping an eye on the driveway through the bow window above Marie's craft table, Gleeva applies a coat of clear fingernail polish, blinks back the tears. She misses her grandmother working at this table, turning out a steady stream of new clothing creations for Gleeva. Marie wanted Gleeva to learn how to transform the Goodwill clothes the way Marie did, but Gleeva got bored with the process quickly. Gleeva preferred reading books curled into the corner of the den with the steady movements of Marie at the craft table in her periphery and the sound of Clifford sanding branches and twigs in the basement.

Gleeva can still see her grandmother adding lace collars and golden buttons, opening and closing pliers to take apart costume jewelry, freeing rhinestones, plastic bumblebees, metal daisies with yellow centers, red lady bugs. Marie, shoulders hunched, squeezing tiny beads of white glue that dried clear under the decorations she chose for sweaters and skirts. Marie humming along with the music from a record spinning on the turntable, Marie's lifetime favorite singer, Engelbert Humperdinck, singing his hit, "After the Lovin.'"

In her senior year, Gleeva had taken some lovin' behind the metal bleachers of the Hillsboro High School football field. Hillsboro High was in another valley forty miles south of Freys. Clifford never sat in the bleachers there or attended a football game at that field. He never visited the sprawling, modern school with the central air conditioning, a theatre stage with an orchestra pit and velvet seats, rows of shiny, new microscopes inside the biology lab, and a dark room for photography. He never saw a place with streetlamps, stop lights, parades, fancy restaurants for candlelit dinners, and a community Christmas tree.

When Clifford asked Gleeva about high school, she described the combination locks in the hallway lockers that no one could open, the horrors of cafeteria food, what some of the teachers didn't know and should have. She made Hillsboro High sound like a place it wasn't. In truth, Gleeva adored it there, especially her English and History classes. At Hillsboro, she discovered she had a gift for the French language. She made friends, real girlfriends who invited her to sleepovers and grain alcohol parties, even though she was never able to attend at the last minute. When she joined the school newspaper, her stories quickly became a regular part of the front page. Everyone thought she would become a famous journalist someday.

As for the boys behind the bleachers, Gleeva took the chances she was handed in that other valley, that other town, that field of wet grass. She laid back and opened her silken thighs for the boys she thought were handsome and nice enough, and there was no shortage of boys willing to show up behind the bleachers with condoms hidden in their varsity jacket pockets or tucked inside their socks to hook up with the beautiful, smart, and mysterious Gleeva Augusta.

Gleeva lapped up their urgency, how they stroked her breasts, the breath hot at the base of her neck. When some of them went at it hard, her heart pounded. She relished the warmth and the soreness between her legs as she crossed the parking lot toward Connie's car, the acrid smell of latex still on her fingertips. It was all her idea, every bit of it. Clifford was never going to get any lovin,' and there was nothing Gleeva could do about that. She wondered if the body part Clifford needed for lovin' had formed in the way it should have. She had her doubts.

Gleeva's classmates knew she had a twin brother, of course. A "hideous, deformed" brother rumored to be the mother's punishment for sinning with a married man, a traveling shoe salesman. Gleeva never wanted a different kind of brother. Clifford was not hideous in any way. He was perfect. And it wasn't their mother's fault, no matter what the pastor in Freys preached. Their mother had been too young to know better, too young to get pregnant, and too young to give birth without dying.

Clifford often told Gleeva she was "a true beauty," assured her she was funny and witty and brilliant, that she would make her life a great success, that she should apply for a college somewhere very far away from Freys and Hillsboro too. The last subject Gleeva and Clifford talked about in the shared darkness of their bedroom had been Gleeva's future.

"I think you should go to college, Gleev. You can go anywhere. You could start with some correspondence courses to get ahead on credits. It's not too late. You could go to England. Oxford. Cambridge." Clifford's breathing had been rapid and wheezy that last night. It was his heart, flat as a pocket watch, and those small lungs of his. Plenty of other organs inside of him were probably letting him down, too, all of them the wrong size and shape.

"Okay, Clifford, I'll get some college books from the library this week, and you and I can look them over together."

In the morning, when she didn't hear Clifford's raspy breathing, Gleeva knew she was alone in that room for the first time in her life. She crawled out of bed, ran down the hall toward the den, switched on the light, picked up the phone, and called Connie. Then she left the front door wide open, walked across the street, and sat down beside the creek water until everything was all over.

Gleeva's nails are dry by the time Connie's headlights turn into the driveway.

"You look so pretty. Happy birthday!" Connie is wearing one of Marie's creations, too, a red sweater with a green rhinestone collar. The familiar scent of her Shalimar perfume has consumed all the air inside the car. "I guess we're both Christmassy today."

Curving their way down the mountainside, Connie and Gleeva harmonize with Connie's standard car tunes. At first, Glen Campbell is a county lineman. When they reach flat ground, he is a glittery, dream-ridden cowboy.

"We're not going to try the new diner in Freys today, birthday cherub," Connie says with a wink.

"We're not?"

"We're going to Hillsboro for a Big Mac. The McDonald's in Sherwank burned all the way to the ground last week. Arson, they say."

Gleeva opens her mouth to object. She hasn't been back to Hillsboro since high school graduation. After she graduated, Connie and Gleeva began driving to towns north of Freys instead. By then, Gleeva had had enough of Hillsboro.

Connie pulls over to the side of the road and tilts her rearview mirror upward for a complete view of the mountaintop. Gleeva sighs, swivels around, lifts her chin toward the heavens and the house. Connie won't hit the accelerator again until she does.

"It's really leaning now, Gleeva. It's become way too dangerous for you to stay there. Your room at my Waldorf Astoria has a freshly blooming amaryllis in it, white as snow, your favorite flower color. You should move in there tonight on the occasion of your birthday. We can get some boxes at the liquor store in Hillsboro and start packing your things."

"Maybe," Gleeva mumbles.

"What about Hillsboro then, at least?"

Gleeva's stomach lurches, but the idea of a Big Mac and a familiar drive with good memories wins her over. "Let's go."

Connie cracks her window, lights a cigarette from her Virginia Slims pack. "I'm no baby, I'm a high-class lady!"

"Is there really such thing as a Grand Fury car?" Gleeva asks. "Where did that come from?"

"I just wondered. You worked at Uncle Bernard's lot. I thought you might have seen one there, that's all. And by the way, Clifford would say if you keep manipulating a rearview mirror like that, it would bust off and then you won't be able to see behind you anymore."

"Yeah, I know, I can hear him saying that too. Maybe I don't want to see behind me. I might catch a glimpse of my fat ass. I can hear him saying that I am right, too, about you moving in with me on your birthday, and there is a Gran Fury, I think. G-R-A-N. No D."

"Really? That's even stranger. And why "Fury"? Why should a car be named after rage?"

"You're overthinking this, Gleev. What's this about?"

"Just curious."

"I don't know why they named a car 'Fury,' but I can tell you where the word 'Fury' comes from for your birthday gift, along with your Big Mac. Greek mythology."

One winter, when the twins were young, Connie got hooked on Greek mythology. She borrowed books from the mobile library, read them, and retold the myths of Ancient Greece to the twins from the first frost to spring's thaw whenever she came to the house to visit. When Connie lost interest in the myths with the coming of warmer weather, it was heartbreaking for Gleeva and Clifford. The stories had been so full of wondrous names, magnificent creatures, epic battles. Every now and then, Connie's knowledge of mythology still bubbled up from the underworld.

"Do tell," Gleeva says as a frown rises and falls from her lips. Excitement never hits as high as a mark as when she shared life with her brother.

"The Furies were three foul-smelling hags with bat wings, tar-black skin, torches, and whips. They carried cups of venom and serpents slithered in and out of the locks of their hair, hissing and darting their tongues. The Furies wore boots like huntress maidens."

"Monsters?" Gleeva asks.

"No. Goddesses. They ascended to Earth to punish the wicked."

"I wish they'd been beautiful, hypnotizingly so."

"That would have made for a better story. You two always had a lot of ideas that would have improved Greek mythology for the betterment of mankind."

Hillsboro's McDonald's has a long line at the drive-thru. Gleeva's mouth waters at the sight of the gaudy, yellow arches. At the other end of the street, the green doors of the Trinity Fellowship Church gleam in the sunshine. In the church's front yard, life-sized, plastic Mary and Joseph lay on their backs together, face up, getting a little breather before they have to be on display, trading stories about the shapes of the cloud billows.

"Another blonde-haired Mary," Gleeva says. "Ridiculous."

"Yep."

"Let's go see him," Gleeva suggests.

Connie's hands rise into the air and plop back down on the steering wheel, something she does when her patience is running low. One car in front is apparently ordering lunch for an entire office building. Connie glances at Gleeva.

"Reverend Enders? Why in the world would you want to do that?"

Gleeva shrugs.

Connie lights up another cigarette.

They inch along.

Three cars away from the order screen, the church doors swing wide and Reverend Enders steps outside into the sunny December day with an additional figure for the nativity scene under his arm, a man with a deep purple turban and ebony skin. He carries the man down the steps toward the lounging Mary and Joseph. The reverend's long, white hair, once dark as tar, whips behind him like a winter scarf.

"Those darn Wise Men didn't even visit the stable. Did you know that, Connie? They arrived months later. There are so many lies about Christmas."

"I think Reverend Enders has one of the Kings there," Connie says. "See the crown?"

When the reverend places Mary next to a brown cow on the slopping churchyard, she leans forward, but it is Joseph who gives the reverend the hardest time. Every time Reverend Enders positions Joseph across from Mary, readying him for the admiration of a tiny and miraculous life heralded to appear in twenty-four days, Joseph tips, falls forward like the Lenin statue felled by a Red Square mob, and lands face down in the empty manger.

As young children, Clifford and Gleeva attended Christmas Eve services given by Reverend Enders. At that time, he was the pastor in Freys. Marie insisted on one day of church a year. The reverend's legendary deep voice shook the glass in the chapel panes and the blood-switching chambers inside a little girl's heart. With impossibly long strides up and down the chapel's center aisle, arms beseeching the heavens above, a fist known to splatter podiums, Reverend Enders always packed the pews. When he left Freys for Hillsboro, the town mourned. No replacements for Reverend Enders arrived. Eventually, the town elders gave up searching, turned off the water and the utilities to their tiny, white clapboard chapel, and padlocked the door. No one could replace that kind of inspiration. Enders was one of a kind.

"Where should we eat?" Connie asks as she maneuvers out of the McDonald's lot. "Want to see your alma mater?"

"Sounds good."

It wasn't much, but Gleeva was pleased when she thought about it afterward. The reverend stopped mid-motion, turned as the two women drove past. He didn't miss Gleeva's head of raven-black hair when she leaned forward to set it on fire in the sun. A snarl passed in the shadows behind his pastoral smile. When he turned his back and cupped his mouth to answer a call from a parishioner on the other side of the street, his shoulders dipped a tick and a tock toward the edge of a cliff.

On the morning of the final Christmas church service in Freys, Reverend Enders had stopped mid-sermon beside a pew. Clifford was seated at the end. Marie always thought it was a good idea for Clifford to sit next to the aisle because he often got sick to his stomach when he was away from the house and the mountaintop. The teachers did the same thing in school. Clifford's desk was always close to an exit with quick access to a toilet bowl.

"You cannot sit in the house of the Lord and not look at him," the reverend spoke into Clifford's ear, loud enough for all to hear.

Clifford's body stiffened beside Gleeva. When he began whimpering softly, Gleeva looked over at Marie, but Marie remained still, staring straight ahead toward the front of the chapel and the cross with the life-sized, wooden body of a limp Christ. Her lips were moving in fervent prayer. Gleeva could tell Marie was scared in a frozen stiff sort of way.

Gleeva reached for her brother's hand at the same time as Reverend Enders reached for Clifford's head. He yanked Clifford's head as far right as it could go to bring the savior into view. For a few minutes, the congregation remained quiet, but then some of the youngest children couldn't help it. They began one by one to giggle at the sight of that boy with his head stuck looking one way.

After that, Marie and the twins didn't return to church, and Marie never mentioned God or Jesus or church or Reverend Enders ever again. Gleeva knew Marie wished she'd never made them go to church at all, but, like a lot of things, what happened that day wasn't Marie's fault.

Connie and Gleeva gobble their fast food in the parking lot of Hillsboro High. Delicious. It doesn't disappoint.

"It's fun to see this place again, Connie, but I think I am ready to head home."

"You got it."

When they pass Hillsboro Liquors, Connie spots some free boxes on the porch. Those go into her hatchback trunk. Connie buys two bottles of celebratory amber ale for the drive back to Freys. By the time they are back on the top of the mountain, it seems too late to start packing.

"I'll be over early in the morning, Gleev. We'll start in the kitchen. Happy birthday!"

Gleeva is exhausted. She undresses, drops a nightgown over her head, brushes her hair, leaves it loose on her back instead of braiding it as she usually does. The moon is full, and she must be ready. She's always imagined sliding down under the shine of a full moon. That's the way it plays out in her dreams, anyway. She wonders if her silk nightgown might float her down like a parachute. Maybe she will have time to see what's in the middle of trees after all.

When the rumble starts, underneath the house, then moves inside the blocks of the basement, the heart of the house's foundation, Gleeva hurries to the den. She snatches the phone receiver to listen to the world as a dial tone for the last time. She thinks of Hillsboro, the football field, that way the lights hummed into her temples, the cold grass, how another person's flesh can burn hotter than your own. She is sorry about how sad Connie will be, but she doesn't call her. What would she say?

When the house lurches violently toward the cliff, Gleeva grins and drops the phone. She skips toward the back of the house, toward the two twin beds with a twig table wedged between them, toward the open window, toward the ledge where Gleeva intends to jump at the last minute.

She wasn't expecting to hear Connie's car horn, for headlights to lift gray from the treetops, to see green again.

"Gleeva!" Connie screams.

Gleeva imagines Clifford beside her when she leaps as the bedroom caves in behind her. Her bare feet find solid ground beyond the window frame. The fingertips of the valley of Freys. Fingertips that have been waiting for many years to catch her. The branches murmur as they pass her between them, all the night words and the peals of twin laughter return to Gleeva tenfold from the places in the middle of trees where the echoes of some memories are granted the chance to last forever.

—

Connie is getting used to the weather being horrendously hot all the time. That's what Florida is, stagnant and suffocating. On the mountaintop, she enjoyed the steam from coffee tickling her nose, warm stoneware in her palms, but in this climate, she ices her morning coffee. Still, it is a comfort to live in the same retirement community as Bernard.

She had two stacks of letters and a hundred and thirty-seven new emails the last time she checked. Every week, the emails and written correspondence arrive in greater numbers. What a blessing.

Connie takes a swig from her mug, chomps an ice cube, touches her keyboard. Gleeva pops up, a bright glow in the center of the home screen. Gleeva, as the newspaper photographer captured her the morning after the Augusta house fell over the cliff, her arms wide, chin tipped toward the village of Freys, eyes closed under long, dark lashes, her delicate, bare feet dangling below the billows of an unsoiled white gown, hair a waterfall cascading over her breasts: "The First Recorded Crucifixion at the Hands of Mother Nature."

People began arriving to the streets of Freys almost immediately. "How do we get to the miracle in the woods?" No one knew how such a thing could have happened, how Gleeva ended up hanging in a tree in such a way, a vision clothed in tranquil grace. After a few weeks, logging crews were hired to chop dense trunks and clear brush to create a walking pathway through virgin forest to the place where Gleeva had come to rest. In all that time, Gleeva's body didn't change. She remained pink-cheeked, hair combed and lustrous, the fabric of her gown bright, flawless. When it rained, she remained dry. No one took her down from the tree. No one dared to touch her. She was breathtaking.

Now visitors travel from all parts of the world to touch tree bark, watch sky through branches, search for some unique blessing, some quiet forgiveness perhaps, a form of earthly peace all their own, and the Angel of Freys is generous. Connie carefully records the testimonials on the website she manages in Gleeva's name. She posts the stories and the pictures of those who have regained something of themselves, large or small, sitting on twig furniture reclaimed from the woods, basking in shade cast by the tree that cradles the Angel of Freys.

—

Several months after the Augusta house tumbled over the cliff, early morning visitors to the miracle in the woods discovered a sobbing, slobbering Reverend Enders. They sliced through a seat-belt noose and lowered him down from a thick-limbed tree across from the glowing Gleeva. The reverend wept pitifully, cried out, stumbled in wild circles. Realizing that the reverend had been blinded, the people present led him to kneel under his daughter's feet as he begged them to do.

There were plenty of human witnesses to his confession of the taking of Gleeva and Clifford's twelve-year-old mother, the cries he muffled in the carpeted aisle, but the woods of the Valley of Freys held no echo for the voice of Enders. His words fell silent, dropped heavy as boulders around his feet. The people present described how all around Gleeva's body, rays of sunlight burst from forest trunk and branch and how in the brightness of that moment, the Angel of Freys turned from human flesh to stone.

Elias Wolf

Elias Wolf is a perfect name for a vampire, and the Elias
Wolf who lived in my hometown of Putnam, West Virginia, certainly
looked the part. Tall. Rail thin. Lustrous, black hair tapping his shoulders.
Skin earthworm pale. Dark brown eyes. The kind of dark that hides pupils
and makes it hard to know if a person is looking you in the eye or not,
though our Elias looked everyone in the eye. And, like all the Wolf
brothers, he had unusually long teeth. He might have looked the part, but
Elias wasn't interested in anything with a strong heart coursing blood. He
was only interested in things that were already dead.

Elias flunked out of my high school class by choice. I still saw
him at school because he would saunter through the school's main doors
midmorning, make himself comfortable on one of the library's sofas, and
read all the daily newspapers back-to-back. When we happened to be in
the library together, we discussed the top headlines of the day. Elias knew
a lot about the world outside of Putnam. He was a brilliant guy. I had a
tragic crush on him I kept inside my chest, buried like a second rib cage
nestled under the one I was born with.

Freed of the annoyance of formal education, Elias embarked on
a full-time career tuning cars at his brother's filling station. In the evenings
he strolled along the side of Bald Knob Road, stabbing the earth at regular
intervals with one of his grandfather's walking sticks. If a person wanted
to leave Putnam and go anywhere else, you turned either left or right onto
Bald Knob Road. It was the only four-lane road we had. Everyone in
Putnam was accustomed to driving past Elias's tall frame clad in a long,
ivory raincoat two sizes too big for him that he'd acquired for three dollars
and sixteen cents, according to Meg Myers, who ran the Goodwill. When
my grandpa and I passed him, Grandpa would honk his truck horn four

times, and I would stick my head out of the window and wave. Then we'd watch Elias in our rearviews flash those long teeth of his, chuckling and saluting us. We'd laugh then too. Not at him. With him. In Putnam, people didn't laugh *at* each other. It was hard enough hanging on inside the carcass of an old coal town.

One day I stayed late at school even though ominous clouds were falling like bricks on the mountain peaks encircling Putnam. As the newly elected chief editor of the high school newspaper, I thought I was special. That's how you are at seventeen. Grandiose. I read every word of every article the staff turned in, wringing their work dry with my edits, trying to put myself on the path to becoming somebody someday. By the time I looked up from my desk, the clock read 4:37.

Outside, I eased my bike from the rack. The pungent smell of pine needles and chimney smoke warned me a rip-roaring storm was closing in. I wasn't worried. My bike tires had deep treads. I would take the shortcut around the little league fields and picnic groves of Plum Orchard Park, even though that meant a dirt path that morphed into a muddy river when it rained. That path was the fastest way home to the cozy house where I lived with my grandpa. I started peddling hard to beat the storm.

I made it a quarter of the way around Plum Orchard Park when thunder cracked. A jagged dagger of lightning sliced open the sky, a knife through a bedsheet. I ducked instinctively, turned my bike left, and pedaled up the hill toward Bald Knob Road. Grandpa never worried about me in rainstorms, but lightning was a different matter. A bolt struck his house once when he was a little boy. No lives were lost, but everything they owned was.

When I got to the top of the hill, Elias was there, standing over something heaped up on the side of the road, wind slapping his coattails like a whip. He looked up at me as lightning split the sky open again, appearing more vampire-like than ever in such violent weather. I was glad to see him. I had missed him in the library lately. I kept getting stuck in the chemistry lab trying to figure out how I'd messed up another experiment. I hated all varieties of science.

"Hey there, Ryder Sycamore Clement," he greeted me as I wheeled my bike over and tapped the kickstand down.

More thunder, followed by a flash of heat lightning.

"You say that like I don't know my own proper name," I said, crossing my arms over my chest.

I was watching Elias blink because I didn't want to look at what was lying still at his feet.

"I said it because you possess one of the coolest names of all time," he answered. "Ryder. Sycamore. Clement. Damn."

"Well, Elias Wolf, Elias Wolf isn't exactly run of the mill. Your proper name is so grand you don't even need a middle one."

That made him laugh.

"There's lightning," I continued. "Don't you think you should head home?"

When he shook his head and knelt in front of the body, I had no choice but to join him in assessing Putnam's most recent homicide victim.

"Ah, poor girl," Elias whispered, patting her neck gently.

An outsider would have said she was just a common, white-tailed deer, and she was, except there wasn't anything common day about that white-tailed deer or any of the animals who shared those mountains with us. We had lots of white-tailed deer, and every one of them was special in their own way. This doe was particularly delicate. She was the prettiest doe I'd ever seen. Silky, chestnut coat. The graceful limbs of a prize-winning racehorse. Velvety black nose. Impossibly long eyelashes you'd expect on a white-tailed deer.

She'd been hit in her back quarter, back legs crushed flat as hotcakes, tail ripped clean. A jagged tear across the length of her underbelly leaked a glistening, mahogany organ surrounded by a waterfall of pinky-white, iridescent intestines that reminded me of a string of bloated pearls. I could tell she was a fresh kill because her eyes, golden as a jar of local dandelion honey, were bright and focused as if she had expected to find me and Elias together on the side of that road.

"Maybe you should drag her a bit further off," I suggested. "Need help?"

"She's good where she is."

Elias's hands were bloody. He never wore gloves. He'd already dragged the deer a good distance. There was a long path across the cinders on the shoulder of the road, but not far enough for my liking. I listened for the squeal of distant truck tires.

DelMarco Lumber's careless drivers had been slaughtering living things along Bald Knob Road for decades. DelMarco bused their employees in and out. Nobody local got hired by DelMarco. There was always another truck overloaded with felled tree trunks heavy as baby elephants ready to come barreling down the mountainside, headed to a sawmill in Troy or Salem, up against a deadline.

Elias's mother was struck and killed by a DelMarco truck driver walking along Bald Knob Road after her car broke down. Elias was eleven at the time, the youngest of the four Wolf brothers. He took it the hardest.

An investigation concluded that the fatal accident had been caused by dense fog, not reckless or careless driving. Everyone in Putnam knew better.

"Let's just drag her a bit farther," I tried again. "I can help you."

"I just got her positioned how I want her," Elias answered. "I'm ready to take the pictures now. Won't take long."

"You better hurry up because it's getting ready to rain really hard," I said.

Elias stood up, took a few backward steps into the middle of the road. Stopping just shy of the solid yellow lines, he cocked his head to the side to survey his handiwork. The road was still empty in both directions as far as I could see, but I thought I heard the faint sound of tires rolling our way. Elias stepped to the right. Paused. Then to the left. Paused. Back to the right. Paused. Back to the left.

"Come on, you're making me nervous here," I blurted.

Elias jerked his head in my direction as if he'd forgotten I was there. Another thunderclap, a real eardrum burster. Thunder sat right on top of your skull in those mountains.

"Elias. Please hurry!"

"Okay, Ryder Sycamore Clement. I'll wrap it up."

I stepped away from the deer as he reached into his coat pocket for his camera. A vacationer had donated the high-end Nikon camera to the Goodwill while passing through three summers ago. It wasn't unusual for people to make a pitstop in Putnam to see what life was like living in the middle of nowhere where nothing much was happening. The camera was beat up on the outside, but it worked perfectly. When Elias asked Meg Myers if he could pay for the camera in installments, she gave it to him. All she asked was that he put it to good use.

Elias should have become a famous photographer. What he did with all varieties of dead animals was nothing short of a miracle. He had a way of propping up what remained of them, turning their necks just so, tipping their chins until the animal's point of view sailed right out of the photo and pierced your heart. He was a true master at staging guts and gore. Sometimes too much had leaked out, and Elias would have to tuck some of it back inside the cavity. Sometimes there wasn't enough, so he would have to reach in and pull stuff out. Somehow, he always knew exactly what to do.

"How about I take one of you with her first?" Elias asked, lifting the camera lens to his eye, walking toward the doe.

"Why would you want me in the picture?" I asked.

Elias and I both looked up at headlights bouncing toward us. A car climbing up the mountain from the housing development outside of the main part of town where we both lived. Good news. That meant someone we knew who could give me a ride home. Elias would walk back to his house. He never accepted rides. Walked in all kinds of weather. I looked up the mountain toward DelMarco's headquarters. Still nothing from that direction, but I couldn't relax my shoulders.

"I won't use it for anything," Elias said. "Just gives me more practice with my photography skills, that's all. You don't have to if you don't want to."

Raindrops began falling as I kneeled behind the doe, unsure of what to do with my hands. Being a part of one of Elias's famous animal portraits made me feel sadder than I liked to feel about what had happened to his mother, his whole family, what kept happening to our animals, what all of it kept doing to Elias. But Elias had asked me for a favor. I tucked my hands under my raised knee and gazed toward the middle of the road. When Elias clicked twice and lowered his camera, I walked to stand beside him while he finished.

I knew Elias would blow up one of the photographs of this pretty doe to poster size, run off a stack of copies at Goodwill in exchange for free car maintenance for Meg, and spend Sunday morning up at DeMarco headquarters plastering the posters all over their buildings and trucks. Then he'd drive his brother's pickup truck out of town to DelMarco's billboard along Interstate 379, set up a ladder, climb up, and paste this poster to the billboard under the large red letters: *DelMarco Lumber: Building a Solid Future Together.*

Elias had been making the posters for three years since he quit high school. The posters weren't doing anything to change DelMarco Lumber's ways as far as I could tell, but they had done Elias some good. He smiled more often now. Laughed some. And so did the rest of the Wolf family, even Elias's father.

After his wife was struck and killed, Mr. Wolf hired an attorney, filed suit against DelMarco for wrongful death. When the case was dismissed for lack of merit, Mr. Wolf contacted state news sources and some national ones, too, like *20/20* and *60 Minutes.* A handful of journalists arrived to interview the family and photograph where Mrs. Wolf had lost her life, but none of them ever ran the story. DelMarcos was rolling in the dough. They could pay people off. When Elias started with the posters, DelMarco officials took the path of least resistance. They simply tore the posters torn down and threw them away.

Elias was drying off his camera with a handkerchief. He was finished photographing the pretty doe.

"How's it going at the gas station?" I asked him.

"It's oily," Elias answered. "How's the newspaper business, Chief Editor?"

My heart jumped.

"Yes, they elected me," I said, shrugging. "Probably because no one else wanted to do it."

That made Elias laugh again. I felt proud of myself.

"Got any plans for the paper during your tenure?" he asked.

"I'm thinking about it. How about I run another story about your posters? The paper didn't do anything about them last year."

"That's a nice offer, but I am trying to stay clear of all things Claymont School District," he said, winking.

Four distinct honks sounded in the air. It was Grandpa coming up the mountain, looking for me. I was so lucky to have Grandpa. It has always been me and him. I was four months old when my parents died in a boating accident. I had no memory of them. I couldn't imagine what it was like for Elias, looking down that road at approaching headlights, knowing it couldn't be the one person he wanted it to be—his mother, out looking for her youngest son. I hung my head.

When I looked up again, the pretty doe was still watching us. She seemed so alive. I could envision her standing up, tossing her head playfully, and leaping into the woods across the road, elegant as a prima ballerina. How I wished she could. Elias would close the doe's eyes before he left her. He always did that. It was the respectful thing to do.

"You sure about not running another story about your posters?" I asked him. "They are so amazing."

"I'm sure, Ryder Sycamore Clement, and by the way, you will be the best chief editor that paper has ever had, the best they ever will have," he said. "You've got everything it takes and more."

A lump blossomed in my throat. I tried to think of something to say that would communicate I was flattered in solely a professional way, but I couldn't come up with anything. Thankfully, Grandpa pulled up and rolled down his truck window.

"You two look like a couple of drowned otters," he teased, grinning wide, white mustache leaping up. "Elias, can I give you a lift?"

"No thanks, Mr. Clement," Elias answered. "I'll be okay."

"Please," I said. "The temperature is diving."

"Thanks anyway," Elias said, shaking his head, the ends of his long hair dripping steadily.

"See you in the library then?" I asked.

"Definitely."

Elias smiled at me as another bolt of lightning split the sky, illuminating those magnificent teeth of his. Linking his arm around mine, he escorted me to the passenger door while Grandpa hoisted my bike into the truck bed. Grandpa climbed inside the cab, cranked his window shut, and sighed. Elias stood on the side of the road beside the pretty doe and watched as we made a U-turn and began heading back down the mountain.

Grandpa said, "I wish he would get his high school diploma and head out of town. Go to college. He's so smart. He could always come back."

"Think he will leave?" I asked.

"No," Grandpa said.

"Why not?"

"Elias doesn't want to let go of this place," he said.

Even though deep down I believed the same thing about Elias, I hoped we were both wrong: that someday Elias would be able to leave Putnam for a different kind of life in a completely different kind of place.

When I got home, I hurried to my room to change out of my wet clothes. Outside my window, the storm had passed. Across an inky sky, tinged deep purple, the celestials were beginning to wake up and wink. I searched for the moon, found a shimmering sliver. When I pulled my sweatshirt over my head, on one sleeve, the faint red imprint of Elias's open palm, his long, slim fingers. I draped the sweatshirt across my desk chair so that when I went to bed later, I would be able to stare at Elias's handprint in starlight.

———

It's easy for things just to go on like they go on in a town like Putnam, and time to slip right by, but I am not in Putnam, and I know four years have passed. I know I am inside my college apartment at Marshall University in Tennessee, an honors student in journalism, when the strong, acrid smell of a raging forest fire wakes me from a deep sleep. There isn't a forest anywhere around for hundreds of miles.

I hurry to the window and scan the section of the main road I can see between the two dorms across the street. The fibers of Elias's long, ivory-colored coat appear illuminated from within in the milky gray morning. His long arm plants a walking stick on the earth's surface every few steps. He stops, turns, tips his chin up toward my fourth-floor window, and waves. Then his shape vanishes. I don't remember waving back, but I must have because when the phone rings, I am frozen at that window with my hand raised in the air.

"Morning, Ryder," Grandpa says, his voice husky. "Something has happened to Elias."

"What?" I gasp.

"He died in a fire that destroyed all the DelMarco buildings last night and a good swatch of the forest around it too. I'm so sorry, Ryder. Still smoking up there. I'm out here in the front yard watching the plumes coming off the mountainside, bawling my head off."

I hang up the phone because a million bees are buzzing me deaf.

The official investigation into the fire and Elias's death is over by the time I return to Putnam about a month later. It is Thanksgiving Day. The conclusion: Elias Wolf started the fire and accidentally lost his life in it too.

Grandpa has turkey, stuffing, mashed potatoes, and piping hot gravy ready when I walk through the front door, dining room table set with white china, yellow roses circling rims. Ceramic pilgrims. Cornucopia of dusty, plastic fruit. How it has been every Thanksgiving of my life. The two of us sit down and begin pushing food around on our plates.

"How are your classes going?" Grandpa asks. "I can't believe you are a senior already."

I don't feel like small talk. I'd been thinking about the fire and what happened to Elias nonstop day and night for weeks.

"Elias intended to end his life," I say. "I am sure of it."

Grandpa jerks forward in his chair, sets his fork down beside his plate. I have never seen his mouth in such a flat, tense line, but there it is. Baggy eyes too. I wonder if he's been eating. If he has been sleeping. I know I haven't been.

"You don't look so great, Ryder," he observes.

"I was just thinking the same thing about you."

This comment lifts Grandpa's lips a millimeter. Not a smile exactly, but he looks more like himself.

"Elias used dynamite, right?" I ask. "Elias was way too smart to do anything careless with dynamite."

"Agreed," Grandpa says, nodding.

"Where would he have gotten his hands on dynamite anyway?" I ask, gagging on a small spoon of buttered peas.

"A few crates were missing from that private mining operation in Chatram."

Grandpa picks up his fork again. It hovers and trembles between us. He places the utensil back down.

"There's something else," he says, reaching his hand across the table, blanketing my wrist, patting it. "I was going to tell you after dinner, but it appears we will have to face this food together another time. Elias left an envelope here for you a few days before the fire. I wasn't home, but Frank Cowley was out behind his house at his compost, and he saw him going around the back of the house with a letter in his hand. I found it between the kitchen door and the screen."

I shoot to my feet. Grandpa pushes his chair away from the table, walks to the kitchen for the envelope. It seems all our movements are in slow motion.

Upstairs, I close my bedroom door, then crack it back open an inch or so.

On the envelope, Elias's printed letters: FOR RYDER.

White dots drop in my peripheral vision, droves of doomed meteors.

I place the envelope unopened on my bed and drag the box from my closet I packed before I left for my freshman year in college.

Inside, the sweatshirt with Elias's faint handprint and a stack of his posters I'd managed to rescue and save over the years. Grandpa never complained about driving me to DelMarco Lumber late on Sunday evenings to check for new posters. He never asked me why I wanted to save them either. If he had, I wouldn't have had an answer. Sorting through them again, I still don't have one. Not exactly, anyway.

So many maimed, murdered animals, posed perfectly, stare back at me: skunk, porcupine, fox, raccoon, hedgehog, wild turkey, several white-tailed deer, including the pretty doe from that night with Elias on the side of Bald Knob Road. At the bottom of the box, a handful of newspaper clippings about Mrs. Wolf and the investigation that followed her death. I place the posters and newspaper clippings on my desk, drape the sweatshirt over my desk chair, set the empty box back inside the closet, and shut the door.

I open Elias's envelope standing at my bedroom window. There is the photograph of me kneeling behind the pretty doe. I am looking to the side of the camera's eye. A cold mist glistens on my cheeks.

I can still hear Elias's boots crunching back and forth over strewn gravel that night, searching for the best angle to capture that shot.

When I turn the photo over, in Elias's freehand this time, it reads: *To Ryder Sycamore Clement. Love, Elias Sedric Wolf.*

"Elias. *Sedric*. Wolf," I whisper.

Sedric is nothing short of a legendary middle name, but Elias Wolf of Putnam, West Virginia, didn't need a middle name.

As for the "Love" part, I am sure he included that to soften the blow. He cared about me in the same way he cared about his family, his town, his mountains, all the animals whose eyes he so reverently closed. The same way I care. The reason he knew I would never let Putnam go, either. I hope that thought came to him near the end—that he could count on me.

Outside, a gusty wind whistles and howls. The final leaves of autumn are letting go, falling in a familiar rhythm I recognize every year and forget about until I see it again. This night a nearly full moon glows over the roof tops of Putnam. The distant shapes of the downtown clear and precise. Pointy top of the Methodist church steeple, domed roof of the high school, stadium lights at either end of the football field, and beyond that, the back of Bald Knob Mountain rising above us all.

Queenie

Queenie lived in an Airstream silver bullet trailer at the edge of a precipice on Black Hawk Mountain. Far below, deep in the throat of a gorge, Beech River slithered silently by. As far as anyone in my village of Concord knew, Queenie never left that precipice during the seven years she remained among us. No need for supplies or human intimacy of any kind.

Queenie and her trailer arrived on July 25, 1961, the day a section of the Black Hawk Mine collapsed and flooded. I was eleven. Women wailed and coffins lined up in the church cemetery but the horror of the catastrophe, five men lost and multiple injuries, wasn't the same for me as it was for most of the other inhabitants of Concord. My father wasn't a miner as his father had been. He went to medical school and returned to Concord to become the town doctor.

There were only two grand houses in Concord, both owned by the Phoenix Company. Phoenix also owned and operated Black Hawk Mine. Dad and I lived in one of those houses. My friends lived in small houses, shared cramped beds with siblings. Mr. Franklin, the overseer of the mine, lived in the other grand house next to ours. He instituted longer shifts, shorter breaks, paltry pay raises, and, worst of all, many of the old timers blamed him for the collapse and the flood in the mine: despite their protests, he had authorized new work on a vein dangerously close to an abandoned shaft known to be filled with ground water.

Our house had a turret with a surround of stained-glass windows, alternating diamonds of peach and turquoise, a deep, wide plank front porch, intricate gingerbread trim decorating the upper eaves and two chimneys. The inside rooms boasted fine furnishings, oil paintings, lace curtains imported from Belgium that rippled with elegance on windy days.

Apparently, my mother cherished those curtains, but she didn't enjoy them for long. She passed during my birth.

On the morning Queenie arrived, Sheriff Lots and one of his deputies went to investigate something near the top of Black Hawk Mountain reflecting the sunrise. They discovered no tracks leading up the mountainside, but they found an old woman in black garb. She explained she was just passing through. Inexplicably, her trailer appeared well rooted into the ground, with tall grasses and wild vines already climbing up the sides. The woman seemed harmless, so she was left in peace. The name "Queenie" soon attached to her, perched as she was on a mountain precipice resembling a throne.

A rumor soon began spreading that Queenie was the soul of the Black Hawk Mountain, that the mine accident had uprooted her, and either she didn't know how to get back inside the mountain, or she didn't want to. Folklore wasn't unusual in Concord, but it had always been set in the past.

"Do mountains have souls?" I asked Dad.

"No," he answered right away, as was his habit. He was in the parlor seated beside a brass floor lamp with two roaring lion heads for feet, reading the evening paper before dinner prepared by Mrs. Finch. It annoyed Dad when I bothered him once he had tucked himself behind newsprint, but it was the time of day I could get his attention.

"You don't think Queenie is the soul of the mountain like everyone else?"

"No, I certainly do not. I am a man of hard science, Violet. Queenie is a human being who wishes to live alone, as is her right, and that is all she is."

"But she did show up here overnight. How did that trailer of hers get all the way up the mountain? There's no road. No one heard or saw a thing."

I leaned over, placed my fingertips inside the gaping mouth of one of the lions. I had this fantasy that someday one of those parlor beasts would bite down, but I wasn't afraid. My reflexes were fast. I would escape harm. It was a taunt of sorts, a secret game I played.

"You are smarter than that. I am sure there is an explanation. Whatever that is, it is none of anyone's business."

"Sheriff Lots asked around in some nearby counties, and no one has ever seen or heard of anyone like her."

"That proves nothing," Dad huffed, clucking his tongue, then lowering his paper so he could frown at me.

He looked more tired than usual. Eyes bloodshot. He was still treating men who had been injured in the mine collapse.

"A mountain is an inanimate object like a slab of wood." Dad waved at the logs beside the fireplace waiting to be burned.

I wanted to frown back at him, but I didn't dare.

"But wood comes from trees. Trees are living things. They grow. They drink water. Maybe trees have souls too."

Dad raised his newspaper back into reading position, tipped his chin. "The subject is hereby permanently closed."

The coming of Queenie was the beginning of good fortune in Concord at a time when we needed it most. When a drought hit West Virginia and surrounding states, rain continued to fall steadily on Concord and its nearby farms. When a hurricane swelled Beech River until it jumped its banks, the flood waters galloped across land, arrived at Concord's town limits, and halted. Dogs, cats, hamsters, pets of all kinds began living longer. Apple trees doubled their harvest. We had an abundance of butterflies in our flower gardens. The fish from Beech River tasted sweeter. Most people, except Dad, thanked Queenie for these blessings.

Even though instructed by grown-ups that Queenie had a right to privacy, the desire to see her exerted a strong draw upon the youth in Concord. In the years that followed, it became a rite of passage to make the trek to Queenie's place at least once during teenage years.

At fifteen, I finally went to see Queenie. After four years of nothing but secondhand stories, I was sick of ignoring the pull of my gut to see her. I admitted to my diary that I wondered if she was calling for me to visit her. Predictably Dad wasn't happy about it, but he could tell by the set of my jaw that I wasn't asking for permission.

I hiked there with two of my closest friends, Darla Pickford and Sarah Martin, on a sunny day in early May. We faced a steep climb we knew would soon have our legs burning, so we got an early start. We made a straight row of paper-doll girls in bell bottoms, flowered peasant tops, and choker necklaces. We hiked silently, for the most part, save some nervous chitchat about the boys we liked and the girls we were jealous of.

Halfway up the mountainside we rested, thinking we'd have a picnic, nibble the sandwiches we'd packed, sip thermos water. No one felt able to eat or drink. We were a trio of combustible nerves. If it had been physically possible, we would have sprinted the rest of the way up that impossibly sharp incline. Once underway, a desperation to get the whole thing over with descended heavily upon us. This was *our* chance to tamp down the same misgiving that prickled along every spine in Concord until they were able to put their pilgrimage to Queenie's place behind them.

Days, months, seasons had passed with Queenie remaining a complete enigma.

"I kind of want to turn back," Sarah admitted, balancing her sandwich on her stomach. She was sprawled on her back, staring up at clouds puffing across the wide expanse of blue sky like a locomotive. The air was still where we were; grasses, branches, and leaves appeared glued into place. I ignored Sarah's remark. A growing part of me wanted more than anything to turn around and let my feet fly down the mountain too.

"When are you going to lose the Pipi Longstocking braids?" I teased Darla as a distraction. Darla was practicing handstands. "You've had those things poking out from the sides of your head since fourth grade."

Darla popped to her feet. Turning towards me, she shielded her eyes. "Never ever."

"Aren't you guys just a little afraid?" Sarah asked in a shaky voice.

Darla and I exchanged worried glances. Sarah tended to be on the panicky side at times. She'd lost an uncle in the mine accident.

"Nothing scary or bad has ever happened to anyone who visited Queenie," I told her.

"I know," Sarah mumbled.

"It's been so long now," I continued. "It's not like anything is going to change today. Everyone says they don't know what all the fuss is about."

I was only speaking the truth. Descriptions of Queenie had remained vague. An old, eccentric woman who liked to sing. Sometimes visitors never saw Queenie, only heard her singing from inside her trailer. Even those people said there was no need to go back because there was so little to see.

"Violet is right," Darla backed me up. "We are going to see what everyone else sees. A lot of 'nothing much.'"

"There's a first time for everything," Sarah said. "The whole mine never collapsed before."

"Technically, the whole mine didn't collapse," I said, immediately aware of how much I sounded like Dad. "There was a pit wall collapse on one level of the mine. The investigators said it will likely never happen again."

"Really?" Sarah's tone turned sharp. "How do *you*—how do *they*—know? No one can predict the future."

"Let's just get going already," Darla said, tossing a cookie toward a squirrel who snatched it and sniffed. "If we hurry, we can be home in time to go see a movie tonight."

"Great idea," I said and began packing up with Darla. "They are showing *Breakfast at Tiffany's*."

That news made Sarah sit up. She'd been wild about *Breakfast at Tiffany's* when the three of us saw the film the first time. I wasn't crazy about it. New York City seemed like a fairy tale. Still, a second viewing wasn't a bad idea. Maybe I'd change my mind about New York. Maybe I'd move there someday.

An hour later, physically spent, we hobbled up to a small grove of dense trees not far from Queenie's place. From the tree grove, we could have hurled a stone and pinged Queenie's front door. One of the wilder ideas about Queenie was that if you ventured any closer to her than the grove, you'd be struck by lightning, and the echo of your teeth chattering would rise up out of the hollow that was the Black Hawk Gorge for all eternity.

The first thing we saw was a bunny who hopped out from under a holly bush. The three of us Nervous Nellies startled and jumped. The bunny eyed us, twitched her whiskers. Turning tail, she bounced in the direction of Queenie's place. Next, a robin sang out clear as a bell.

"If birds and bunnies aren't afraid, then we shouldn't be either," I whispered.

Darla nodded a bit too exuberantly.

"I'm not afraid anymore," Sarah added unconvincingly.

We parted thick leaves to gain a clear view of Queenie's place. Sarah's hand flew to her mouth to hush a gasp. Queenie was outside. She had her back turned toward us. She was singing while polishing her front door with a crimson cloth in steady, even circles.

I couldn't imagine that the silver on her trailer could be glossier than it already was. Just a few direct glances at the trailer had already rendered me sunspot-blind, but perhaps Queenie's trailer was like Genie's magic lamp in *Aladdin*. If Queenie rubbed her trailer in this exact way, then the trailer would grant her wish. Maybe that's how she'd been bringing good fortune to the people of Concord.

The thing that stuck me the most, though, was how naturally the silver trailer belonged on the side of Black Hawk Mountain, as if it had grown out of the soil.

Queenie herself had brilliant white hair lopped off unevenly, close to her scalp. At first, I thought her outfit was composed of strips of black fabric stitched together and fitted tightly to her form, which was female, tall, thin, and small-breasted, but when the wind suddenly stirred, the strips plumped up and beat against her sides like a crow drying off after a cloudburst. I realized her body was covered in massive, purplish black feathers. My mind raced toward a rational explanation, but the feathers were much too large to be the feathers of a crow, and her limb moved as a wing flapping.

The air was filled with Queenie's singing. An entrancing sound, as others had reported. Part of me worried it was a spell that would render us unable to remember what we were about to witness at the top of Black Hawk Mountain, but it was impossible not to fall in love with that voice. My friends were already swaying back and forth, eyes shut. I felt as though I was floating, sore feet dangling limp in the air.

Queenie's slow tempo, husky alto yodel reminded me of thunder's echo when it rumbles back from a distant valley, seeming to say, *Here I am, I haven't left you.* I also thought of Beech River, the low note lullaby of the current when times of high water ceased: a river song I had listened to all my life from underneath my bed covers, assuring me the waterway was tucked safely between her banks once more.

Exactly how long the three of us stood mesmerized by Queenie's song, I am not sure, but it did come as a great shock when, suddenly, she straightened her spine and reached for the handle on her trailer door. I snapped back into reality. Was this how it was going to end? A cold rushed into my belly. I longed to see her face, and now my chance was slipping away. I was sure she'd sensed our presence in the tree grove the second we arrived there. It would be her choice whether we would have the opportunity to see more of her or not.

"Please turn around," I pleaded under my breath. "Please, please, please."

Sarah reached for my hand, grabbed it, began squeezing the life out of it. "Maybe we should just go," she whimpered.

"No," I hissed.

"But we've seen her now," Sarah whispered. "She sang and everything."

"Go ahead and leave if you want," I whispered, dropping Sarah's sweaty hand. "You can wait for me halfway down. I just want to see if maybe she'll turn around."

And then Queenie let go of the door handle. Her arm fell to her side, began swinging back and forth like a grandfather clock pendulum. As she turned around to face us, she did so in movements so gradual that the world slipped into slow motion along with her. My heart wound down to a clip and a clop, clip, clop. Darla remained at my side while Sarah retreated a few steps.

Queenie's eyes were larger than any human eyes I had ever seen. Glittery, black as anthracite. She raised her chin, glanced at Sarah over my shoulders, gave Darla a once-over, then settled her gaze upon me. I knew I was in the presence of the soul of Black Hawk Mountain and that I'd never be the same. Her trailer glowed brighter and brighter as if, any minute, it would burst into a star. My heart skipped wildly. The hairs on my arms stiffened, stood straight up.

Seconds later, Queenie disappeared inside her trailer. I was gasping for air by that time. We turned and ran.

I wheezed once we slowed down, "Her eyes were huge and shiny as glass!"

"I don't know," Sarah surprised me by jumping right in, sounding all together composed and downright cheerful. "I didn't notice her eyes. Her hair was really short. She had a friendly smile."

"What about her outfit?" I tried again. "What was that?"

"She was wearing a long dress," Sarah answered. "The kind old ladies wear in the summertime. She looked okay to me."

"The dress hung on her like a sack," Darla said. "She needs a belt, but she didn't look too bad. What was the matter with her eyes?"

"She looked like any old woman," Sarah added. "Maybe we shouldn't have bothered to walk all that way."

"Agreed," Darla said.

"But she looked weird to me," I sputtered. "What about how she flapped her arm like a bird?"

"What?" Darla said. "I didn't notice that."

"Me either," Sarah said.

Had I let my imagination get away from me? I began coughing to clear my throat.

"Are you alright?" Sarah asked, her cornflower-blue eyes flying open.

"Are you choking?" Darla asked, stopping to swat me hard on the back.

That swat made me cough even more. When Darla swatted me again, I fell to my knees.

"Violet!" Sarah was in a true panic now. "What's the matter?"

I managed to push myself up off the ground, though my legs were trembling.

"I'm fine," I announced in a forceful tone. "It's just spring allergies. Gives me asthma. The sooner I can take my medicine, the better."

"I never noticed you had allergies," Darla said, hands on her hips, head cocked.

"How about a bet?" I suggested, forming a grin. "When we get to the sign for the town limits, we race to the Esso Station. Whoever wins gets to go to the movies tonight, free, buttered popcorn included. Deal?"

"Throw some Sugar Babies in and it's a deal," Sarah said eagerly, though she looked worried.

"I'm in," Darla said. "But it's Good & Plenty for me."

Sarah was skipping her way toward the start of the race, with Darla and I trailing behind. Her chances of a free movie ticket were high. She was a fast runner. I struggled all the way to the town sign, panting like a dog.

"Hey, you don't look good," Darla said. "You wait here with Sarah. I'll go get your dad."

"No. It's just this asthma. I'll take medicine as soon as I get home."

I'd have to think of something later to explain this sudden asthmatic condition of mine because one of them was bound to ask Dad about it.

Sarah won the race to the Esso Station. Relief flooded over me when the three of us finally parted. I dug deep and found enough energy to walk the rest of the way home.

I'd been aware of the black bird that had been tailing us all the way from Queenie's place and didn't dare look skyward for fear of tipping off my friends. But I stopped now to watch as the bird flapped upward and perched atop the turret of my house, a beady-eyed gargoyle, her caw anguished and familiar.

The roofline and outline of my house and its identical twin, as it appeared to me that evening, had turned into two hideous monsters. If I had had anywhere else to go, I would have. Why hadn't I seen them this way before? Their structures, against the darkening sky, were all wrong for Black Hawk Mountain's gentle, moss-green valley of rounded hills: everything about them brutal and out of place. The stark, sharply cut angles, the oversized windows as alarming as gaping stab wounds. The turrets, something I had loved all my life, were the worst of all. Nothing but silly, showy appendages. Grotesque tumors. And then the adjoining backyards, the stone pathway linking the two dwellings permanently together. A pathway trellis laden with wisteria. Lavender blossoms I long admired had taken on the appearance of the fingers of a cascading poison. I hurried to my room. Sank onto my bed.

That evening, before the movie, I gathered myself together and went to find Dad in the parlor. He was watching the doorway as I entered the room, ferocious lions still salivating near his feet. His newspaper sat untouched on the table beside him. There was a squat, cut crystal glass of amber liquid on top of the newspaper. Dad rarely had a drink. He nodded once and cleared his throat.

"How did it go today?" he asked. "You look pale. Did you drink enough water during the hike?"

"Yes. It was a long walk. Queenie was outside."

I padded over to the fireplace mantle to stand instead of taking my customary chair across from Dad.

"What did you think of her?"

"She was interesting-looking. I don't think she's just an old woman if that's what you are asking."

Dad cocked his head at me. His lips disappeared into a thin, straight line as he folded his arms across his chest. "What was she then?"

I can't say he was mocking or teasing me. He unfolded his arms, folded them again, crossed his legs, uncrossed them, turned his head to look out the front window where there stood a massive oak in the front yard still holding my childhood swing. The clock on the mantle ticked and ticked.

"Did you ever think that we shouldn't live in a house like this when no one else does except Mr. Franklin?"

Dad's eyebrows arched. "This house is part of my compensation for providing medical care to the miners and their families at a discounted rate. Phoenix wants them to have the best medical care possible."

"So Phoenix can have workers who can keep making truckloads of money for Phoenix," I said. "You've said many times that the miners themselves aren't paid nearly enough."

Dad stood up. "I care about the people of Concord. You know that."

"They work underground, Dad, get injured and sick with things they would never get if they weren't miners. And sometimes they die."

"I can't stop the mining industry."

All I could do was shake my head. For the first time in my life, I was ashamed of my father.

Three years later, Mr. Franklin suffered a darkly biblical death. I was a senior in high school when a lightning bolt rained down upon his driveway one morning. The momentous crack woke me. Our house was engulfed in bright light. The mighty beams holding the house together shuddered. Roof rafters groaned. The turret windowpanes screamed a million tinkling deaths back and forth to each other. Dad ran to Mr. Franklin's aid, but it was too late.

Shortly after, Phoenix closed the Black Hawk Mine, profits from coal mining being down everywhere, and Queenie disappeared as mysteriously as she'd come. With giant boulders now blocking the wound on her side, the former entrance to the mine, she no longer had to watch over the mining families of Concord. That's what everyone believed, maybe even Dad, though he never admitted it.

Homecoming

Jillian Reese is sipping a venti Starbucks Green Tea Frappuccino on a bench in the Men's Department of Nordstrom. So far, for the occasion of her fiancé's return after a three-year deployment in Afghanistan, she hasn't garnered the energy she needs to begin searching for something special to wear on the day she welcomes him home. Her plan is to continue sitting and sipping until inspiration strikes.

Jillian practically grew up inside this store: trailing behind her mother's shoes. Brown snow boots with black fur trim in wintertime. Pastel, strappy sandals in the hot weather. When she was a child, department store mannequins were different. Then, they looked like real people. Male mannequins in pleated shorts and short-sleeved golf shirts with muscled arms hanging relaxed by their thighs. Overly animated child mannequins frozen in action shots as if by camera flash. Plastic boys and girls kneeling on sleds, catching primary-colored beach balls, or plopped down on shiny, alabaster knees, tying bandanas on dog mannequins. Jillian remembers gripping their hard, little hands. Tracing the impressions depicting the fingernails. Pretending they could all be one big, happy pack of friends, running around the store after hours, climbing up onto counters, eating bowls of ice cream in the café.

Jillian examines the store mannequins posed around her now. The preference of this decade is that store mannequins must not resemble living human beings at all. Most of them have no heads. In place of heads, plateaued rows of smoothly severed necks top the plastic bodies scattered throughout quiet, carpeted sales floors. The mannequins that have been allotted heads have no faces. Only hills and valleys suggesting eyes, a nose, lips, a set of teeth.

What happened to all those bright-eyed, realistic, cheerful mannequins from her childhood? Are they in some back storage room now, smushed together, staring into each other's necks, noses poked into ears, layered with dust? Or were they gathered up and crushed at a recycling center? Jillian clears her throat, hoping to unearth some store personnel, a human being who might know the answer, but the store appears emptied of hired help. Jillian uncrosses her legs. Her left leg is numb. Her whole body feels numb. Brain too. She's been detached from the real world for over a week now, watching her own body going through the motions of someone else's life. Jillian sighs. Groans.

Jillian still remembers the day her mother stopped so abruptly in the Women's Department on the third floor that Jillian plowed right into the back of her. A mannequin with shoulder length, messy brown hair, peach lips, and a row of smiling teeth had captured her mother's attention. Of course, she got a cross "Jillian!" and a scolding glare. Shopping was serious business with Mother.

"I think this lady could use an appointment with Velma, but her smile is just perfect, so lovely, and isn't this an elegant coat?" Dorothy Reese had purred. "If I had all the money in the world, I would own a winter-white coat just like this one."

Jillian, left with a ticker tape of her own thoughts, had reached up to stroke the coat's soft fabric, smooth as horseback. The coat wasn't white, though. It was beige. White was freshly fallen snow. White was powdered sugar on funnel cakes. And the mannequin's mouth was completely out of whack. No different than the dentures that resided inside Velma's mouth, her mother's hairdresser, lending a horselike quality to both women.

Jillian glances down at her Starbucks cup. At the age of twenty-seven, she has finally secured a good-paying job as a paralegal. She can afford treats like this now. And hanging in the hallway closet of her own townhouse, a new, belted, black cashmere coat ready for winter's bluster. Burberry. Not winter white, but her fashion-crazy mother, who moved to Paris years ago, would approve of the coat no matter the color. It has a designer name.

Since Jillian's engagement, her mother has been begging Jillian to come to Paris. To see the sights, of course, but also her mother wants to buy her a couture wedding dress from the city of lights. The promise of a Parisian wedding dress is no longer exciting and glamorous. Now, the whole idea feels ridiculous and self-aggrandizing.

Nearby, one of the new-age mannequins, a glossy, yellow suggestion of a man, waits stoically for someone or something beside the entrance to the Men's Fitting Room. Poor guy. Stark naked. No head. Below his broad shoulders, arms that end where elbows should be. Truncated. Lopped-off. Stumps. Such repulsive words. Someone should come around and dress this poor guy. That's the least they could do. Jillian leans forward, gags audibly, then tosses her unfinished Frappuccino into a trash can. The drink tasted off from the first sip. Sour. Something spoiled about it.

Jillian is engaged to Kyle Richardson, a former Lenape High School star quarterback. A Marine who happened to be in a Humvee near a land mine that blew to hell and took most of his right arm with it. It has been nine days since his accident. Jillian has been receiving steady updates from Kyle's mother, Tess, via text message since it happened.

She checks her phone now. No new messages. Scrolling up, she rereads some old ones from her future mother-in-law.

Kyle is stable. Bleeding under control. Pain managed. Thank GOD!

The other Marine didn't make it. DEVASTATING! Kyle's in shock. To be expected.

Kyle should be up to talking to us soon.

The doctors say Kyle will heal quickly. He's very strong. The US military has the most state-of-the-art prosthetics. Just above the elbow is a fortunate thing. Confirmed that he has full movement of that shoulder. Thank God for our blessings.

Kyle will be back in the States by the end of the week. Still isn't up to talking but his nurses say he is doing well, and he sends his love.

We asked about bringing Roscoe, but the request was denied. No civilian dogs allowed on base.

Jillian folds her hands in her lap and tries to picture herself at the base standing with Kyle's mother and father, his four brothers, and little sister, Alice. It's true that Roscoe should be there too. Kyle is crazy about that dog. Probably launched a million neon tennis balls far and wide across cornfields, plowed to stubble for the black lab to gallop after and retrieve, tail wagging his whole body.

Jillian shakes her head.

It's unforgivable to think of fun and games at a time like this. How dare she recall Kyle's arm arching back like the arm of a Roman gladiator as the Colosseum erupts with cheers. She wishes she saw golden javelins, paper airplanes, tomahawks, sparrows, or frisbees flying through her nightmares. Anything other than what she does see during her restless nights: Kyle's right arm tossing those bright tennis balls for Roscoe or Kyle's right arm hurling a simple, brown ball farther and better than any other boy from their hometown ever had. All those Hail Marys that delivered the Lenape Tigers to victory, obliterated state records and some national ones too.

Jillian rereads the last text from Tess:

We'll pick you up at 7 a.m. on Friday. I asked again. No Roscoe. Alice wants to sneak him in. I told her he barks too much.

Jillian stands up, turns her back on the Men's Department and its soulless mannequins, and walks toward the other stores inside the mall.

On Friday morning, Jillian and Kyle's family wait at a grassy area with picnic tables for the arrival of Kyle's aircraft. Jillian glances up at the heavens. A gray, humid day. Rain threatening. Wind picking up. Clouds slung low and heavy-bellied.

The Air Force base reminds Jillian of the Playmobile Airport her younger brother Seth used to have. Plastic airplanes. Doors and hangars that opened and closed. Landing wheels that rotated. A giant's child would have a lot of fun at an Air Force base. The child could plop down right in the middle of things, tattoo the earth with a jagged crack. She might pluck one of these transport planes off the tarmac and make the giant, gray whale of a thing soar. Shred up these rain clouds. Maybe she could pinch Kyle's plane out of the ominous sky and set it down safely right in front of Jillian's nose.

Military personnel stream past: navy blue or drab olive-green fabrics, sharp corners, ironed cuffs, expert tailoring, shoes shining without the light of the sun. No stooped backs. No tilted chins. Brisk salutes here and there. The occasional exchange of a sentence or two. A general lack of loose hair. Crewcuts. Tight buns. Caps. Heads that turn to acknowledge Jillian's group with respectful nods. Wide-eyed as Seth's Playmobile people.

Kyle's parents are talking with the parents of other returning servicemen and women, exchanging notes on location of service, length of missions. Kyle's brothers and Alice listen intently. Watching their parents, they nod and smile. Jillian can't seem to focus on the exchange of words. It is difficult to breathe.

Since the news of the accident, Jillian has been going over the features of Kyle's face from her memories. She's been dusting, smoothing, touching up, and resting her lips upon the clay bust of Kyle she tends to inside her brain. Kyle's patented, sheepish grin. His twinkling, crinkling eyes. How he looks when he is teasing her, telling her one awful joke after another.

She has never seen Kyle in agony, but Kyle must have cried out when the accident happened. He must have screamed: his features contorted by the pain and horror of it. In those initial moments of blood and gore, Kyle would have looked like someone Jillian has never seen.

In his official Marine photograph from five years ago, Kyle appears stoic and, because she knows him so well, also amused by something, though now she can't imagine what that could possibly be. Didn't he know something awful like this might happen to him if he enlisted in the Marine Corps? Even then. Even on that day when they were both so young. Neither of them thought anything like this could happen to their life story, but they should have. If only she had talked him into a technical school. Something that had nothing at all to do with the military and never would.

Jillian glances down at the dress she bought to wear to this homecoming and frowns. She is a monstrous, iridescent termite trapped inside a hill of industrious, sensibility-dressed worker ants in this white dress with the crimson flowers from ZARA. In the store's dressing room, the flower petals had appeared more muted, the whole dress more tasteful. But here, among monochromatic people and identical brick buildings, her choice of attire is nothing short of ridiculous. No need for black. Kyle isn't dead. Others have suffered so much more. But no need to look like she's about to attend a luau on her Hawaiian honeymoon and she's cheerful as hell about it. If only she could ask one of these military people if she could borrow a sweater or a jacket. Anything colorless.

She needed professional advice at ZARA, but just like Nordstrom that morning, no employees as far as the eye could see. When Jillian stepped out of her fitting room, a woman was standing there, about Jillian's age, gawking at the beam emanating from her iPhone. She was waiting for a friend to decide on a bikini. Jillian smiles bitterly now as the conversation replays.

I hate to bother you, but I was just wondering what you think of this dress.
I think it looks great on you. Love the red flowers.
Maybe it's too bright.
No, no. It's a rich color. A party or…?
No, no. Not a party. My fiancé is coming home after a deployment.
Deployment?
A military deployment. In Afghanistan.
Afghanistan?
You've heard of Afghanistan, right?
Yeah, I think so. Yeah, sure. I have. I have.
My fiancé is a Marine, and he was there.
Doing what?
There's a war there.
We're in a war? An active war? I didn't know that, actually. Er, sorry.
It's fine.

Where is the war again?
Are you fucking kidding me?

Jillian slammed the door to her fitting room and changed quickly as the two women whispered. Tamping down the urge to scream or worse, she stomped to the register, paid for the dress, and left.

She should have phoned her mother before going to the mall in the first place. Together they could have sorted out what Jillian should look like at this moment, standing on an Air Force base waiting to greet Kyle after such a long time apart, after all that has happened. At least she would have gotten that much right.

Jillian glances over at Tess Richardson. She is being so brave. Talking, smiling, even laughing with the others. Tess has always been nice to Jillian, but with four sons younger than Kyle, and Alice, Tess doesn't have much free time. Jillian should have texted her about what she was planning to wear. Tess is wearing black slacks, a gray blouse, pearl earrings, no makeup. Perfect.

"The plane will set down in about fifteen minutes," someone announces. Everyone cheers and claps except Jillian. Her mouth is stuck shut. Her arms are too heavy to lift.

Jillian strains to hear the drone of distant engines. She can only hear the snapping of flags on the tall metal poles nearby.

She can't know exactly what she will feel when she sees Kyle again, but she knows what she won't do.

She won't look at that side of his body where she imagines his shirt will be folded and neatly pinned or where there may be the crisscross of a truly white bandage peeking out.

She will set her eyes on his face instead.

She will hope like hell it looks like his face.

She will smile no matter what he looks like.

She will let his mother go to him first, his father, his siblings.

Then it will be her turn.

She won't embrace him.

She won't wrap her arms around him and hug him to her because what if he tries to squeeze her back and he can't, or it's awkward, or it hurts, or it's humiliating for him?

She will wait for Kyle to make the first physical move.

If he doesn't, if he can't, if he falters, she will open both of her palms wide.

She will place them gently onto the middle of his chest where his heart is.

Then she will reach her lips up toward Kyle's perfect mouth.

Dollhouse

One afternoon during every summer vacation, Deirdre is expected to slide into the passenger side of her grandfather's latest model of Subaru station wagon. The day will be a stormy day, when mountain hiking, swimming, and fishing are out of the question. "It's Great-Uncle Ralph Day," her grandfather will announce cheerfully, releasing the emergency brake with a pop. He never includes Great-Aunt Ethel in the anointed title of the annual visitation, but that is how Deirdre thinks of the day. Great Aunt Ethel Day. She can't wait to see Aunt Ethel.

At the end of the lane of dirt and cinder, just past Madge's Store and the Estella Lumber Mill, there will be Uncle Ralph in his bed. To be clear, there will be his feet, which are all Deirdre sees of the actual man. Just two tiny tombstones under the cloak of a gray woolen blanket.

One time, when Deirdre was five, she did see more. Aunt Ethel led her into Uncle Ralph's bedroom, where he sat in a corner chair, watching Deirdre's grandfather change his bedsheets. Aunt Ethel gripped Deirdre's hand so tightly it hurt. Underneath bushy, gray brows, Uncle Ralph's dark eyes never wavered from his younger brother's chore of tucking and smoothing. Deirdre whispered, "Hello," because she thought she should. When Ralph didn't swivel his neck or avert his eyeballs, Ethel's arm fell heavy across Deirdre's shoulders, and the two vanished from the room.

This visit, Deirdre is waiting for Ethel in the living room of the house as she always does, positioned on the edge of a loveseat cushion. To her right, Uncle Ralph's bedroom, about three yardsticks away, door cracked open wide enough so a person can slip through sideways. Deirdre never rests her back against the scratchy, burgundy, and gold damask of the loveseat. Once, the fabric must have been refined, elegant, but now it reeks of damp dog, pot roast, and mushy carrots. If only there was a real dog, and not just this sour reminder of Charlotte, the cocker spaniel, whom a logging truck smashed flat as a pancake a few Christmas mornings ago.

Inside the kitchen, to Deirdre's left, some cut of fresh, local beef roasts inside a cast iron dish in a wall oven. Between every lunch hour and dinner hour, meat sizzles and spits in that kitchen. Uncle Ralph insists upon well-done, daily beef. Deirdre summons the alternative smell and sounds of native rainbow trout frying in a stainless-steel pot, iridescent skin, pink enamel stovetop, her grandmother's kitchen several miles away. Some thoughts are strong enough to overtake reality. Inside her mind, Deirdre begins an incantation: "Trout, trout, trout."

The living room's other appointments match the formal, Victorian style of Deirdre's present perch: thick, gold-toned oriental rug with a meticulously combed fringe, glossy, cherry wood coffee table, ball-and-claw feet, polished copper toenails, two wing-backed chairs upholstered in the same raised, intricate brocade as the loveseat, cut crystal lamps centered over starched white doilies. The room reminds Deirdre of the dollhouse inside the Gettysburg Wax Museum. During their spring field trip, she and her sixth-grade classmates took turns peering through peepholes that magnified the decorated boxes and their furnishings. Uncle Ralph and Aunt Ethel's bungalow feels the same and all the better for it: just an optical illusion, a trick of the eye.

Aunt Ethel's prizewinning lavender and pink African violets reside in a tiered, wicker plant stand underneath front window drapes. The violets don't appear to be part of the real world either. They never have. Before every visitation, Deirdre's mother reminds her to compliment Ethel about the violets. "They are such challenging plants to grow, requiring just the right amount of sunlight and a healthy, daily dose of humidity. No one knows how to keep them blooming year-round the way Ethel does. Even your great-grandmother couldn't achieve that, although she cultivated some stunning violets too."

Deirdre isn't sure about adequate sunlight unless her mother means African violets prefer tightly closed drapes and artificial light, but there is adequate humidity here for sure. Being inside the bungalow is like being inside the interior of her grandfather's tobacco humidor. And she agrees. Ethel's African violets do not resemble any other African violets. Deirdre tries not to glance over her shoulder at the pots, but she does. She can't help it. They can't be vegetation. They are hairy and fat as if filled with bone, sinew, and vessels. Deirdre sits on her hands and fidgets, watches the stems pulse, longing to pinch just one of the gray-green leaves to confirm it bleeds.

Deirdre waits. Her grandfather visits with his older brother. The porcelain clock on the fireplace mantle ticks louder and louder. Deirdre stares at clock hands, feathery fine as spider legs, grows cross-eyed willing for some movement that will propel her own breathing along, infuse her lungs with air, but the arrow shapes never move even though the clock is deafening. The violets snicker behind Deirdre's back. There is so little oxygen in the room. All Deirdre can do is swallow and pant like poor Charlotte used to do on this loveseat cushion.

"Ethel. Ethel!" Uncle Ralph doesn't scream or holler as much as he gurgles words, stuffing them between coughing fits and spitting. Deirdre dreads the sound of the spitting even more than the motionless pounding of the living room's mantle clock.

Soon Uncle Ralph will clear his throat, cough, and spit. Ping! The sound will reverberate like a peach pit hitting brass. Deirdre's father has explained many times that Ralph keeps an object called a spittoon bedside. Deirdre avoids imagining the contents of the spittoon or how and where her aunt might empty it.

Ethel erupts from the fragrant kitchen now and scurries past Deirdre with a steaming mug in her hand, her steps resembling a woman with bound feet, an urgent, running tiptoe. She offers Deirdre a sideways glance, followed by a tired, weak smile. Ethel is wearing one of her floral print cotton dresses, a white apron, black stockings, and black shoes. If she had a white cap to fasten over her neat hair bun, Ethel could transform into the perfect Mennonite wife so common in this area of rural Pennsylvania. Ethel isn't Mennonite, even though she looks the part. It might be better if she was. Then she would have regular visitors from the congregation. As it is, she is alone here most of the time with Ralph.

Ethel slithers and disappears through the bedroom door, the last droplets of chilled bathwater vanishing down a drain. Deirdre enjoys the passing whiff of cinnamon sprinkled over the surface of a hot liquid. Deirdre's grandfather begins speaking.

"Try sitting up, Ralph. Maybe less tea, more water?"

"Shut up, Mark. Shut up and get the hell out of here. You jackass. Get out of my sight."

These remarks from Ralph are followed by the crash of something against one of the far bedroom walls. Deirdre hopes it isn't the tea Ethel spent time preparing. Ralph can be prone to throwing objects, and he is having a very bad day. Ethel didn't give Deirdre a hug when she and her grandfather arrived earlier. That is never a good sign.

Deirdre's parents have talked about how Ralph worked longer than any human being should have deep inside the Butte Dam Coal Mine.

There was a pending lawsuit against the mining company at some point, too, seeking help with medical bills, so Deirdre knows it was the mine that made Ralph sick in the beginning.

During some visits to the bungalow, the inside of Ralph's bedroom remains mercifully peaceful as Deirdre's grandfather tells Ralph about a bountiful sweet corn crop or the maple syrup camp's new copper vats, interspersed with soothing murmurs from Ethel, which sound like a cat purring on a lap to Deirdre sitting alone in the living room. On those good days, Ralph eventually falls into a roaring snore and Ethel emerges from the bedroom. She reaches for Deirdre's hand, and they venture in the opposite direction to the kitchen for homemade peanut butter cookies sealed inside a purple tin embossed with an image of Queen Elizabeth II's Coronation Day.

Queen Elizabeth II wasn't ever beautiful, but on that occasion, she did look lovely; dark, glossy hair, rosy cheeks, crimson lipstick. Sipping chocolate milk, sitting across an enamel table from Ethel, Deirdre can examine Ethel's features more closely. Unlike the English Queen, Ethel must have been very beautiful once: pale green eyes, slender nose, high cheekbones. Admittedly, the past is easier to imagine on days when Ethel doesn't have a black eye aged olive green, a bandage taped over puffy lips, or the pinkish glow of a paw print along the hollow of her throat.

Ethel's teeth are perfectly straight and white too. Surprising joy surfaces in her smile whenever she has the opportunity to watch Deirdre chewing her homemade cookies.

"I wonder which set will murmur today. Last summer, it was the Diamond Cup from Occupied Japan, or was it the Royal Vienna from Germany?" Ethel had asked the last time the two sat across from each other in the kitchen. Her lips were moving, but Ethel was really watching hummingbirds suspended like tiny, skittish helicopters around an outdoor feeder. Even though Ethel was talking to herself, Deirdre had answered.

"No, it was the Limoges from France stamped: *Strawbridge and Clothier.* The summer before that, it was the gold-rimmed cup with pink peony blossoms from Bavaria. Remember? I love them all, but you really don't have to give me any more dishes. You have given me so many already."

Ethel had stood then, opened the pantry door, and switched on bright, blinding bulbs that illuminated shelves stacked with thin papery teacups resting inside delicate, matching saucers. Deirdre knew there was no sense in refusing another gift from Ethel, and anyway, Deirdre never could. Something inexplicable drew her body toward the porcelain pantry.

No one would believe her except Ethel, but whenever Deirdre stands back, folds her arms over her heart, cocks her head to the left to examine the shelves, always one cup trembles, nods its rim forward like a chin, and chooses itself. They both see this happen. They both hear the tinkling. Ethel wraps the cup and saucer carefully in lavender-scented tissue paper for the journey to a new home with Deirdre.

Today, sadly, there will be no peanut butter cookies and no chocolate milk, and no teacup to take home. Uncle Ralph is having his worst day ever. Deirdre is ashamed because she is disappointed, and she feels sorry for herself. She has grown to love her blossoming collection of teacups. At home, she displays them on the dresser top in her bedroom, dusts them every week, rereads the names of the faraway, exotic places where they come from.

Besides the outline of Uncle Ralph's feet at the foot of his bed, Deirdre sometimes looks her great-uncle straight in the eye, but just one eye, a glass eye sealed inside a clear glass jar underneath his bed. When Deirdre was younger, Ethel would scurry into Ralph's bedroom and scoop the eye jar away if she wasn't too distracted to remember it was there, peering out at a child on a loveseat, her hands folded politely in her lap as in an overly formal portrait. Now that Deirdre is older, twelve this year, Ethel doesn't bother.

Through the narrow opening in the doorway, Deirdre inventories other items stowed under Uncle Ralph's bed: a baby-blue bedpan, a box of tissues, a round Big Ben alarm clock with a shattered face. Today, Ralph is tossing back and forth, rocking the bed, squeaking the frame. Below jumping box springs, his eye bobs and quakes inside its jar of water, a buoy on top of choppy sea. Every now and then the spinning pupil pauses in Deirdre's direction, winks once, then turns away.

The moment Uncle Ralph's draped toes vanish, Deirdre stops breathing. The bottom of the bed has morphed into a strange landscape: an unrecognizable desert inside a familiar frame. Deirdre feels her heart for the first time that day: as fast as her hamster's heart must have been beating the time it got its feet caught in an exercise wheel. The tiny, silvery bells on the wheel sounded like fairy music. Deirdre thought Rhoda was just having some extra fun, but then she dropped dead.

"Now, Ralph. Stop that. What are you..." Deirdre's grandfather's voice is higher pitched than usual.

Ralph and Mark look nothing alike. It is difficult to believe they are blood brothers, though they are: Mark, slim, fine-boned; Ralph, broad, strapping; Mark, educator, poet, natural gardening enthusiast; Ralph, big game hunter, log splitter, brute.

"Get out of here, Ethel!" Deirdre's grandfather cries.

Several heavy thumps against bedroom walls, but no Ethel. The tasseled lampshades inside the living room shake. Two African violets tumble to their deaths. White-dotted soil spills over vacuumed oriental. It reminds Deirdre of blood when it pours out more rapidly and spreads a lot farther than you expect a thick liquid could.

Glass crashes behind the bedroom door now. More wall thuds, followed by the groans and grunts of the two men struggling, and then a mechanical *CLICK-CLICK.*

Someone is choking.

"Ralph! Stop!" Deirdre rises at the sound of Ethel's voice, so desperate, so terrified.

When the shotgun sounds, real blood flies out of Deirdre's nose, even though she is nowhere near the danger. She is safe in here, in this living room, with the deafening clock, the hands that don't move, and the throbbing violets.

Next comes the heaviest of thuds yet, then silence.

Deirdre watches as a print of a covered bridge slides down the living room wallpaper toward the radiator like a tear.

Deirdre's grandfather appears at the bedroom door, wide-eyed and flushed. He swings the door open halfway, blinks at Deirdre, his mouth frozen in an oval shape, the same as the mouths of the caroler figurines her mother displays at Christmastime. Behind his shoulders, Deirdre glimpses the thin arms and trembling hands of her great-aunt still gripping a shotgun raised to her shoulder, nozzle pointed now at what must be Uncle Ralph's body on the other side of his bed, dead on the floor.

Deirdre's attention falls to something scurrying over the carpet toward her. Not a ghost. Not a mouse. No. The square toe of her grandfather's thick work boot has kicked the eye jar over, fanning liquid and jettisoning the orb in Deirdre's direction. Deirdre scoops up the eyeball, cold and wet, and turns toward the kitchen.

Outside, the hummingbirds have run away. Deirdre hops the back porch steps and begins running down the middle of the dirt and cinder road. It is almost a full mile to the Village of Estella. Madge will be sitting inside her store on a wooden stool behind a register. In a glass case, assorted candy: Atomic Fireballs, Owl Bubble Gum Cigars, Tootsie Rolls, Charms, and Black Licorice Pipes. The pipes are a stale and bitter candy. Outside, someone will be filling his truck with gas from one of the round, red pumps that look like life-sized cherry lollipops from a distance.

Further along the road, a Mennonite convalescent home where

Deirdre wishes Ralph could have lived all these years. An American flag will be curling and unfurling at the top of a shiny brass pole in the yard.

When the paved road and the green entrance doors of the lumber mill come into view, Deirdre walks into the woods. There, under tree monoliths, she drops to her knees, begins clawing a hole through fragrant pine needles. The earth is dense and heavy with orange clay. Deirdre winces and plunges further, hurling earth from side to side, howling, snot flying, digging blind by the end. Finally satisfied, she sits back, lifts blackened, bloodied fingernails to her nose, inhales nutty sweetness, dabs her eyes dry with her shirt.

A salmon-colored string drops out of nowhere at the bottom of the grave, wiggles: an earthworm, turner of dirt layers, seamstress of air and nutrients into soil's fabric. The little miracle tunnels and is gone by the time Deirdre pushes the glass eye deep into the bottom of the hole with her thumb, pupil down, so it can see where it is going.

Due North

Daniel Troyer and Faye Croft have been walking farther and farther from the shapes of their neighborhood every day. The weather has warmed. Evenings stay bright. After suppertime, there is nothing to do at the dead end of Clover Street. Dirty dishes harden inside the kitchen sink at Daniel's house; his mother, Candy, deep into reruns of *Hollywood Squares*, gin, 7Up, and ice tinkling inside a metallic tumbler. She has a case on the center square, Paul Lynde. By the time the lighted squares extinguish and the wide-open pastures of another oldie, *Bonanza*, pan into view, the two friends will be nearly a mile away from their homes.

Faye's father, Jeremy Croft, sits inside the house next door, reading his feathered copy of the King James Version of the Holy Bible. The den where he reads is cave-quiet, save the ticktock of the mantel clock and the man's growling gut. His taste buds flickered and fizzled out when he lost his wife to breast cancer. He subsists on God now, pouring over verses every evening, black coffee plus three shots and several more of Jameson Irish Whiskey by his side.

Jeremy Croft warns his daughter Faye that God dwells only within the pages of the Old Testament. Jesus can't be trusted. He talked too much about something dubbed the "good news." God's son was the original sugar-coater, running around the desert wrapping up pretty packages. "There's only so much mercy to go around. Look what happened to your gentle, dear mother."

Daniel's father, Lance Troyer, hasn't found God yet, not as far as anyone around the town of Hillsborough knows. What Lance Troyer did find was his son's twenty-year-old, fourth-grade student teacher. Daniel liked Miss Dixon before everything happened between her and his dad.

She decorated times table cards with Power Ranger stickers, brought homemade Rice Krispie treats on Fridays.

Last July, just as the sun was peeking over the rooftops of the businesses along South Main Street, Lance Troyer, Miss Dixon busy in his lap, drove his wife's candy apple-red Pontiac Firebird out of Hillsborough for the last time. He left town with his clothes, his fishing pole, his shotgun, and everything in the family bank account.

"At least he didn't take Cougar," was all Faye could think of to say to Daniel the day his father left. Daniel did love his dog, Cougar, more than his dad. Daniel had nodded, crying quietly. That was also the first day the two began their routine of walking away together. Once supper ended, it seemed no one was keeping an eye on either of them, so they just went.

At first, they would walk as far as the Timber Dump on top of the hill behind Clover Street and turn back, but soon they began following the one-lane dirt road that led away from the dump.

Tonight, when Daniel pulls his dad's old compass out of his shorts pocket, Faye frowns. Daniel has become obsessed with that thing, but Faye doesn't have the heart to try to convince him to get rid of it. He likes it too much. He found the army-issued compass, two tins of Wintergreen Skoal, and an unused Victor mousetrap in one of his dad's emptied dresser drawers. Daniel tossed the chewing tobacco, which Faye sniffed and agreed was putrid, along with the mousetrap, into the yawning belly of the Timber Dump on the night of their first escape together.

Daniel's dad had it in for mice. Daniel routinely emptied the bait from the traps he set inside 203 Clover Street. Sometimes, Daniel would miss one, and he'd have to dig a grave or bandage a tail or a limb. He caught on quickly that medical procedures on mice work best before you open the trap. Tending to the rescued mice in his bedroom, Daniel admired how their whiskers tilted back and forth like miniature, merry chopsticks. The mice didn't exactly love Daniel back, but they didn't bite once they were free again and could romp around on the shag carpet.

"If we use this compass and stay due north, we can make it to the Eskimos, see their igloos, chew on whale blubber, ride sleds pulled by wolves, stay there, learn a trade, set up shop. I bet it's All-the-Ice-Fish-You-Can-Eat-for-Free up there in the great wide north," Daniel says now, like he does every evening. Faye marches beside him, struggling to match his fast clip. They are on their way back to the dump, then they'll go down the hill and on to home.

Daniel chews bubblegum like a hog. Huge, pink bubbles explode. "Daniel, I'm going deaf. Stop it."

"Come on. That's not loud enough to make you go deaf."

Faye glances over at Daniel's eyes, rolling dramatically above his bony shoulders.

"Stop rolling your dumb eyes. And slow down."

Faye wishes she'd grabbed a leftover hotdog from her dinner with her dad and whatever was left at the bottom of the chip bag. Last time Faye surveyed the refrigerator at Daniel's house, all she observed was a jar of murky, green liquid that used to contain Spanish olives, ketchup, mayonnaise, and a jar of Smucker's Concord Grape Jelly, all sitting in the same places they were last time Faye opened the door. The only difference was the mayonnaise had turned the pewter color of an old nickel.

The dump road is a rough, winding walk, the surface chewed up from truck tire treads. It rained hard last night, transforming the road into a serpentine of flapping, splashing birdbaths.

"I thought birds didn't like to be out when it's getting dark like this," Faye says. "We better not stop at the dump tonight. It's already dark. We should go straight home."

"Maybe," Daniel mumbles, head down, watching the compass arrow hop.

"We went exactly forty-three minutes past the dump tonight. That's the farthest we've gone. We still didn't find anything, Daniel. Nothing."

Daniel doesn't answer. Faye elbows him. He's hypnotized himself again with that silly compass. She's thirsty and hot, sick and tired of walking and walking and seeing nothing but pastures gone to seed, junked-up cars, and beady-eyed crows.

Still no answer. Another elbow.

"Daniel!"

Daniel blinks blankly over at Faye.

"There's nothing back there. We need another plan." Faye stomps once for emphasis. "Seriously."

"There's got to be a train track that runs back there," Daniel says. "One of these days we'll find it and head as far north as it will take us. Be patient. Did you know you can ride a thousand miles on the Iditarod Trail with your wolves?"

Faye moans and squints into the distance, trying to spot the silver, diamond-shaped sign for the Timber Dump. Once they reach that, it's sixty-seven steps to the dump's rim. Sometimes, they race those final steps.

"I've told you dogs pull the sleds, Daniel, not wolves, and I'm totally out on the blubber-eating thing. My legs are aching. Aren't yours?

71

We should have brought some water. I'd rather go south, live in Florida or Louisiana, a Cyprus forest, a bayou. Some place with a tree house that we need a canoe to get to, where there is a voodoo princess who stirs vats and hexes people if we ask her to," Faye finishes breathlessly.

She is thinking particularly of Gloria Trent, a classmate in school. She hates Gloria Trent. Her perfect blonde hair and all her new shoes. She'll put a hex on Gloria Trent.

"You wouldn't like it deep in the South," Daniel says. "You hate bugs. They got bugs as big as cats, rats with red eyes and razors for teeth, hungry alligators, and no water. If you think you're thirsty now, just wait. My uncle Todd says Florida is about out of water. Our best plan is to hop on a train and head for Alaska. We should start hiding clothes out near the dump. We'll bury stuff little by little so no one suspects anything."

"Suspect anything? No one goes to the dump on foot except for us. It stinks to high heaven. Even the truckers back up, tilt their beds, and hightail it out of there."

Faye knows she sounds cross, but she can't help it. If she could only sit down. When they finally make it back to the rim of the dump, Daniel doesn't look good. His face is chalky white.

"Are you okay?"

"I'm fine, I guess," Daniel answers.

The Timber Dump does stink, it's true, but it's always fun to see what ends up there. She and Daniel have a game. Whoever spots something new in the subterranean landscape first wins. If they find a new addition at the same time, the game continues. To cheer Daniel up, Faye pulls a flashlight out of her pocket and begins the familiar sweep.

"Ready?" she asks.

First, she illuminates the baby blue Volkswagen bug, nose down, silver fender coppery with rust. Then she rolls the circle of light over a tossed washing machine and dryer, mangled metal bed springs, filthy mattresses, busted swing sets, office chairs, file cabinets missing drawers, rotting wooden benches, tires, outdated chunky computers, high chairs, a forest-green tricycle with no seat.

"Ah!" Faye screams and drops the flashlight.

Daniel throws himself belly down just in time to save the flashlight from tumbling over the edge. The walls of the dump are steep. You'd slide down fast, but you would never be able to climb back out. Daniel jumps up, gripping Faye's flashlight.

"Faye?"

Faye grabs the other end of the flashlight, but Daniel doesn't let go. She gives the flashlight a tug. He tugs back.

"Daniel, there are *eyes* down there," Faye squeaks.

When Daniel sees tears on Faye's cheeks, he stops tugging, but he doesn't release the flashlight.

"Come on, Faye," Daniel whispers. "You know you didn't see eyes."

Faye's temper flares. She releases the flashlight and runs down the hill toward home. Daniel watches her black hair flap up and down like a soppy work shirt on a clothesline. Faye is scared of a lot of things. He's not scared of anything.

He shuts off the flashlight and listens. In the distance, a semi's horn wails. The rats are scurrying. Rat scurry is a sound that could be mistaken for long fingernails scraping back and forth across a mesh window screen, but not close to a dump with a sky swapping lilac for purple. Rats tunnel and leap as daylight fades. This evening is the same as every other evening on the rim of the dump, but just in case, Daniel calls out.

"Hello? I come in peace. Anybody down there? Do you need help?"

Hearing no response, Daniel looks upward at faint, distant flickers appearing one by one. Sometimes he is afraid that stars are "fictional," a term Miss Dixon taught him, but either way, real or not, something as pretty as constellations doesn't belong over a place as ugly as the Timber Dump or a town as boring as Hillsborough. Daniel suddenly wishes his no-good, two-bit dad would show up because he misses Daniel, his son, his only child, with all his heart and has been searching everywhere for him. That silly wish doesn't last long.

Come to think of it, the rat scurry does seem extra loud tonight.

"Hello? Is someone in trouble down there?" Daniel tries again.

Eventually Daniel flicks the flashlight back on, starts at the blue Bug, passes the circle of light over the familiar objects the way Faye did, but more slowly. There is plenty of stuff down there to hide behind if a person really wants to hide. When Daniel spots eyes, amber ones, his heart leaps too at first, but then he laughs. The eyes belong to something blind and long dead. A ratty, old deer head that someone got tired of looking at on their wall. It would be a cool thing to hang on his bedroom wall in Alaska, but he can't drag something that big that far.

With faint hope, Daniel searches for Faye's silhouette coming back up the hill. Maybe Faye doesn't have what it takes to help bring their dream journey to a happy ending. It's been bad for her, worse than for him. Daniel couldn't see how someone as sick as Faye's mom could walk, but Mrs. Croft walked to her mailbox every day, even on the day she died.

The skinnier she got, the bigger the teeth grew in her head. Eventually, when she smiled at Daniel, she looked like a set of dentures on a broomstick. Daniel doesn't bring it up to Faye, but whenever he sees a woman who resembles Faye's mom before she had cancer, he sends an ESP message to the woman's brain: Is something growing inside your boobs you should know about?

Faye is out of breath and sweaty by the time she makes it back to Clover Street. Although she wished otherwise, she knew Daniel wouldn't follow her. These days he doesn't listen to anything important she has to say. Always the boss. Eventually, Daniel will learn he doesn't know everything about everything. Faye knows plenty, and she knows what she saw up there at the dump. She could go and tell Mrs. Troyer what she saw, but Mrs. Troyer gets snappy when you pry her away from the Cartwrights and their Ponderosa ranch. Anyway, Daniel can run fast if he gets himself into trouble.

Instead of going inside, Faye plops on Daniel's back porch steps. Luckily, Daniel's mom left a glass bottle of 7Up, half full, under a reclining lawn chair from her afternoon's sunbath. The 7Up is warm, and there's some picnic-ant float, but it's still good. Faye gulps the soda; kicks open a pizza box leaning against the garbage can: two crusts with Mrs. Troyer's coral lipstick on them. Faye rips off the colored parts and saves the crusts for Daniel. Once he sees those eyes, he'll come flying.

—

The shrill screeches of seagulls bother some people, but never Faye. She is calling back to them in perfect pitch, locking the doors of Buccaneer's Bounty for the evening. Faye operates the beachfront gift shop year-round; the business of selling sunscreen, umbrellas, foldup chairs, skim boards, paddleball sets, buckets, and sand shovels has been picking up recently. It is early May. The weather has warmed. Evenings stay bright.

Several tourists are holding their phones in the air a few inches in front of their noses, recording Faye's conversation with the gulls. People come to Buccaneer's Bounty just to find Faye. She's a star on social media, or so her customers tell her. Faye never had any use for computers or electronic devices. Long ago, the world inside that web crowned Faye "the Witch of Sunset Beach."

Now that Faye is nearing forty, her given title works even better than it used to. Tourists are delighted with what stands before them: unruly, waist-length black hair streaked with glossy, silver bands, an ankle-length, black dress of multiple, jagged layers, red leather boots, heavy, amethyst eyeliner, and the oddity of a snow-white mouse in an ebony bird cage. After years of hauling heavy boxes of store merchandise, Faye stoops forward almost a full foot, naturally, gracefully. Even without a broomstick or a wart on the tip of her nose, Faye fits the part of an enchanting witch. It wasn't Faye's idea to become a witch, although she would be willing to admit that she had brought it upon herself.

The local writer's guild is working on a collaborative children's book about their beloved resident witch, for it is children who love Faye most. The witch patiently poses for pictures with the little ones, pays complete attention to every upturned, sun-touched face, drops surprise prize bags into tiny hands: cinnamon candy hearts, faceted gem rings, bouncy balls, temporary tattoos, kaleidoscopes. And in every bag, a plastic compass.

When curious children ask Faye how to use the compass, she answers. Practice and you'll find your way. The candy hearts turn the children's tongues bright red. Something that never fails to delight them. They ask the witch if she ever combs her hair. Is she over a thousand years old? Why doesn't she fly on a broom? Where is her cauldron, her black cat, her cackle?

"Every witch is different," Faye replies. "I don't have a cat, but have you met my mouse? You can pet him if you'd like. I can see he likes you already."

"It's a white mouse! Where's his tail?"

"It's a secret."

"Are you married?"

"No, but what do you think of Zoltar? I'm considering him. He's very handsome. Have you seen him on the boards inside his fortune-telling box, wearing that fancy, purple hat of his with the peacock feathers?"

"You're teasing. He's plastic."

"Don't be so sure. He is a good fortune teller, but I'm a better one."

"What's my fortune?"

"At a stroke past midnight tonight, a shiny crow will fly past your windowpane, and you will grow a whole half-inch just like that."

"Now me."

"This year you will make a special friend who will always keep your secrets safe."

"Do you know what the seagulls are saying?"

"Only sometimes."

"Do you turn into a seagull instead of a bat?"

"Not that I know of!"

Jeremy Croft moved Faye and himself to Sunset Beach two years after Daniel went missing, purchased Buccaneer's Bounty for a song from a man anxious to retire. It took two years for the authorities to halt their official search and declare Daniel Troyer: presumed dead. Faye didn't complain about the move. She was anxious to get away from Daniel's empty, unlit bedroom window. Daniel's mother moved to Wisconsin to live with her sister after she lost her son.

All those years ago, waiting on the Troyer's back porch for Daniel to get back from the dump, Faye chewed and swallowed one of the pizza crusts she'd been saving for Daniel, then counted to five hundred, something Daniel always did when he needed to think. Then she ate the other crust, considered more counting, but by that time, she was too angry. She stomped into her house, woke her father, and spilled the beans. "Daniel's up at the Timber Dump, and I think there's a big animal that got stuck down in the dump, like a cow or a bull."

Faye was still furious when her father called her name from the base of the steps a few hours later. She'd been pacing her bedroom floor, staring out the window at police car lights swirling red, white, and blue into black sky over the Timber Dump. The dancing colors looked like the pictures of the Northern Lights Daniel had shown her. *See Daniel, you can see the same stupid stuff right here in Hillsborough.* She was expecting her best friend to materialize any second in the backyard. When he did, she was going to run outside and kill him.

Downstairs in the kitchen there were two police officers with belts and shoes as shiny as black mirrors. They told Faye that Daniel wasn't up at the dump, and they hadn't been able to find him anywhere in the surrounding area. Faye told the officers about the eyes and everything she could think of about Daniel's dream of reaching Alaska, the Eskimos, riding the trail, learning a trade, the Northern Lights, even chewing the whale blubber. She could hear Daniel's mom outside, a wailing cry.

In the weeks that followed, the Timber Dump was dredged and emptied. No big animals were found, dead or alive; the only human remains: a newborn's skeleton. That opened a second, unconnected investigation.

For a while, the police visited the end of Clover Street every other day. Had Faye thought of anything else? Had Daniel ever mentioned any specific city names or rivers, or how about a lake, a campground maybe? Would she describe those eyes again?

Faye got used to the officers, stopped noticing the blinding shine of their leathers, how straight-backed they were. Sometimes Officer Leadon played Monopoly at the kitchen table with Faye and her dad. Eventually Officer Render took Daniel's dog Cougar home for his own kids.

Once in Sunset Beach, Faye developed the habit of disappearing herself inside the public library. The library was air-conditioned and quiet. People left her alone there. It didn't take long for Faye to discover what she needed. In one of the basement stacks: *The Book of Spells for All Young Practitioners of Magic*. Faye checked the book out, sprinted home with it, copied the spell for *Finding a Lost Person* into her diary, and got straight to work:

1. *Bless your front doorstep with sea salt.*
   (Easy, just evaporate seawater)
2. *Visualize the person as you last set eyes on them.*
   (An almost 11-year-old boy wearing navy-blue shorts, a yellow shirt, straight auburn hair, green eyes, freckles, a gap between his front teeth, Band-Aid on his left knee)
3. *Write his or her initials in the sea salt with the tip of your tongue.*
   (D.J.T.)
4. *Carve the initials in a blue candle with a knife tip. Blue is the promise of a safe voyage.*
5. *Burn the candle all the way down to the very last fabric of wick.*
6. *Say the lost person's name aloud fifty-seven times. Then say: This person was never really lost.*
7. *Visualize them stepping through the open door of where you sleep.*
8. *Perform all seven steps only under a full moon.*

Faye has remained faithful to the spell since the day she found that book twenty-five years ago. To be fair to the powers of magic, there have been times when Faye thought the spell might finally be taking hold. One year, a rare spring snow fell in Sunset Beach all day. It was April 3rd, Daniel's birthday. Another year, the same brochure advertising an Alaskan cruise arrived four times in the same week inside Faye's mailbox.

The most recent hopeful day happened last summer. Faye was returning from lunch when Gus, who flipped burgers at the stand next door, hollered to her.

"Hey Faye! Some guy was just here looking for you."

"Who was it? What did he want?"

"Wouldn't say."

"What did he look like?" Faye's breath had stuck to the sides of her lungs; her heart dropped cold and heavy to her toes.

"Don't know, Faye. That's all I got."

"How old was he? What color was his hair?"

"I'm working over here, Faye, in case you haven't noticed."

"Which way did he go, Gus?"

"Jesus Christ. What's the big deal?"

Faye closed the shop immediately. She scoured the boardwalk, hiked the beach back and forth until it got dark. Then she collapsed on the bench by her shop door and fell asleep until dawn. No one woke her.

—

The tourists have finished photographing the Witch of Sunset Beach; the shops along the boardwalk are darkening their lights one by one. Even the seagulls have taken their leave. It is time for the witch's evening beach walk.

Waves are breaking rough and lovely, erupting a fine mist all along the line where land and sea come together. The horizon appears infinite, something that happens when flat, pale sand, a stark, rolling sea, and the descending rays of the sun collide.

Those lingering on the beach watch the dark fabric of the witch's clothes, whipped by the wind, draped birdcage bumping rhythmically against her thigh, long hair lifting, sailing skyward, surf breeze flipping it over, then tamping it down again. They follow her swaying figure as it grows smaller and smaller on the horizon, as all things that leave us do.

"Go home, Faye," Daniel whispers to Faye.

Daniel leans in closer to his laptop screen, examining the feed from the live webcam of Sunset Beach. The wind is punishing flags and kites, rattling the signs above shop doors. A gale storm is predicted to make landfall all along the coast in the next hour or so. Faye never cares about weather conditions. She walks straight into the heart of storms.

Daniel's cell phone has remained silent next to his coffee cup all day while the temperature climbed to a high of twenty degrees in Fairbanks. Nothing from all those job applications, but that's not surprising. Daniel is the only soul alive who believes that Daniel Troyer is finally clean and sober. He reaches into his pocket and pulls out his dad's old compass, cradles the compass in his hand, watches the red arrow quiver and tip.

He has to stop parking across the street from the house where his ex-wife lives with his kids, slouching down in his half-dead truck, gaping like a weirdo at their basketball hoop, their bikes, the plastic playhouse he dropped off on Christmas Eve once that is supposed to look like a log cabin. If he doesn't stop lurking in the shadows, they'll only remember their father as a spook, a nut job. He sees their hands pushing curtains aside in upstairs windows, peeking out at the shitbag they got for a dad.

When the computer screen blackens, Daniel smacks a key. Up pops Sunset Beach under a black sky. *Man, it's getting bad there.* The sky has morphed into something murderous. The clouds, electric with lightning, flicker their warning. Daniel sends a concentrated ESP message.

Go home, Faye. Now. Please. For me.

Daniel sighs, shifts his gaze to the window of his efficiency apartment. Outside, snow has begun another silent falling.

Starscraper

Whenever Eva is alone in her bedroom, she trails the sharp tip of a stolen steak knife over her thighs. She is getting better at this. Her drawings possess more depth and definition than they once did, and recently some of the creatures who live under her skin have begun speaking directly to her in words she can understand perfectly. If this is happening, then Eva must be drawing them as they really are. The Skin So Soft lotion her mother orders from Lois the Avon Lady hides the etchings well, but even during periods of necessary invisibility, Eva senses a cement foundation settling in by millimeters, windowpanes shuttering through gusty storms, frames warping beneath the weight of spring damp, the tickle of tiny footsteps clambering up fire escapes, sprinting across rooftop balcony playing games or chasing cats.

Unfortunately, Eva is not in her bedroom now. She is in the kitchen with her mother.

"It's such a good thing you are doing, Eva, tending to your skin so regularly. We all must make the best of the skin we come wrapped up in when we are plopped into this world. We can't just peel the skin off our bodies and install a new sheet. There is a new sample cream from Lois, by the way, on the coffee table in the living room. Smells of freshly squeezed lemons, I believe she said. Won't that be refreshing?"

Eva's mother stands huddled over stainless steel, scalding Tim's dinner plate. Steam chugs up from the sink bowl, a locomotive bursting at the seams, trying to scale Mt. Everest with a single engine. This daily ritual inside the Hollings' house reminds Eva of the book her parents used to read to her before she could read to herself, about a dinky blue engine that pulled a long line of heavy railway cars up a very steep hill just by thinking she could. *What a dumb-ass book.*

The plate Elizabeth Hollings is currently washing, along with its accompanying silverware, remained unused throughout the dinner hour. Even so, the dish must still be scoured and sterilized. Items removed from kitchen drawers or cabinets are immediately suspicious. It is possible that Eva's father sneezed a few times between the tossed salad and the salmon patty entrée, but what really concerns Eva's mother is those stealthy germs that float around in the air all the time. Eva's mother is a germophobe.

Eva can't really remember the last time her older brother, Tim, showed up for dinner. Why her mother continues to set a place in front of his vacant chair is beyond her. Tim's not big on food anymore. That's only one of the problems.

"Eva, are you sure there isn't anything dirty left on the table?" her mother asks her daughter for the third time.

"No. There isn't anything left on the table at all, Mother," Eva responds, nudging a few crumbs with her pinky finger across tablecloth and onto glossy linoleum floor. "Today, in geography class, Mr. Mandes told us hundreds of people have died so far trying to scale Mount Everest."

"That's nice. What was Timothy doing, did you say, that prevented him from joining us for dinner this evening?" Mother asks.

"He has a big biology exam tomorrow," Eva lies.

"Oh, yes, well, I am sure there's a lot of memorization required for that."

"I figured out why," Eva continues.

"Why what? Why biology requires a keen memory?"

"Those people were brainwashed by a little blue engine."

"Eva, make some sense, please, for once. What are you talking about now? What engine? What people?"

In addition to being a germophobe, Eva's mother is also a full-blown neat freak. Biweekly tidying of the contents of kitchen drawers and cabinets is executed with a brand of perfectionism found only in prison kitchens where everything must be accounted for before the cooks and dishwashers can return to their cellblock. In addition to new drawer liners, her mother counts aloud, drill sergeant style, verifying the existence of twelve of everything in her kitchen. That inventory includes twelve sterling silver steak knives with "naturally shed" deer antler handles.

Eva had no choice but to steal a steak knife from someone else's kitchen. Her mother's steak knives are seriously creepy. Eva never saw anyone roaming around a forest searching under trees for fallen antlers. People do not discover unattached horns scattered on the ground amid snakeskins and tumbled bird nests. *Naturally shed? Please.*

Stealing the steak knife had been a cinch. Two doors away at the Long house, the kitchen is a shit show. No one ever knows where anything is inside that house. Mrs. Long would only notice if her television suddenly went missing. Eva's true challenge had been hiding the knife, or what Eva thought of as "How to outwit a mother who rummages through everything when her daughter is out of the house attending school, flute lessons, or playing with Judy Long at her house." It just so happens that Elizabeth Hollings is also a nosy body.

"Eva, why aren't you over here drying these dishes?" Her mother's voice retains a hint of her South Carolina upbringing, curlicue tendrils that slip off the final syllable of a word like a soprano's Sunday church solo.

This is a bad day. Eva has to think of something to get out of this room.

"I can't dry tonight, Mother," Eva answers, expecting her voice to echo back from some faraway, aseptic cloudland. "I have a big test tomorrow too. I think Judy is going to call me. She wants to study together."

"Okay, I'll dry tonight."

The truth about Judy Long, Eva's best friend and neighbor, is that Judy bores Eva to the brink of death. It's because Judy was born with so little imagination. Even so, Eva walks to Judy's house mostly every day. There isn't a better place to go, and having almost no imagination isn't Judy's fault. Judy is sweet-natured, shares junk food, and has a pet, a black cat with golden eyes named Minx. Minx transforms into a miniature, purring chainsaw when Eva plays with her, which is as often as possible, and she licks Eva's sore thighs with her pleasingly rough, salmon-pink tongue.

There used to be another reason to spend so much time at the Long house. When the girls were younger, Eva and Judy played Barbies for hours. Eva never tired of making up extravagant stories about their lives, even if Judy didn't add much to the plot lines. Now in middle school, Eva and Judy are too old for dolls, but without Barbies, time drags. Even Judy seems bored when they are together. Eva is considering hauling some dusty board games up to the Longs's picnic table, the only uncluttered horizontal surface the Longs have.

Eva used to play games with Tim. Stratego mostly, but Tim doesn't really go for games anymore either. Like food, Stratego, and all the smart strategies Tim taught Eva about winning that game, how to be the first to capture your opponent's flag, have been relegated to features of his past.

Closing her bedroom door behind her, Eva sighs, breathes deeply. No one should ever take dry, cool air for granted. Immediately, Eva spots handprints on the carpeting. Her mother has been crawling around on her hands and knees, peeking underneath her bed again.

Eva has seen those movies where people hide money under bed frames or slice mattresses and poke pistols or daggers inside. Beds practically sit up and call from the corners of rooms everywhere: *Come over here and search me!* Eva knew she had to be smarter than that when she hatched the plan that would prevent her mother from discovering the stolen steak knife.

Eva had considered taping the utensil underneath one of her desk drawers, but you can't trust tape. It gets tired: lets go. The pockets of everything in Eva's closet, even the never-been-worn ski jacket at the very back, were also out of the question. Her mother turns the pockets of all clothes hanging in all closets of the house inside out on a regular basis, leery of lint. On those days, Eva discovers a row of panting, cloth tongues waiting for her behind her closet door and on her desktop, unearthed contraband: Bazooka comics, dried dandelion heads, thumbtacks.

A knife, being three-dimensional, cannot successfully be concealed inside a book either, unless it is one of those fake trick books. An Edgar Allen Poe short story she'd read had teased Eva for a short while with the idea of prying up a wooden floorboard, but that would be obvious, and there was no guarantee of a secret compartment underneath. Also, Eva's bedroom ceiling is solid plaster, not a drop ceiling like the one in Tim's basement bedroom.

In the end, Eva carved a trough into the green felt inside her flute box. This was a stroke of brilliance. The flute box is something her mother never touches. Her mother is never going to open the lid of a box containing an object harboring saliva. The only thing her mother cares about, relevant to Eva's flute and its box, is that Eva replaces the starched, cleaning hanky with a clean one once each week.

Eva settles her back against her dresser now and opens the flute case. She wets the tip of the steak knife with her tongue and begins drawing the basement of the high-rise that always starts at the very bottom of her right thigh. The structure is not an earthbound building. It rises higher than anything mankind has witnessed in the natural world, including Mount Everest. It is the Starscraper.

Eva scales the building from the outside as a rock climber would. She doesn't need contraptions to assist her, no grips or ropes or safety belts. The building reveals little dents in its masonry, just the right size for

Eva's feet wherever she needs them, and there are sturdy window ledges to grab on to. The ledges appear to be of brick and mortar, but they certainly don't feel like commonplace building blocks. They have the texture of warm hides, the Guernsey cows that live inside her grandmother's barn.

As she ascends, Eva leans from side to side to peek inside the rooms that materialize one by one. Some window frames are shaped like the glowing constellations Tim used to find for Eva in night skies. Some rooms are stuffed with Christmas trees pulsing multicolored lights. Others have music boxes that play top hits from the current billboard chart by request. Often, inside one window frame, there is a Ferris wheel. Who doesn't adore a Ferris wheel? You can see so far away when you are at the top.

Yesterday, a white German shepherd thumped a glittery tail as Eva approached one of the Starscraper's rooms. It was a representation of Jill, of course, a dog Eva used to have and misses. After the Jill room, there was a porcupine in a room who winked one amber, glassy eye at Eva. Eva recognized the porcupine as a character from an old picture book and remembered why she was so fond of him. Every time the animal tipped a teacup toward his snout, his monocle popped off, and he would make up a new word like "Bumgle!" What is inside the rooms doesn't always make perfect sense to Eva, and that is why they always make Eva perfectly happy.

Today, as Eva sketches, she discovers a window with an upper sash of rose-tinted glass. The carved frame mimics one of the bleeding-heart bushes in her grandmother's garden. Bleeding-heart bushes are magical in an earthly sort of way: plants that bloom living valentines. Spectacular.

Inside the bleeding-heart room a cozy, orange fire dances a merry chorus line inside a hearth; Eva swings her legs over the windowsill and steps inside to a chair waiting just for her. Set upon the side table, a scone and a steaming cup of tea. Eva knows this kind of fire. There have been other fires in other fireplaces in other rooms of the Starscraper just like this one. This is a talking fire.

"Hi, fire," Eva trills toward licking flames, opening the conversation right away. "Sorry, I don't know your proper name."

"Eva! It's you at last. Please sample that dessert. Not a dessert, no, strike that, not really, it's more than a dessert, a new recipe. It's a lemony thing—well, not exactly all lemon. By the way, lemons should be squeezed and sliced. They should be juiced and tasted in a way that is exquisite, not slathered on the body. Don't you agree that constitutes a terribly weird notion, the notion of a lemon lotion?"

"Yes, it is, just about as weird as steak knives with real deer antlers for handles," Eva answers.

As the fire laughs along with Eva, the tips of its yellow and orange flames jump up and down, disappearing in and out of the fireplace flue.

"Tomorrow is shaping up to be a very good day for you, Eva. I predict a trip to the East Mall, an egg roll from the cart by Boscov's, extra duck sauce and hot mustard, and not with your mother. Don't burn your tongue again. I can't decipher quite yet who might accompany you, but I think you're going. Most definitely. The odds are good. At least I think so. Do I have a proper name?"

All talking fires believe they can see into the future, and they do mean well. They try very hard, but they aren't reliable fortune tellers. In any event, a trip to the mall is something nice to imagine.

"I don't know. Don't you know if you have a proper name?"

"It seems I do not know."

"Might there be a swing outside the window today?" Eva asks, hoping two parallel ropes might materialize outside the bleeding-heart window frame.

"There could be," the fire answers. "Let me see what I can accomplish."

The fire blazes into a crimson roar that glows lava-red inside the tea inside Eva's cup. *Talking fires think they are magicians too. They try very hard, mean very well, but are only moderately successful when it comes to magical tricks as well.*

Surprises appear outside the Starscraper's windows at random times: swings Eva can slip onto, sail up very high, drop very low, roller coaster thrilling. There have been purring, black cats, like Minx, slinking past for scooping and cuddling, and drawing tablets and markers, and dark chocolate ice cream cones dangled from the window above, along with books Eva begins reading and finishes on future visits.

The fire's black lips pop in and out of sight. The little mouth reminds Eva of a game she played at a carnival once with Judy. Rubber gopher heads popped in and out of different holes. The idea was to whack as many heads with your mallet as you could. Eva loved smashing those heads, but Judy didn't really have the heart for it.

"What's so funny?" the fire asks. "Have you a new joke?"

This fire's voice is a female one, an older woman, Eva would guess, someone's kindly flute teacher perhaps.

"I was thinking about Judy trying to bop gopher heads that one time."

"At the carnival, yes, our dear Judy. Care for some bubblegum? I am afraid the swing has gone missing today. Try that lemony thing before the gum, that somewhat desserty thing. I am curious. It's a new recipe, as I mentioned."

Following a pop and a hiss from the fire, a mound of Bazooka bubblegum appears beside Eva's teacup.

"You did it! You made bubblegum!" Eva exclaims with an equal mix of genuine admiration and surprise.

"Glorious! Now try that lemony thing, please. I can't wait any longer."

Of course, the sort of desserty thing is deliciously lemony and not exactly lemon, tasting of lemony lime pudding or key lime pie at first, almost too tart but then moist cake, sweet and soft, then whipped, satiny buttercream icing. On the final swallow, Eva's whole mouthful turns into a generous gulp of icy cold, refreshing lemonade, ending with a hint of mint and raspberry.

"Unbelievably scrumptious lemony, sort of a desserty, drinky thing," Eva compliments the fire.

She lifts the tea mug to her lips, blows twice to cool the steaming liquid.

A telephone blares.

"Dammit, I have to go," Eva says.

Eva takes one sip of tea, stands up, and pockets the gum. As the warm liquid falls into her stomach, another warmth wraps itself like a scarf spun from the softest yarn around her shoulders. Eva closes her eyes; soaks in this perfumed embrace, not really perfume, more fresh-mowed grass, soft under feet, the kind that springs back when you run barefoot under summer twilight. The fire's embrace.

"No worries," soothes the fireplace. "You'll be back soon."

"Do you wish you had a proper name?" Eva asks just before she goes.

"Yes, I think I should have a proper name. I would relish that, I think."

"I'll think of a good one and tell you when I come back," Eva promises.

"I'll be here."

Whenever Eva exits the Starscraper, she does something between floating and falling. The first time she had been terrified she might descend too fast, crack her skull, or boomerang her spine, but now she knows she will float down onto her own two standing feet. Eva stretches out on the woven hearthrug in front of the talking fire, flattens her back, points her nose toward outer space, and closes her eyes.

"Happy flolling," coos the fireplace.

"Good word. See you in a few hours."

"Eva, it's Judy," Eva's mother is calling from behind the kitchen door at the end of the hallway. Clapping her hands too.

"Be right there."

Eva slips the knife into the flute case, squirts lotion, rubs her right thigh clean, and heads to answer the call.

"Aren't you coming over?" Judy asks. "I have something critical to tell you."

"Okay," Eva answers, hanging up.

Judy says that often. Usually, it is nothing critical or even unexpected, but you never know.

At Judy's house, Mr. and Mrs. Long are watching *Hey Lucy*, eating Jiffy Pop popcorn, sipping Tab, and smoking. Mrs. Long's knitting needles nod and click soothingly: another pair of duckling yellow baby booties. She has been creating booties for a local hospital nursery for years. Mr. Long is telling Mrs. Long again how talented she is. This is where Judy gets all her sweetness from, right here in this living room.

"*Bonjour,* lovely Eva," Mrs. Long issues her customary greeting.

Eva waves through the smoke screen, wonders how many other children wish they could swap parents with their best friends.

"Let's go outside to the swing set," Eva suggests to Judy, helping herself to a silver package of iced blueberry Pop-Tarts from the kitchen counter on the way out. No one has bothered clearing the dinner plates, the double sink contains a replica of the Leaning Tower of Pisa. Floor tiles stick to the bottom of Eva's flip-flops, and there's the aroma of something sour, turned milk or rotting fruit or both maybe, at a standstill in the air. What a perfect kitchen.

"Didn't you eat dinner?" Judy asks, latching the screen door.

"Salmon patties," Eva explains.

Judy groans. She has suffered through many a meal of Eve's mother's infamous salmon patties. Fishy and greasy, but at least they aren't very large or filling.

"Gross," Judy says.

Outside in the Longs's backyard, a rush of gratitude washes over Eva at the sight of the rusting pink and white metal swing set. Judy received the set as a present on her fifth birthday. Two swings on it, so Judy and Eva didn't have to wait in line. The girls have been campaigning for the perpetual life of the swing set ever since. Every year when spring returns, Mr. Long levels the set, sands the rusted spots, and paints it.

Then, he marches his way through another summer mowing and carefully trimming around its spindly legs with a smile on his face.

Eva and Judy manage to squeeze their bottoms into the swings. They can't swing anymore for fear of uprooting the whole set, but they can rock gently forward and back, twist the metal chains tight and let go, spin themselves into two dizzy tops. Sometimes Eva rests her back on the slide, head at the top, feet on the grass. Once, she was afraid of the height of the drop. Now her body is longer than the entire surface.

"They were talking about Tim again on the bus, according to Gabby," Judy begins.

Eva rolls her eyes. This is nothing critical. This is everyday news.

Gabby, Judy's older sister, and Tim, Eva's brother, are both juniors in high school. Gabby is the ideal nickname for Abigail Long. She enjoys gossip, especially about Tim. Eva has decided that Gabby is overwhelmingly envious of Tim's superior brain. Gabby aspires to be a female Albert Einstein, but Tim always gets the best of her on AP Chemistry, Biology, and Calculus exams. Tim teases Gabby relentlessly: tells her he is dedicating his scientific life to sewage treatment plants, to the science of how to process shit stink-free, things like that. Eva gets a kick out of those moments.

"Gabby said people were saying that Tim was sitting in the back of the bus the other day, making no sense, all glassy-eyed and talking to his thumb about radon levels in the earth's atmosphere."

"Radon? What day was that, specifically?' Eva asks, sounding defensive, but she can do that with Judy.

"I don't know. Sometime this last week."

Tim was in a similar condition a few hours earlier when Eva went downstairs to tell him dinner was ready, although there was no conversation going on with his thumb. This is admittedly a new development, but Tim has been heading this way, heading towards doing things such as having serious conversations with his own human digits.

Judy walks her swing sideways to drape an arm around Eva's shoulders.

"I was thinking, Eva, what about leaving an anonymous note on a teacher's desk at school? Mrs. Rubley seems cool, or maybe you could just walk into church and leave a note on a pew? Aren't ministers supposed to help people?" Judy suggests, toeing some feathery dandelion heads, exploding them into feathery white fireworks.

"Judy, please don't ruin the dandelions. They are so pretty. And what could I possibly say? Greetings. You should look inside my brother's drop ceiling, basement bedroom, 53 Carlton Road, right away? He'll know it was me. He'll figure it out. He'd never forgive me."

"Okay, Eva."

Suddenly, Eva feels exhausted. If she were back with the talking fire and the tea and the lemony thing, she could close her eyes and drift away toward something like sleep.

Last Saturday, Tim surprised Eva. He had been up and around unusually early. Eva found him outside on the driveway, packing his car, sliding the garden shovel into his trunk. When she noticed the red plastic box holding vials of chemicals for field tests, she begged to go along.

Eva knew her role well as far as Tim's excursions to local quarries were concerned. Follow behind, drop rock samples into paper bags, write down the identifying names Tim spells out for her, make sure each bag receives the correct index card. There wasn't going to be much conversation, but it was going to be a good day, and it had been a good day.

"Tim, how's this drug experiment going? How much longer?" Eva asked during the car ride home from the quarry, hoping Tim would take some time and think before he answered, but he didn't.

"Eva, I am fine. I am just experimenting. I am expanding my mind so that I can expand the world's concept of science exponentially."

Eva had turned away, swallowed hard. Outside the car window, the invisible hand of the wind rippled a field of tall grasses.

"I guess I should go, Judy," Eva says, pulling herself out of the swing. Thanks for the tarts. See you tomorrow. Oh, here."

Eva empties her pockets of Bazooka.

"Bazooka, hey thanks. By the way, your thigh is bleeding," Judy says.

Eva plucks some furry lamb's ear from Mrs. Long's garden, dabs her thigh, and gives Judy a wave goodbye.

Back inside her bedroom, Eva quickly re-sketches the Starscraper's basement on her right thigh, begins adding building floors as quickly as she can, but the room with the talking fire and the hot mug of tea and the lemony thing isn't where it was before.

"Shit," Eva hisses.

She could really use some more of that tea and a nap in such a soft chair. She sniffs what could be fireplace smoke and climbs faster, trying to think of a fitting name for a fireplace who bakes.

———

Earlier, when Eva was supposed to tell Tim it was time for dinner, she knocked loudly, but no answer came from inside his bedroom. She knocked and knocked. He had been inside the room all day. Those are the bad days. Eva's parents routinely avoid the basement now. Once a week, her mother leaves the vacuum cleaner at the base of the steps. Tim occasionally drags it into his room, turns it on, and lets it run standing still.

Eva's father used to shoot pool in the basement, but not anymore. Her dad is seldom home. He travels with work, and when he is home, there are outside chores to catch up on and mounds of mail to open. No time to move colored balls around a green felt table.

Eventually, Eva stopped knocking on Tim's door and rested her forehead against it, letting her brain cartwheel away, roll down hillsides, leap into quarries, race itself to the customary finish line. There are bad days, but there are good days too. At least Tim goes to school and to work. He still plans and performs field tests. There are active laboratory experiments underway on the dry sink beside his desk. Tim gets straight A's. Tim is brilliant. Tim's dreams don't resemble anyone else's dreams. Tim's brain doesn't resemble anyone else's brain. Tim is unique. Tim is one of a kind. Tim is infinitely indefinable. Tim is more mysterious and magnificent than Albert Einstein ever was.

Eva pushed the door open a few inches with her shoulder. Tim was sitting at his desk with his back to Eva. This wasn't unusual, although he wasn't leaning forward, reading or writing. His head was cocked backward. Odd. Eva stood still, held her breath. Watched. Waited.

Tim didn't move. His back didn't rise and fall. There was nothing. Nothing.

Eva's heart knifed her clean through, but she did it. She slipped through the door and entered the dim room.

"Timmm," Eva whispered into her brother's ear as she brushed her lips over the back of his ear.

This was a trick a star fairy named Andromeda taught Eva long ago, the Ear Whisper Trick. Andromeda lives on Eva's left thigh. Andromeda is one of Eva's favorite creatures. She isn't afraid to talk about anything, and unlike talking fires, she sees into the future with precision.

"First thing you do, put your lips on the back of your brother's ear. Always make sure it is warm before you turn him around," Andromeda had advised.

"What if it's not warm?" Eva inquired.

Andromeda pushed a lock of her turquoise hair out of her eyes, fluttered her ivory wings, iridescent as opals, cocked her head to one side.

"If that happens, call for me, and we'll decide," Andromeda responded, singing some of the words without even trying as she always does.

Tim's ear was warm against Eva's mouth, hot even, but Eva didn't want to turn him around. She began to whimper. She shook Tim's shoulders from behind instead. She decided she would simply stand there and shake his shoulders until she couldn't anymore. Finally, Tim groaned. Eva grabbed on to the back of the heavy oak desk chair and spun.

Tim rolled into view with his eyelids shut, eyeballs darting back and forth under blue-veined lids like furious tennis court volleys. Foamy spit bubbled from the corners of his mouth, dribbled down, dripped off his chin onto a stained Moody Blues concert shirt. The shirt hung wide as a house over what was left of Tim's bony chest.

"Timmm," Eva pleaded, sniffling, hot tears popping, sailing through air.

Tim opened his eyes, glassy yes, the old tried and true druggie stereotype, but he recognized Eva. That much she could tell.

"Tim? What should I tell Mom about dinner?" Eva squeaked.

"Tell her I'm busy," Tim replied, with a weak smile.

—

Eva follows the smell of fireplace smoke to a top floor of the Starscraper, far above cloud cover, and still, no bleeding-heart room, no talking fire, no cup of tea, no comfy chair, and no lemony thing. The good news is that her parents went to see a movie. She should have enough time to sketch the fire escape. From there, she can cross from her right thigh over to her left thigh by way of the ice tunnel. Diamonds of all shapes and sizes will be scattered and frozen into place inside the tunnel walls, their facets created for the sole purpose of reflecting moonlight. Crystalline shapes will spin on the tunnel's floor. Eva loves that part, an enchanted game of Spirograph, drawings drawing themselves, coming to life, swapping colors underneath her bare feet.

Eva sketches the metal rungs of a fire escape ladder, climbs out of the building, and hopscotches through the ice tunnel, enjoying cool, frosty air, thinking about building snowmen and sledding and hot chocolate with marshmallows, how first snowfalls never fail to come back. Eva doesn't believe that all snowflakes look different. *There must be some snowflakes who are identical. It's just that there are too many of them and they layer too fast for people to prove otherwise. And anyway, snowflakes have a right to have secrets of their own.*

On the other side of the tunnel, it is nighttime, the normal course of things. Eva stops, looks skyward, begins waiting for the luminous thread that will drop into her fingertips from an overhead star.

The first time Eva made the journey through the ice tunnel to her left thigh, she had been terrified to accept the gift of a star thread, even though she knew it was meant for her. It had seemed so fragile, a shimmery filament no bigger than a single strand from a spider's web, but Eva took a chance on trust. When Eva wraps a star thread around her wrist, it grips back and pulls her body up through the chill of black space toward a starry someone who happens to be searching just for Eva at just that moment.

Tonight, the journey through galaxy air is as swift and gemstone brilliant as always, like corkscrewing through the center of a massive kaleidoscope. The well-dressed gentleman fox who owns a collection of velvet tuxedos of every color, including some colors Eva has never seen before and therefore cannot name, awaits her. The red fox has been preparing for Eva's visit. He is the one who cast the line that reeled Eva to his side.

The fox has something new in his sunken living room he wants to show off. The living room is decorated with Asian furniture, sculptures of Buddha, paintings of red and gold dragons, incense sticks emitting violet smoke tendrils.

"Isn't it lavish, Eva?" Barnaby says in his cheerful, British accent. "Or is it a bit too much?"

A new hot tub has been installed. Barnaby is sitting on a black lacquer, circular sofa, soaking his toes, tapping the empty cushion beside him, inviting Eva to join.

There is something decidedly Asian about the shape of Barnaby's eyes, so the surroundings where he resides fit him. He wears the best-smelling cologne, has impeccable teeth, and a shiny, groomed tail with a pinkish cast. One of these days, Eva will work up the nerve to ask Barnaby if she can brush his tail. It looks very soft.

"It's lavish in a very good way, Barnaby. Too much? Never. I love it."

Eva drops her sneakers on a rattan mat by the front door, joins the fox, slips her feet into the hot tub.

"How's the temperature?" Barnaby asks.

"Perfect. Thanks for having me."

"Sure thing, sure thing. Did you remember my Pop-Tarts by any stroke of luck?"

Eva giggles, pulls blueberry Pop-tarts from her shorts pocket. The fox already has his paw extended, licking his beautiful chops. He's addicted to iced blueberry Pop-Tarts, and this is completely Eva's fault.

"Iced blueberry? Jackpot! My favorite."

"Have you seen Andromeda lately, Barnaby?"

"She's flown by the window a couple of times today. I'll tell her you miss her," Barnaby answers.

"This hot tub is the best thing you've added to your room yet."

"I am thinking of adding a jukebox, one with a rainbow that arcs from one end to the other," Barnaby says. "Or maybe that's too predictable, maybe something other than a rainbow. What do you think?"

"Definitely not a rainbow. Maybe something that starts as one thing and changes into something else, you know, like a butterfly or a baby, but not a butterfly or a baby," Eva suggests.

"Hmmmm."

The red fox adores music and is quite accomplished at humming. Humming is his special talent. He never misses a note. When he begins humming a current radio hit about a red rubber ball sun shining up in the sky, Eva recognizes the song and joins in, pondering the lyrics and providing harmony.

Across the room, on his kitchen table, Barnaby has arranged a stunning vase of dandelions in all stages of life. When they finish their duet, Barnaby swishes his tail in the direction of the centerpiece.

"Don't forget to take those flowers with you when you go, Eva."

"Is the worst over yet?" Eva asks Barnaby. She has to shout to be heard above the merry splashing of four feet in a frothy tub. "Will Tim get back to being himself soon?"

As usual, Barnaby doesn't miss a beat. "We shall meet the future together, Eva, you and I," the fox calls back to her. "Come back as soon as you can. I've got it now—the perfect jukebox. You won't believe what I've come up with. Lavish it will be with beguiling, bemusing, bewitching music the likes of which you have never heard before."

The Shadows Outside

In the summer of 1976, my father lost his hometown for good. It was my fault, but to be fair, I was only eleven when I did him in. Before that, we were a family living contentedly, I thought, in a small town tucked into the Pennsylvanian coal region. My name is Nicholas Stepaniak.

My parents and I left Shamokin once a year, in August, so my mother could shop in a big city. It was a four-hour drive to Pittsburgh. Admittedly, the retail offerings in the Shamokin area were dismal. Other mothers seemed okay with the offerings inside the Dry Goods Emporium in Genesee Falls, but Dad never seemed to mind the annual trips to Pittsburgh and neither did I. Mother purchased her entire wardrobe from Kaufmann's Department Store, including shoes, purses, Evening in Paris Perfume, hosiery in various suntan sheens, and leather gloves.

Mother did all the talking when we ended the shopping day with a visit to Klavon's Ice Cream Parlor. Dad, who looked like Cary Grant with even thicker, curlier, blacker hair, sat beside her, square-shouldered, grinning, and bobbing his chin at the waitress. He wasn't flirting. He did that bobbing chin thing with everyone. It was a very encouraging gesture.

"Where are you folks from?" a name-tagged Lillian or Rita or Judith would inquire, followed by a pink lipstick smile.

"We are living in Shamokin at the moment," Mom would respond. "My husband, this is Marek, is in banking."

He was in banking, my father. A fixture inside the lobby of the National Bank of Shamokin on Coal Street. Hollywood charm behind a broad, oak desk with a silver nameplate pivoted toward revolving entrance doors: *Mr. Marek Stepaniak, Assistant Manager.* I have wholeheartedly agreed with Dad about almost everything my whole life, including his opinion that his broad, oak bank desk bore a striking resemblance to a coffin.

At home he used the guest room closet for his bank clothes: dark suits, ties, silver tie bars and pins, a collection Mom swelled to outlandish proportions for him over the years thanks to the Gentlemen's Accessories Section at Kaufmann's. His shoes were also stored there: three pairs of burgundy shoes rotated throughout the workweek. I liked the holes on top of the shoes shaped like bird wings. While inside his closet, those shoes were never empty, thanks to fragrant cedar inserts.

"Dad, why do your bank shoes need those wooden things? My shoes don't have those, and it's not like they cave in."

"Technically, the wooden things are called 'shoetrees.'"

"Shoetrees? They don't look anything like trees."

"True. Not sure they do much good either, but they come free from that friendly Florsheim guy. What would you name them, Nicko?"

"Feet molds?"

For some reason, that suggestion really cracked Dad up.

Most of the buildings on Coal Street were red brick: the bank, Lucky Tubs Laundromat, Denna's Pancakes and Pierogis, Petrik's Tavern, and Sonny's Bed and Breakfast. Mom said that everything profitable in downtown Shamokin was the color of a kidney bean, with the exception of Kolvasky's Funeral Home. Kolvasky's gray fieldstone made it stand out like a tooth that belonged in someone else's mouth.

Every kid loved Mr. Kolvasky. He tossed out the best candy during the annual Halloween parade: Owl bubble gum cigars, black licorice pipes, Stallion candy cigarettes, and Nik-L-Nips wax lips that made us look like a town of short, rowdy orangutans.

Mr. Kolvasky spent hours decorating his shiny black hearse for the parade. So many orange and yellow balloons and crêpe paper tails you almost forgot it was a hearse. Almost. He donated the most money to the Shamokin Civic Club every year, so he got to lead the procession every year, and he did it in style. Attached cowbells to ropes. Dragged them, clanging over pitted asphalt all the way to the end of the parade route.

Mom complained about the pace of the parade. "It's like watching a locomotive running out of steam." She dared Dad to ask Mr. Kolvasky "…if he has a gas pedal in that hearse of his."

I know Mr. Kolvasky just wanted to make the parade last longer. It cheered everyone up. We couldn't wait to see Mr. Kolvasky's costume. A grinning ghost conductor one year, a devil with orange horns the next. Clown with fluorescent purple hair. President Lincoln. Marilyn Monroe blowing a whistle for some reason, and one time Cyclops with a drippy eye, puffing on a kazoo.

Mr. Kolvasky might have lacked some taste around the edges, I'll admit that, but I didn't care. I looked up to the guy almost as much as my dad. They had the same sense of humor. Mr. Kolvasky always belly-laughed whenever Dad patted his bank desk in the lobby and said, "Good afternoon, Hank. I believe you may have dropped something out of the rear end of your hearse."

Shamokin had veins of coal running through a mountain that rose like one of the Great Pyramids above our main street, our parades, our asphalt roofing shingles, garage doors, silver mailboxes, school swing sets, church steeples, baseball diamonds, sledding hills, sidewalks, howling dogs and Christmas tree lights. At the top of the mountain stood a gaping, black mouth that led into the heart of the Glen Burn Anthracite Coal Mine. The mine was loaded to the gills with black "diamonds." I never really understood the idea behind calling coal black diamonds. In Shamokin, everyone worked hard, but no one wore diamonds or got rich.

My family's serious trouble with Shamokin began on the day of my sixth birthday, July 26, 1971. I was standing on the seat of a wingback chair, poking my head through curtains decorated with the airplanes of World War II. My bedroom window faced Ash Street. In the distance, a dazzling snake of fallen stars was sidewinding itself down the side of the mountain toward my house. When the lights got closer, they transformed into a row of yellow, glow-in-the-dark orbs bobbing merrily up and down like yoyos suspended on the longest clothesline you ever saw.

Once the lights reached the sidewalk, some of the miners with their cap lamps sensed me there, mesmerized inside a window frame, and turned to wave. Their eyeballs, brighter than sun on snow in their blackened faces, scared me the first time I saw them.

Mom must have heard me hopping: chair legs up and down on the wooden floorboards as I waved back, because she appeared beside me looking cross. Later, loud, argumentative voices from my parents' bedroom kept me awake. After that, I still waved to the miners from my bedroom window, but I did it quietly.

A few years later, just before it was my birthday again, I questioned my mother about that wingback chair in my bedroom. I freely admit that I came into this world with an undying curiosity about wings of all kinds. That's something I can't explain, just one of life's mysteries.

"I don't get why they call it a 'wingback chair.'"

"Those parts on either side look like folded wings, don't they?"

"But they are frozen in place. Aren't wings supposed to flap?"

"Those wings are supposed to block cold drafts."

"What if it's a hot day and I want to get some breeze?"

"Nicholas, when you grow up, you can become the famous

inventor who invents a chair with moving wings."

I must tell you. There were some aptly named wings in Shamokin. The stunning, lily-white wings painted behind the pulpit inside St. Cornelia's Roman Catholic Church on Water Street. Every Sunday morning, the pulpit angels hovered over baby Jesus and his mom, Mary. I suppose everyone thought those angels were beautiful in an impossible, heavenly way with their flaxen hair, endless lashes, turquoise eyes, and glittering, ruby-red lips. I never trusted them. They looked jealous of Mary. Their eyes drilled into the top of her head, bitter because they weren't the mothers of a savior. They were angels. They would never be mothers at all. The longer I sat there, the meaner the angels looked.

But their wings! Those creations were another matter entirely. So artfully crafted. They reminded me of the wings of large birds, birds of prey, eagles and hawks. I studied the arc of the gold-tipped, overlapping feathers, closed my eyes at intervals to imagine the wings beating their mirrored rhythm, drumming down drafts.

Would these angel wings work? Would they carry the angelic bodies into the air, whisk them through stained glass and up up and away to the glory of heaven? Could these winged church ladies peel themselves away from plaster to swoop over the top of our human crowns, angel toes dangling in my father's thick curls, knocking hats off the women just for kicks? Dad and Mr. Kolvasky would have laughed to see something like that. Me too.

The answer is no. I suspected as much then, but I know for sure now. The wings inside St. Cornelia's, as lovely as they looked, were much too small and set too far underneath the angels' shoulder blades. In order to fly, the angels would have needed wings twice as large, extending from their armpits and not from the middle of their backs. The angels of St. Cornelia's could have flapped and flapped all they wanted, but they were never destined to soar. They were bound to nosedive into our laps, spill our communion wine, splash us from the baptismal font.

By the time I turned eight, I was still admiring angel wings at church every Sunday morning, but I had lost interest in what was outside my bedroom window at night. If everything had stopped there, we might have never left Shamokin, but it didn't. That fall I entered the third grade, and we were assigned our first challenging homework; tasks that required real concentration, not just color the scarecrow and bring it back in the morning. Kids began bragging about how they did their homework underneath their kitchen tables, how fun it was to pretend they were deep down inside the mine. They gobbled snacks, chewed bubble gum, kept flashlights, water guns, and all kinds of contraband down there.

Mom hauled me out and into the blinding, fluorescent lights of our kitchen the first time I tried it. She said it was too dark and cramped underneath a table for homework. She said being under there would ruin my eyesight, my posture, and my grades. She was cross again. I knew my mom was right, but I still felt mad at her, deprived of something.

As far as homework, I did my assignments without help from my parents. I was good at schoolwork, but nobody is good at everything. I struggled mightily learning to tie my shoes. I was hopeless at dribbling, throwing, and catching a ball of any kind, and I was clumsy. The following autumn, I broke my arm. I had no business trying to hop up and down on a pogo stick. One morning before school, I said, "Mom, I was wondering if you could call Mrs. Pestrock. I need to borrow some mining clothes from somebody and a hat and equipment because the fourth grade is dressing as miners for the Halloween parade. We're using charcoal on our faces. I have that but—"

Mom's head flew back and our eyes locked.

"Under no circumstances will you be joining your class in the parade this year, and you are not tying your shoes tight enough!"

She bent down and tied my shoes for me, yanking the laces so tight I wanted to scream, but I didn't. I'd never heard such a hissy, low voice coming out of her. The snarl on the side of her mouth had sucked my real mother out of the room. Before that voice could find a way to come out of her again, I grabbed my lunch box and hobbled out the front door.

At the end of Ash Street, I couldn't take another step. I dropped to my knees and crawled into a hedge thick as a stone wall that ran along the side of the Pestrocks' carport. I tugged and pried at the knots in the shoelaces, but I couldn't get them loose because the cast on my arm kept getting in the way. A screen door slammed. I peeked out at Manny Pestrock's two sneakered feet jogging towards me. Manny was always late for school. He was the youngest of six.

"Manny!" I called out.

Manny stopped dead and sniffed the air like my uncle Leon's bloodhound Hubert. I stuck my head out of the hedge again and waved. Manny crawled into the bushes with me and tried to take stock of the situation. He smelled like pancake syrup.

"Nick. What are you doin'?"

Manny Pestrock was galaxies cooler than me. He excelled at sports, physical movements of all kinds. We weren't close. We sat in different classrooms. His mother didn't make him join the Boy Scouts or take trombone lessons, and my mother didn't allow a steady diet of comic books and episodes of *The Three Stooges*, but Manny and I had lived five doors away from each other our whole lives, so we were still friends.

Manny was wearing a Pittsburgh Steelers jacket. I believed in Manny's dream of becoming the quarterback for the Steelers when he grew up, but after that morning, I wished for this future for Manny fervently.

"Manny, can you untie these?"

I slid my feet toward him. When he didn't move, I glanced up. Manny was staring at me. I wouldn't have blamed him for making a jab at me about not being able to untie my own shoes or use a pogo stick. One tear escaped down my chubby cheek and dropped into the dirt between us. Manny gave me a quick pat on my back, hunted around, found a sharp-tipped stone, dug at the knots in the laces, and released my feet.

That was the thing about all those Shamokin kids. They looked real tough, didn't have the cleanest language all the time, hands all buggered up from picking stones from the coal piles for pocket change, but if a person was really down on his luck, they knew it.

That year, on the day of the Halloween parade, Mom called Principal Wallace's office and reported that I was sick with a fever. I didn't march with my class, but she did allow *The Three Stooges* and a whole box of Nilla Wafers. Apparently, Mr. Kolvasky was a smash hit as Frankenstein that year.

If you are wondering what the straw was that finally broke the camel's back, that happened a few years later. As I said, I was eleven. When you turned eleven in Shamokin, things changed for you. That's when you could ride down into the Glen Burn mine for the first time during the week of the spring carnival.

Of course, I was dying to go. I had heard about what it was like inside the mine since as far back as my memory went. My friends and I had been talking about finally getting to go down for years. The anticipation was creeping up on me from every direction.

I faced Mom one day after school armed with a handful of A+ test grades and a letter from Principal Wallace congratulating me for achieving gold honor roll again. I had to butter Mom up. She didn't even like butter, but she liked hearing about my scholastic achievements. She talked often about the colleges I would tour when I got old enough, about the different scholarships she and my father were confident I would receive.

"Mom, please, just this one time, in the name of hard science. There are real, prehistoric specimens down there. Whole, extinct fish with all of their bones and the fossils of tropical plants, real mushrooms growing right out of the coal veins. Did you hear, did I tell you, that my science teacher told us there might be a whole dinosaur preserved in one of the back rooms on level five? Jack Unger said his dad might let us see it. His dad's actually *seen* it. They've been hiding it from the mining inspectors because it's our own town secret, our own secret dinosaur. Please. I am begging you. Just this one time."

Mom was a deliberate, decided person. Her opinions rarely changed. That afternoon she spent a few centuries looking over my school papers. When she set the stack back on the kitchen table, she picked up a teacup painted with lavender roses, drew in careful, even, endless sips. I wanted to scream. I guess that's how she felt all these years watching Mr. Kolvasky set the pace for the Halloween parade.

At long last, she placed the cup back into its saucer as daintily as you can return porcelain to porcelain and looked at me standing there, hands planted firmly on my hips, sweating through my shirt. She was cross again, but her voice sounded normal, and her mouth retained its shape. The message was the same old tune.

"Nicholas Benjamin Stepaniak. If you ever, *ever* ride down into that mine for *any* reason at all, in the name of hard science or God himself, you will *kill* your own mother. You will break my heart to pieces. It is as simple as that. You must decide what you want."

Not long after that declaration, we left Shamokin for good, relocating to the town of State College, where my parents had met as university students.

As we packed up everything we had in the world, everyone we knew in the world stopped by to say goodbye. I mostly stared, lost sleep, shed an inch of my roly-poly waist, but I knew my mom wouldn't change her mind even though I was suffering. Dad knew it too. Shamokin wasn't going to change, but we were.

I only cried a few times. Like when Manny came with a present. You guessed it: a Pittsburgh Steelers sweatshirt. I wept like a baby when Mr. Kolvasky arrived with a paper lunch bag full of the best candy ever. Later, when I found his business card buried at the bottom of the bag, I bawled again.

One night about a week before the moving van was scheduled to arrive, I woke to the sound of voices and beer bottles clinking in the kitchen. Mom was setting up our new house in State College, so it was just Dad and I left in Shamokin. Any time my mom went away without us, like when she visited her sister in New Jersey, Frank Pestrock came by. He and Dad talked about the stuff they did together growing up, the baby fox they caught and kept in an abandoned garage for a month, how

Mr. Pestrock had been the best quarterback in all of Pennsylvania during their high school years and Dad his most reliable wide receiver. Frank called Dad, "…the dude with the Velcro hands."

At the sound of their laughter, I slipped out of bed, tiptoed across the living room floor, now barren, cold, and dusty, and settled myself beside the kitchen door, closed to contain Mr. Pestrock's chain-smoking to the extent possible. Not that it mattered anymore. Mom wasn't coming back.

"Franko, I just hate to leave you," Dad said, sounding pretty choked up.

"You're not going that far. Pauline will be happier. No one said she had to like it here like we do. We grew up here. She gave it a good go. Your Nicko is one smart little cookie. He'll get to go to a better school. Hey, there, come on now, Marek. It's not like we're dying or we'll never see each other again."

On the other side of the door, kitchen chairs screeched back across linoleum and there was the sound of big hands thudding embraced backs. When my dad honked his nose, my tears fell like liquid fire.

"How about another beer?" Dad asked, sniffling, clearing his throat.

"Have I ever refused a cold one?"

There was the pop and click of metal caps rolling across the floor. It had always delighted me how Dad treated our kitchen like a bar when Mom went away. I had a feeling that was going away too.

"Listen, Marek, I hate to ask you, but I need to anyway. Got no choice. Any chance you can pull some farewell strings with my loan request that's been growing moss under Mr. His-Nose-Is-Up-His-Ass's desk down at the bank? I'm in a bit of trouble here. I need the money."

"Is your dad getting worse?"

"He is. Oxygen round the clock. You know how it is. I can't work many hours right now. That's the thing. Doc Rivers says my back can't take it. If there's anything you can do before you go…"

I knew Manny Pestrock's grandfather had black lung. Most every miner in Shamokin got some form of that disease eventually. Inside the walls of St. Cornelia's, their coughs rattled the rafters, handkerchiefs raised to cover mouths, white linen seeping with black sputum.

"You know I will, Frank, and if you need to borrow some money from me for a patch here, I can scrape some up. You know that. All you have to do is ask."

Chairs screeched; backs were slapped again. Two grown men sobbed without trying to stop in a kitchen with nothing but beer.

When we moved away from Shamokin, I thought we would go back and visit often. I was wrong. I was a kid, though, so life went forward. My school in State College was better in some ways. We had newer books, and there were more classes to choose from, but I missed my friends and the adult faces I knew: black lines sunk deep into creased eyes and the folds of necks, mouths smiling, palms extended, encouraging me to share the news of my day. Adults didn't shake hands with kids in State College. The first couple times I instinctively extended my hand after we moved there, I heard a gallery of cartoon hecklers in the back of my brain. State College was a nice enough place to live, but it would never be Shamokin.

My parents lived contentedly enough in State College, especially my mother, who decided to take night classes and finish her marketing degree. She got a part-time job selling women's fashions in a store on College Avenue. My dad found another bank job. Sadly, his new bank desk was ordinary, and he was never quite as funny after we left Shamokin. I am sure I was the only person who noticed that about him, and that just makes me feel even worse about being the reason he had to leave his hometown.

Eventually, I fulfilled my mother's dream and went to college. Studied aeronautical engineering at the Massachusetts Institute of Technology. No surprise there, I guess. I stayed at MIT until I was awarded a PhD. Then, the State University of Pennsylvania made me an offer I couldn't refuse. I returned to State College as a professor with a hefty research grant, bought a house three streets away from my parents.

I still dream of the steep, olive-green mountain that ascended to the entrance of the Glen Burns mine, the flock of landed, white birds on the flat field just beyond Coal Street that weren't birds but tombstones, hundreds of them, and one of them is for Manny now.

Manny never found his way to the lineup of the Pittsburgh Steelers. He didn't make it out of the mine either when a fire broke out on level eight during the mid-1980s. Six miners were trapped and buried alive, including Manny and Mr. Kolvasky's youngest boy, David. The headline in the *Centre Daily Times*: "Disaster and Grief Grips Shamokin." In the footage on the television, I recognized people, reheard names of the families I knew well, and wept. The mountain collapsed a secret dinosaur and some great men that day. That meant six funerals for one small town and the angels of St. Cornelia's. I'll never forgive myself for never going back to visit Manny before he died.

Unlike with Manny, I visit Dad several times a week. He has a sunny room in the Memory Care Unit of the Mountainview Convalescent

Home in State College.

"Hey there, what's the date today?" Dad asks the same question, phrased this way, every time I enter his room. He rarely knows who I am anymore. I suspect he is just trying to be polite by asking a question.

They do a fine job here. Dad is always clean-shaven and showered. This morning I see he has eaten most of his customary breakfast of scrambled eggs, bacon, raisin toast, and tea. The local paper and, of course, the *Carbondale Press*, rests on his lap as a comfort. He is no longer able to read.

"Today is September 14, 1999, Dad. I am Nicholas, Nicko, your son."

Dad smiles and waits for me to say something else.

Sometimes, I talk about my wife Alice and our two boys. Last week I recounted the story of Josh playing in his first Pop Warner football game. When Josh got his hands on the football, he ran in the wrong direction. Dad laughed hard at that, slapped his right knee like he did when I'd done lame-brained kid things.

"I have a new invention, Dad," I begin now. "Last time I was here, we looked at pictures of birds in flight. You admired the photo of an albatross. I invented a new airplane wing design. It works exactly like an albatross wing."

Dad nods, furrows his forehead, tries to remember. I take a deep breath and dive in anyway.

"I used to love those wingtip banking shoes you had."

Dad sits back in his chair. Shuts his eyes. He often falls asleep. I sip some lukewarm tea from Styrofoam and wait.

"Dad?" I say quietly after a few minutes.

Dad's eyes are rolling back and forth under blue-veined lids. If he doesn't wake up soon, I will leave and drive to Dan's swimming meet. He might not have an event, but he'll be glad to see me. My boys have inherited my dismal athletic ability and my Michelin Man body type. Even so, they participate in sports more courageously than I ever did. I have so much admiration for them.

I try a few soft claps to decide whether I should wait or leave. Dad sits up, opens his eyes wide, takes me in. I hold my breath. Search for some recognition in his eyes.

"Of course! My wingtip shoes. I'd forgotten those. Always had three pairs, as your mother insisted."

I startle and drop my tea.

"That's right, Dad," I sputter. "And your desk at the bank where you worked in Shamokin looked like a coffin."

"I remember," Dad says, smiling broadly now, chuckling in his old way. "What do you hear from Manny? I'd sure like to hear from his dad again sometime. What do you hear about Frank from Manny, Nicko? Any news about Frank?"

Frank Pestrock passed away long ago, but what's the point in saying that now?

"Would you like to take a drive back home to Shamokin one of these days, Dad?"

Dad leans forward, nods his head vigorously. He looks radiantly happy. My heart burns hot in my chest.

An albatross can fly 10,000 miles in a single journey.

We won't need to go that far.

Mystery Box

The summer of the mystery box, my cousin Rockford and I were too old to play all day and too young to find real jobs picking crop at one of the local fruit and vegetable farms. We did offer to share a position. Our argument was that if you added our ages together, twelve years each, you had a real bargain—a twenty-four-year-old laborer with four legs and four arms just raring to go. It was a clever pitch that never got us anywhere. Some kids our age earned a few hours of cash money as helpers at Lilac Lake Scout Camp, but Rockford couldn't swim, and his asthma was always worse in the woods.

Even though times were tough, we managed to squeeze out enough money for the occasional movie, pinball games at the bowling alley, and our fair share of Mallo Cups. Rockford landed a morning paper route. It paid spit, and the before-dawn risings made him grouchy, but it was better than nothing. I babysat here and there. Not often because my name was the last name on everyone's babysitter list. Babysitting made me miserable. I couldn't help frowning my way through it.

We made it to the first of August before our collective boredom hit an all-time high. Frenzied for a surprise, a windfall, a miracle, anything to set the day apart, we walked into town and decided, on a whim, to combine our pocket change and buy one of the mystery boxes inside Larry Tanner's Second Hand that were so popular that summer. It was either a mystery box or two slices of greasy pizza from DiNunzio's Pies, and we were sick of DiNunzio's by then.

"Let me remind you that *you* are the person who said these boxes are the biggest rip-off ever," I challenged Rockford as we stood, arms crossed over our chests, eyes roaming back and forth across the shelves strung with multicolored, blinking Christmas lights displaying a dozen or so boxes of various sizes and conditions.

Larry Tanner's Second Hand was no bigger than a two-car garage. The roughly built, splintery shelves lining the walls leaned against each other to remain upright. In the middle of the store, lopsided picnic tables piled high with everything under the sun. Pots and pans, shoeshine kits, pocketbooks, men's wallets, bird figurines, clown music boxes, pool balls, alarm clocks, stuffed animals, plastic curlers, yarn balls, fishing poles, and all kinds of "gently used" shoes.

The mystery boxes, wrapped in either Christmas tree paper, silver birthday balloon paper, or tan paper grocery bags, were sealed shut with overlapping layers of clear packing tape: contents as secure as the vault at Fort Knox. A crooked sign with fluorescent orange lettering read: *No lifting, poking, sliding, jostling, or touching of any kind. Hands off! All boxes $10.00 each. NO RETURNS. ALL SALES FINAL. Treasure lies in the eyes of the beholder.*

"I thought they were a rip-off," Rockford admitted, "but Jimmy Cooper found a Topps baseball card signed by Babe Ruth in one of them last week, and if it's authentic, it's worth a shitload. Now that dumb shit might be a rich dumb shit."

It was true that Jimmy Cooper wasn't one of the smartest students in school, but that's not what Rockford meant. Rockford didn't like Jimmy Cooper because Jimmy teased Rockford relentlessly. He'd been hurling slurs Rockford's way for seven years. *Innertube Belly. Gut Boy. Blubber Butt. Lard-ass.*

Rockford had never been skinny but over the years things got worse with his weight as things got worse with his dad. Rockford's dad, my uncle John, had a serious drinking problem. Uncle John hadn't lived with Aunt May and Rockford for a long time, but he was still a part of our little town. When he wasn't locked up for stealing something, he was either falling off the bar stool over at Hank's Place, stumbling down the middle of a street, or puking in someone's front yard.

"Hey, Rock," Larry's wife Helen chimed in from a corner of the thrift store, seated in a plastic patio chair, chomping her way through a pint of unwashed strawberries, blowing dirt off one berry at a time before popping it into her mouth. "If you keep using filthy words, I will have to ask you to exit the premises."

I glanced over as Mrs. Tanner hunched forward to paint a toenail, bare feet propped up on two magazine stacks. The scent of Mrs. Tanner's acrylic nail polish mixed nauseatingly with her rose milk perfume, a perfume both of my grandmothers wore and every other old, papery woman I knew. Mrs. Tanner wasn't that old yet. I didn't know why she wanted to smell old before her time.

"He is very, very sorry, Mrs. Tanner," I said, frowning at Rockford.

Mrs. Tanner tended to be on the touchy side. She didn't tolerate kids coming into the thrift shop just to soak up some free air conditioning. I guess that was fair. Kids usually don't have money to buy anything, but then again, Mrs. Tanner was never in a good mood. My mother said Mrs. Tanner was a sour puss because she'd married a man decades older than her who was only interested in fly fishing.

"He's sorry," I reiterated to make sure she'd heard me.

"I hope you are truly sorry, Rock," Mrs. Tanner said.

"Rock?" Rockford said. "That makes me sound like a famous movie star. Rock Miller. Has a real Hollywood ring to it, don't you think?"

I laughed. Even Mrs. Tanner couldn't stifle a quick chuckle. Rockford was always so funny. When he opened his mouth again, I shook my head, jabbed my index finger at the row of mystery boxes. We had a decision to make.

"Maybe we should pick the smallest one," he suggested. "There might be a diamond ring inside. You know, some wedding that got called off. Or maybe a box big enough for a jewelry box, like the jewelry box you have."

"The one you ripped the ballerina off of because you wanted to give her to your mom for her birthday?" I asked.

"Come on, Aubrey," Rockford groaned. "I was six years old. Give me a damn break."

"Last warning, Rockford," Mrs. Tanner said. "And I am going to tell your mother about this language of yours next time I see her. The last thing she needs in her life is another foul-mouthed no-good Nik."

That last proclamation from Mrs. Tanner had gone too far. Rockford's cheeks turned bright red. He had a right to be mad at Mrs. Tanner. No kid wanted a dad like Rockford's dad. Certainly not Rockford. Rockford didn't want to be anything like his dad. Uncle John was an embarrassment to our whole family, to our whole town. I clenched my fists. I had half a mind to march over and punch Mrs. Tanner in her strawberry-stuffed mouth.

"Let's just choose a box and get going," Rockford said, no doubt noticing that my cheeks were reddening too. I couldn't help myself. I hated it when people were mean to my cousin. What did he ever do to them? To anyone, for that matter?

Instead of the smallest box, Rockford drew a circle in the air around the largest of the mystery boxes and raised his eyebrows. Rockford looked funny when he raised his eyebrows. The hairs were so fair, silvery white like icicles. You could barely see them. Everything about Rockford was pale. His crewcut, eyebrows, cheeks, even the freckles on the bridge of his nose. By the end of the summer, those freckles might be pale gold, but they never made it all the way to brown. When he raised his invisible eyebrows while asking me a question, it made him look like he was terrified.

The largest mystery box was wrapped in Christmas tree paper. I stepped closer to it, leaned forward, and sniffed.

"Smell anything?" Rockford asked.

"Nothing," I answered, "but it's the size of a mini-Igloo cooler. The ones people use to keep fish bait fresh. I bet that's what it is. Somebody's old fish bait cooler."

"Well, which one then?"

"Choose another one," I urged Rockford. "Which other one would you pick?"

"Yes," Mrs. Tanner's voice chimed in again. "Please do choose, Rock. I'm going to add a new rule to this mystery box thing. Absolutely no hemming and hawing. You two are giving me one of my hallucinatory rainbow migraines. I don't have time for that. I am going to the movies with Mr. Tanner tonight."

"That almost sounds like an enjoyable experience," I said.

"I love the movies," Mrs. Tanner gushed, her chair squeaking as she scooted forward to spit a strawberry stem into a trash can.

"I meant your rainbow migraine," I said.

"You better watch yourself too, Miss Aubrey Lockhart," she said, raising dark, colored-in eyebrows at me. Made me think of the old comedian Groucho Marx. "Don't be a smart mouth like your cousin there."

"Ignore her," I said to Rockford.

We continued examining the boxes one by one. I had a hunch. I pointed to one the same size as a box of Pop-Tarts, tan paper grocery bag wrap, the most beat-up-looking thing on the shelf.

I asked Rockford, "Remember when we saw that *Indiana Jones* movie last summer?"

"Not the holy grail scene," he whined, rolling his eyeballs so dramatically I envisioned them popping out of his head and me reaching out to catch the gross, warm, wet little orbs to save them. "We aren't looking for Jesus's favorite water cup here, Aubrey."

"I know that, but the theory kind of fits."

"That box is a dirty trick. It's there to make us think we are being clever by choosing the ugliest box. I bet it's a box of assorted Band-Aids so old they don't even stick anymore."

"Maybe," I said. "But I have a feeling. That one is calling to me."

Rockford raised his eyebrows again, added some tongue clucking. "Next thing you'll be telling me is that you can talk to spirits," he teased.

"You got a better idea?"

"Smell that box if you have all this ESP, hocus-pocus, mumbo jumbo, sixth sense stuff all of a sudden," he said. "Go ahead. It's going to smell like Band-Aids. I'm telling you. Bet you a dollar."

"Do Band-Aids really have a smell?" I asked.

"Everybody knows what Band-Aids smell like," he answered. "Don't tell me you haven't smelled a Band-Aid or two."

"Okay, that's it," Mrs. Tanner said. "I've had enough of you two. Another mystery box rule. Absolutely no smelling the boxes. Hear me? No smelling the boxes."

She was too late. I had already taken a good, deep whiff of my box of choice. It smelled metallic, like the shoebox of old, rusty skeleton keys my grandpa kept on a shelf in his garage. Grandpa would never find the locks meant for any of those keys, but he kept buying them at yard sales anyway. Keys that could unlock rooms, attics, root cellars, secret spaces inside big, old houses, but where? Which doors? Which houses? Keys to nowhere.

"Changed my mind," I told Rockford. "I don't like the smell of that one. You're right. It's a dirty trick."

"Does it smell that bad?" Rockford asked, trying to sniff the air around the box quietly.

"I just don't like how it smells," I answered. "If you could smell a dead end, that's what it would smell like."

"But I don't smell anything," he said, "not even Band-Aids."

"I said no smelling!" Mrs. Tanner said. "You two are officially kicked out. No mystery box for you. You are in violation of the rules of this establishment. Go on now. Be on your merry way." Mrs. Tanner pointed us toward the door with a wave of her nail polish brush.

I grabbed a box from the shelf. It was about the same size as the ugliest box, but this one was wrapped in the birthday balloons, corners tight and perfect, as if it had been wrapped by one of those professional gift wrappers in department stores during the holidays. I brought the box over to Mrs. Tanner with Rockford trailing behind. Everyone had to make a living, and who could resist an extra-large tub of buttered theatre popcorn or a jumbo box of Sno-Caps? Mrs. Tanner snatched the money I slid under her nose, stuffed it in a manilla envelope she kept underneath her chair.

"I'm not giving you a bag," she said.

"Didn't you used to give away free candy with every purchase?" I asked. "Like a Charms?"

Mrs. Tanner groaned. Removing the lid from a shoebox also stored under her chair, she shoved it toward us so we could choose a flavor, which was very nice of her, I'll give her that. It occurred to me then that Mrs. Tanner wasn't bad-looking. Up close she looked less like Groucho Marx and more like Sally Fields. I wanted to ask her why she had decided to marry such an old, boring man, but I bit my tongue.

"One candy per customer," she snapped when Rockford scooped a handful.

The ongoing heat wave smacked us hard when we opened the door and stepped outside. The bell above the door tinkled the same way it had when we entered the shop.

"This candy is sticky," I complained as we unwrapped the Charms. "Probably outdated by only a thousand years or so."

We began walking in the direction of the neighborhood where we both lived.

"Why did you choose that one anyway?" Rockford asked.

"I like cherry," I said. "You know I like cherry."

"I meant the mystery box."

"We were out of time back there with Mrs. Grump," I said. "I just grabbed one."

I stopped then, lifted the box to eye level, shook it. Something moved up and down inside. A soft, dull thud against the top and bottom of the box. At least it wasn't a box full of air. Rockford stuck out his hand.

"Let me see it," he said.

"We can't open it here."

"Why not?" he asked.

"If it's valuable," I said, "we should keep it a secret until we decide what to do."

"Good point," he said. "I won't open it. Just let me hold it."

I handed him the box. He shook it too.

"It's pretty light," he said. "I hope we didn't blow our money on a box of erasers."

"Think positive," I said. "Let's go to your house and open it in the potting shed."

"Okay, boss."

"Hey you two!" Uncle John called out suddenly.

We turned toward Rockford's dad crossing the street toward us, veering sharply back and forth like a tightrope walker caught in a sudden windstorm.

"Oh no," Rockford whispered.

"Hello, kiddies," Uncle John said, stopping a few feet from us, swaying. I bit my lower lip. He stank of booze, as usual, a sweet and sour smell all wrapped into one putrid package. His sunburned nose and cheeks were as red as raw steak meat. I guess he didn't bother with sunscreen. Rockford had inherited his dad's pale skin. They had identical faces, just at different ages. Uncle John's thin frame bore the same clothes I'd seen him in all summer, blue jeans and a torn-up Lynyrd Skynyrd concert T-shirt. He had a strange look to him. All skin and bones everywhere except for a stomach that popped out like he'd wedged a basketball underneath his shirt.

"What's news?" Uncle John asked, slurring his syllables.

"Nothing at all," Rockford mumbled. "We really have to go, Dad."

"What's the rush?" he asked, grinning, sucking air through the sizable spaces between his front teeth. "Don't have a spare minute to chitchat with your old man?"

"We have errands," Rockford said.

"Errands? What are you now, Rockford? Suddenly an *adult* with *errands?*"

Uncle John laughed at his own joke. He used to dress up as Santa Clause before Rockford and I were of school age. He'd made a good Santa Clause. Really had the *Ho Ho Ho* down pat. He drank some then too, but there were enough good times between the bad times to keep things going okay over at Rockford's house.

"What errands?" Uncle John pressed.

A few cars slowed down as they passed by the three of us, no doubt trying to eavesdrop. I wished one of them was my dad or my mom. I glanced over at Rockford. He was staring down at the sunlit sidewalk, gulping like a goldfish lying on a counter. That was his asthma acting up. It got worse when he was nervous or embarrassed or when he was trying not to cry. I was embarrassed and nervous too. I had nightmares about Uncle John puking on my shoes.

Uncle John switched his focus from the top of Rockford's bowed head to me. I met his stare and shrugged. Same eyes as Rockford. Same eyes as his sister, my mother. The blue color of a gas stove flame. Rockford and I didn't look like cousins. I had my dad's brown eyes and dark brown hair.

I thought about my parents. How everyone in town liked them. How Rockford and Aunt May celebrated holidays at my house. How Dad took Rockford fishing with him, showed Rockford how to fix things like cars and indoor plumbing. When I asked my parents what had gone wrong with Uncle John, Mom said her little brother never found the right path for his life. Never went to college. Never found a job he could keep. Began drinking more and more until the drinking just took over. They always made it sound like it wasn't Uncle John's fault, but wasn't he the one to grab the bottle and bring it up to his lips?

"We have to get going, Uncle John," I announced.

"What do you have behind your back, Rockford?" Uncle John asked, taking a few steps toward Rockford.

"Nothing," Rockford responded in a shaky voice.

"Well, I can see it's not nothing."

"It's not really your business, Dad."

"Not my business?" Uncle John cocked his head to the side, frowned, creased his forehead disapprovingly at Rockford.

"It's a birthday gift for my mom," I interjected. "I can carry it, Rockford."

When I put my hand out, Rockford thrust the box toward me, but Uncle John was quick even in his condition. He snatched the box, began turning it over and over.

"What is it?" he asked, looking at me.

"A candle," I said at the same time Rockford said: "An alarm clock."

"Why are you both lying about this box?"

"We're not," Rockford said. "Not exactly."

"Well, one of you is lying."

"It's just that it's ours," I said. "It's a mystery box from Tanner's. We bought it with our own money, Uncle John."

He'd stopped listening to us by then. All he could do was stare at the box. He'd fallen under its spell.

"I think I'll put an end to this hoo-ha right now," he said. "Let's see what we have here."

Uncle John reached into a pocket of his jeans, scooped out a slender, ivory-handled pocketknife. I gasped.

"Dad!" Rockford sounded panicked. "It's our box. Please don't open it."

Uncle John let out a bellow of a laugh. Before he could flip the pocketknife blade open, Rockford charged into him headfirst like a rodeo bull seeing red, hit him dead on in his beach-ball gut, knocked a full-grown adult man on his can. I'd never seen Rockford do anything like that before. He didn't even own a temper as far as I knew. Even though the world flipped to slow motion and my ears began to buzz, I grabbed the box from the sidewalk where Uncle John had dropped it.

"Come on, Rockford," I said, touching my cousin's elbow to turn him around. "Let's go!"

Rockford shrugged me off, turned back toward Uncle John, who was sitting on the sidewalk, blinking, looking up at Rockford like he'd never seen him before.

"Rockford, come on," I repeated.

Rockford spun around then. I took one more look at Uncle John, and we started running for home.

We went as far as we could before Rockford got too tired and we had to slow down and walk. I considered throwing the mystery box over my shoulder to buy us some time, but I wanted that box. It belonged to us. To me and Rockford. It was our mystery, our chance at something, not Uncle John's. After a few blocks, I glanced back. No Uncle John.

The potting shed at Rockford's house was one of our favorite retreats. Aunt May hadn't used it in years. She worked long hours as an aide at a hospital, and when she wasn't doing that, she was running around like a chicken with its head cut off, taking care of everything inside the house. The most she got done outside was reminding Rockford to mow the grass.

When Rockford and I reached the potting shed, we latched the door behind us and collapsed on the ground. The space was empty except for some ripped-up sleeping bags. Chests heaving, we stared up at the roof peak. I placed the mystery box on my belly, balanced it there. All was quiet outside except for some songbirds calling back and forth and the distant hum of an airplane through sky. When the world stayed like that long enough, I sat up. Rockford did too. I handed him the box.

"I picked the box," I said, "so you get to open it."

In the dim light, Rockford looked even paler than usual. His hands were shaking, but he gave me a quick smile and started ripping at the tape layers.

Our mystery box had begun its life as a box of Earl Gray teabags. The box itself wasn't taped shut, so Rockford unfolded the top, turned the box upside down, and dumped out the contents.

Plastic squeeze purses of assorted gem colors. Emerald green, ruby red, and sapphire blue. They made me think of ironed-out gumdrops. It wasn't the worst discovery, though we both sighed out some disappointment. It wasn't teabags, but it wasn't a diamond ring either.

"Maybe there's money in one of them," Rockford suggested, sounding more like himself. Almost hopeful. Excited.

The purses had been used to advertise various businesses in states far away from our South Carolina coastline town—Midwest states like Wisconsin and Iowa. They had addresses, slogans, and phone numbers printed on them.

"Open one, Rockford. We'll take turns. It'll be more fun that way."

"How do they open?" he asked.

"Pinch the sides together at the same time."

Rockford chose a ruby-red purse from a place called Loppy's Ice Cream Parlor that had been "scooping and squirting" since 1946 in a town called Red Cloud. When he squeezed the purse open, it was empty.

"Lousy name for an ice cream place anyway," he remarked, using the empty purse as a mouth, making it open and close in time with his words. "Sorry folks, but at Loppy's, all our ice cream is lumpy."

I laughed and selected a green purse. A bowling lane in Nebraska. It was empty too.

"Munster Lanes," I read aloud. "Like the old TV show. Can't you see Herman Munster tripping in those big shoes of his, dropping a bowling ball on his toe? Eddie getting competitive. He was a spoiled brat, that Eddie Munster."

"Yeah, he was a pain," Rockford agreed. "The grandfather would have wrapped his body up inside one of the mansion's old, dusty oriental rugs like a hotdog in a bun and rolled down the lane, pushing the ball that way."

"And that scene would be in fast motion like they did in all those old TV shows," I said. "TV was pretty bad in the 1960s."

"*The Munsters* were funny, though," Rockford said. "Look at how they keep playing them in reruns."

"Yeah, and look at how you keep tuning in."

We took turns pronouncing the names printed on the other purses like advertisers do on TV and radio: *Pressssstone's Plumbing and Heat-ING! Pioneer Savings BankAROOO!* I found two measly dimes inside *Maple City Taxi. Let's Go Places Together!* Rockford suggested that might be a taxi service in a place made of real pancakes. When he pinched open a yellow smiley-face purse advertising a dentist, *Miles of Smiles,* he pulled out a tightly folded bill, peeled it apart. It was Canadian money.

"Bingo," he said.

"Is it real?"

"I think so," he said, handing me the bill. "It's a twenty, but I don't think Canada's money is worth as much as ours."

"What should we do with it?" I asked.

"Maybe you should ask your dad," he said. "He sells insurance. Isn't that kind of like working with money?"

"Okay."

"Maybe we broke even," Rockford said. "How's that for being positive."

"Excellent."

I refolded the bill. Rockford's stomach growled.

"I'm starving," he said. "Want to go inside and see what's in the fridge? Might be a frozen Mallo Cup in there we can split."

"I guess I can't," I said. "I told my mom I'd be back around two."

When I stood up to go, Rockford didn't. He continued stacking the purses, knocking them down, restacking. I hesitated as he constructed and wrecked one purse tower after another. Eventually, I sat back down beside him.

Uncle John built the potting shed for Aunt May during better times. Once, it was like an illustration from a fairy-tale book. Wood siding painted buttercup yellow. Red metal roof. Four paned windows no bigger than cereal boxes. Flower boxes that used to sing with color, dark purple and violet pansies, the elfin faces of spring. Fluted pink petunias and golden marigolds during summer months. Above the door, a Pennsylvania Dutch hex sign, a circle as big as the clocks in our school classrooms decorated with primary-colored stars, the promise of good fortune.

In time, the hex sign fell off, the siding faded, the roof dulled, and though the window boxes hung on, they rotted through. At least the inside still smelled of the potting soil Aunt May handed to Rockford and me in paper cups when we were little. Silky soft dirt, black as coal with white dots she told us was flower food. Our job was to tuck the flowers in after she planted them in the boxes. Our fingernails turned black underneath when we helped those boxes. Funny how things that seem gross at the time can turn out to be good memories.

Rockford stopped stacking purses, lifted his chin.

"You don't think I hurt my dad, do you?" he wheezed, choking near the end.

"No," I answered right away. "Definitely not. He's fine."

The phone inside the house rang ten times and quit. Aunt May calling on her work break to check on Rockford. Rockford pulled up one side of a sleeping bag to wipe off his face but decided against it. I didn't have to look over to know tears were spilling every time he blinked. Rockford never had to gulp with me.

"Don't do something like that again. Okay, Rockford?"

"Okay."

Rockford had already started running for home, so he hadn't seen it, but sitting there on the sidewalk, a quivery half-smile had appeared on Uncle John's lips like he was proud of Rockford for the first time ever.

August

The plastic park-service-issued nametag reads *Lonny,* but this is incorrect. Her name is *Lonnie,* Lonnie Gray. It's only a summer job, so Lonnie let the misspelling slip. Anyway, the name she likes hearing the most is the one her grandmother and mother use when the three generations of Shawnee women are alone together. In those times, Lonnie is "Nuttah," which means "my heart."

"Hey Lonnie, what would happen if a smile suddenly got slapped on your face?"

Rick Godfrey jams his square, pimply face into the middle of the window. Calling him a cook, even of the shortest order, would be a stretch. Rick's only job in the snack bar kitchen is punching buttons on a microwave.

Lonnie frowns, pinches the edges of the white paper boats Rick pushes toward her. Turning around, she places hotdogs on the counter in front of a row of shivering kids sipping cocoa from Styrofoam cups. Twin girls, one with eyeglasses steamed opaque, and an older brother have been swimming in the creek that gallops through this section of Canyon Vista State Park.

"How's the water today?" Lonnie asks, sliding squeeze bottles of mustard and ketchup where little hands can reach them.

"Freezing," the boy replies.

That's the standard answer. Inside the park's roped swimming area, the Sehoy Creek's white-capped currents froth and tickle bellies. The water is deep enough for swimming, but tourists who climb down the metal ladder mostly wade in circles like a herd of sleepwalkers. The Sehoy is ice-cold, even now, in the dead center of an August heat wave. Only

119

locals sleep through winter snowstorms dreaming of swimming the Sehoy.

"Here's the trick. Dive in right away. Don't stand there thinking about it. And then, swim hard," Lonnie suggests to the blue-lipped trio.

She looks past drippy, bony shoulders at a *Sorry, folks! We're closed* sign hanging cockeyed in the snack bar window, then down at her wristwatch. Two more hours with this jackass Rick bugging her, staring at her chest every chance he gets. Two more hours until her cousin Bodie swings by in his rickety Ford truck. He better have enough gas to get here. If not, she'll have to jog home and try not to sweat to death.

"Lonnie, you're in outer space again. The young man is paying up," Rick barks through the window.

The boy has placed a row of six Sacagawea dollar coins face-up on the counter. Lonnie reaches underneath for the change tray.

"You look like her," the girl without glasses says, her smile missing two upper front teeth. She points to the coins. "You're pretty too."

"Thank you," Lonnie says. "That's really nice of you."

Lonnie glances at the coins and then at her own image reflected in a silver napkin dispenser: straight hair pulled back, high cheekbones, almond eye shape. There is a resemblance, of course. The girl on the coins looks about the same age too. She's young to have an infant on her back. It must be her baby, though. Why else put it there?

"I haven't seen any of these coins yet," Lonnie says to the boy.

"They just came out last year," he says. "Early 2002."

"My brother collects coins," one twin explains.

Lonnie smiles down at the three upturned faces, masking a familiar rage at the idea that the United States government would use the image of the first, original people of this land for any purpose of its own.

"Hey Lon, I want to see your gorgeous face in gold," Rick says. "Be right out."

Lonnie turns around. Somehow Rick has managed to poke his head all the way through the window. Lonnie gives some thought to a guillotine. Bodie better have enough gas to get here, and he better be on time.

"As if you know what my *face* looks like," she says. "Don't you have something to do in the kitchen?"

Rick frowns, matches her glare.

"Get back to work, Rick."

"Fine. Whatever."

He backs his head out of the window, mouthing: "Bitch" to

which Lonnie responds with a muted: "Fuck off."

The boy's hotdog is gone. Inhaled. He is watching his sister's jaws moving up and down.

"Hey, Rick," Lonnie calls over her shoulder. "It's buy-three-dogs-get-one-free day. Remember? Need another dog out, please."

To her surprise, Rick plays along. Lonnie is rewarded with a wide smile from the coin collector as she serves him a second helping.

It's Sunday. That means dinner at her grandparents' house with her mother, Bodie's parents, and a smattering of other close relatives. At least she'll have Bodie all to herself during the ride over unless his little brothers tag along. She and Bodie need to hatch a plan regarding their recent discovery in the forest. He doesn't want to help Lonnie put it to good use, he made that clear, but she needs his help, so he's going to have to help her. Bodie fits comfortably into a pair of sixteen-year-old Goody Two-shoes. Lonnie is nearly the same age, but she has no interest in being anyone's role model.

—

"I guess you will be turning eleven next week," Lonnie's grandfather, John Hawthorne, says to a ten-year-old Lonnie.

"Ten and not until next month, actually, on September fourth."

Summer is nearing an end, and Lonnie has had her fill of it. She's ready to go back to school, which means getting off Elk Mountain for part of every weekday. There isn't much down in the valley in Montoursville where the school bus will deposit her, but there's more than Canyon Vista State Park, the mobile home park where she lives with her mom and Bodie lives with his parents, their grandparents' cabin a few miles down the road from that.

In Montoursville, there are no farms, barns, cows, vast armies of dense trees, creeks with nothing but round-edged rocks, the constant quiet of forest. Lonnie is sick to death of listening to nothing but the world of small things. If she hears one more insect, loud as a drill set to the side of her skull, she might scream her way to the first school bell of the year.

"What will your school subjects be this autumn, Lonnie?"

"I don't know yet."

Grandpa is a retired high school principal turned organic gardening addict. Lonnie is walking to the lower garden with him only because her mother asked her to, more like croaked her to, from inside the hammock on Lonnie's grandparents' front porch. Mom got home after three a.m. last night, another late shift drawing beer from the taps at the Black Squirrel Tavern. Connie Gray is transforming into a black squirrel herself, the dark rings under her eyes blending into her dark brown irises: charcoal briquettes for eyeballs.

It's been rough. Lonnie's dad, Justin Gray, left when Lonnie was three. Last word, he was living in some province in northern Canada. He occasionally phones Bodie's dad, Bodie Sr., looking for money. They used to be best friends. That was before he married Bodie Sr.'s sister, Connie, and treated her worse than shit.

"I suggest you call the school office and request your textbooks early so that you can read several of the introductory chapters ahead of time," Grandpa says.

Lonnie doesn't want to walk or talk with her grandfather. All he ever does is quiz her with that sour puss of his: the names of trees or the cloud types he has been teaching her since her toddler years, times tables, abbreviations for the elements listed on the periodic table, the names and spellings of all the state capitals in the United States of America in alphabetical order for bonus points. He's never satisfied with the number of correct answers Lonnie or any of the cousins can provide. No human child could ever please this man.

Why did Bodie have to sign up for the middle school cross-country team anyway? There are so many preseason practices. Two good legs can run anywhere. Lonnie hates it when Bodie isn't around, and this August is the hottest August ever. She closes her eyes and imagines snowflakes filtering through the trees. They fall slow and settle silent onto the dirt path underneath her feet.

———

"Smells like Cheez Doodles in here. Hand them over," Lonnie says to Bodie, swinging the whining truck door toward her bony hip and slamming. Rick can finish sweeping up the snack bar alone. He can take out the trash and lock up too. He deserves it. He had showed up an hour late to open the place.

"I know, and I ate them all, but you can lick the bag," Bodie teases.

"Selfish pig."

"You work in a snack shack. You can hog up hotdogs all day long if you want."

"Would you eat anything Rick Godfrey touched?" Lonnie asks. "No stowaways? Where's Donny and Arlo?"

Bodie shrugs, cranks his window down as Lonnie lights a cigarette she swiped from the pocket of a sweatshirt some delivery guy left hanging inside the walk-in cooler.

"You should be nicer to Rick. He's about the only person in the world who will help you with this recent, lamebrained idea of yours because I won't. Don't even think about asking me again. I know you've been thinking about it all day."

"Rick is so disgusting. He's lamebrained enough to think that one of these days I am suddenly going to stop detesting him. He nauseates my soul. I will never be nice to him."

"He's been nuts about you since third grade. He'd do anything for you. Jump off the Empire State Building. Break into Fort Knox. Help you screw up your life."

Lonnie arches her neck back, launches an arrow of white smoke toward the roof of the truck cab. The smoke takes a right-degree turn when it hits solid blockade, races toward the top of Bodie's head in the shape of a witch's bony finger. He coughs and smacks at the air.

"My life? Always so dramatic," Lonnie says. "It's a prank. A joke. That's all. Jesus. And as for Rick, he likes anything that falls into the category: *girl with tits*."

"Maybe. In any event, don't ask him to help you either. This prank is bound to backfire on you, Lon."

"Shut up, Bodie."

"No, I won't shut up, and blow that shit the other way or I swear, I will pull over and dump you out. Where'd you get that cigarette anyway? Smells like a skunk's ass."

When Bodie and Lonnie laugh together, they sound like the two little bandits who stole their grandmother's warm apple pie one Thanksgiving morning, hid in the root cellar, ate the whole thing, and somehow didn't get sick.

—

"Are those your new school shoes?" her grandfather's voice asks.

The only good thing about walking to the lower garden today while Bodie laps the middle school track is that Lonnie can check on the beavers. Last week one was bobbing on the surface of the dam, a whiskered submarine, silent, stealthy, but Lonnie had spied her quickly.

In Lonnie's favorite book, C.S. Lewis's *The Lion, the Witch and the Wardrobe*, children enter a magical land through a door at the back of a wardrobe. All the animals talk in this land. A beaver couple lives inside a cozy burrow with fine china teacups, lamps on doilies, a hearth with an orange fire, ticking clocks, and fat, stuffed furniture.

If Lonnie could dive and see the beaver's house in her grandfather's lower garden, maybe the beaver would invite Lonnie inside. Maybe Mrs. Beaver bakes orange rind scones. Maybe she is waiting anxiously for Lonnie's visit, crocheting, a Parcheesi board set up behind the curtained window. Lonnie could tell her about all the animals she has: two dogs, a cat, one hamster, two gerbils, a goldfish, and Ruth, an ancient rabbit Lonnie believes is a goddess. Her mom has always been proud of Lonnie's adoration for animals of all kinds. She never said no to a pet that Lonnie wanted to bring home. Not once.

"Lonnie, I just asked you a question," Grandpa says.

"Sorry."

"We're going into the chard rows for slugs. I hope those aren't your good shoes you are wearing. It is bound to be muddy."

"Don't worry about it."

"It is not a question of my level of concern. It is a matter of practicality and your mother's restricted budget. These are life lessons for you, young lady. Work hard in school. You can't make a decent life pulling beer taps behind a bar like your mother. Your mother needs to enroll in some sort of technical school. Life doesn't make itself."

"These aren't my school shoes," Lonnie lies.

She almost adds: Mom's too tired. She never gets any sleep, and she *is* making a perfectly decent life. *She's* not the one who up and left.

As Lonnie and her grandfather approach the gate to the lower garden, there is something off-kilter about the August morning. The suspended leaves, usually so full of song, are strangely still. Birds with their throats locked up tight. Something leaden settles around Lonnie's shoulders. She should have joined the cross-country team with Bodie.

—

Lonnie and Bodie have been treasure-hunting the woods of Bradford County for most of their mutual sixteen-year-old lives. The suspense that goes along with being explorers of such a vast, untamed world is perfect for killing boredom. The bounty of their discoveries fills one corner of their grandparents' root cellar: canteens, bullet shells, a gilt picture frame, silver comb, clock hands, one military boot, a fillet knife, shoebox of assorted fishing lures, and a menagerie of antique glass bottles dug up from the remnants of the old Lenox farmstead.

Last Sunday Lonnie had the day off from work, and she and

Bodie made a decent haul from a deserted campsite near Bird Woman Falls. Lonnie found a silver charm bracelet and Bodie dug up an unopened bottle of Jim Beam buried under a tree. They had to hurry out of the woods because, according to the sun's position, they were already late for Sunday dinner. Bodie hummed, then whistled, hummed, whistled, fist gripping the throat of the whiskey bottle, amber liquid rising toward the cap and falling back down.

Bodie was always in a good mood. He had adored life from day one. Loved the mountains. Loved Bradford County. Loved Elk Mountain. His long-range plan was to work in his dad's lumber business after high school and save enough money for a new, cherry red Chevy truck with custom rims. All the years growing up, side by side with Bodie, Lonnie watched for some sign of discontent in her cousin. Never saw so much as one hint.

"Do you like whiskey all of a sudden?" Lonnie asked.

"I like it all right. You gonna keep that?"

Lonnie held up her wrist, made the charms on the bracelet dance: a miniature suitcase, plane, passport, Eiffel Tower, baguette, artist palette, croissant.

"I don't know, probably not. Maybe I can get some money for it when school starts."

"It's pretty. You should keep it. You're good at French, you're not that bad at painting, and you eat a lot of bread."

"I do not. You're the one who eats bread all the time, even stale hamburger buns with nothing on them. You eat anything."

They stopped marching at the same time on the same step forward. People don't spend a lifetime roaming woods and not develop a sixth sense for the contrived hand of man.

"You see it?" Bodie asked.

Lonnie nodded. "Brush pile under the crab apple tree," she said. Bodie handed her the whiskey bottle.

When he tossed a pebble into the pile, the jagged, metal teeth of a jaw trap sprung into view, slammed shut in the center of a cyclone of rising sticks, leaves, and dirt.

"Damn. Let's take that with us," Lonnie suggested.

"What for? That's nothing but a Duke Square-Jaw Trap. Only thing that's good for is snaring a fox or a small coyote maybe."

"I've had this hilarious idea in my head lately," she answered. "As luck would have it, all I need is a trap to make it work."

"My dad's got plenty of traps."

"Yeah, but he'll know if one is missing."

"I'm not screwing with a fellow trapper. What kind of idea?"
"Come on, Bodie. Let's just borrow it."
"No."

—

The almost ten-year-old Lonnie latches the garden gate behind her, turns to follow her grandfather. Stops. She's seen cage traps in her grandfather's gardens many times, but they have always been empty. She's never had a reason to think much about them. The traps were no different than the posts making up the fence or the wooden stakes holding up the vines.

Today something alive is inside the rectangular metal box. Eight eyes on a single, white body. One mouth locked on open. Fangs long and pointy. The animal resembles a strange, angry snake.

Lonnie's grandfather whistles now in the same way he does when he bends over green stalks in his garden to pluck a ripe, prize-worthy yellow tomato or speckled squash.

"Lucky days are here again," he sings.

Waterfalls begin crashing inside Lonnie's ear canals. The black eyes peer out at her, accompanied by hissing and guttural growling. Lonnie's heart claws to get outside.

"There's the little beast who's been eating everything in sight down here, and I can see why," her grandfather mutters to himself. "She's a fat one. I was hoping for that beaver but no matter. Stay back, Lonnie."

Back where?

"What *is* that?" she whispers.

"Opossum."

"You sure?"

—

Lonnie draws on the skunk-ass cigarette again, coughs, crinkles the freckles on the bridge of her nose, drops the cigarette into an empty Hires Root Beer bottle in the console cup holder of Bodie's truck.

"That thing is on the strong side," Lonnie admits, leaning over to pluck an empty bag from the car mat. "I can't believe you didn't save me any Cheez Doodles."

"I never do," Bodie responds, turning onto the gravel driveway that leads into their grandparents' house.

"I hope it's not ham today," Lonnie groans. "I hate ham."

"You say that every Sunday, and it's always ham, every Sunday."

"You think that trap still has some life in it? It worked perfect when you set it off. It wasn't rusty, was it? How many times can you reuse those things?"

"I swear to God. I told you, Lon. I am not getting involved in this. No way in hell. I don't want to hear about it. If you promise to forget we ever came across that cursed thing, I'll drive a bulldozer over to the Lenox foundation. Maybe we can dig up some real Lenox skeletons."

"Weenie," Lonnie says.

"You need to let that whole opossum thing go once and for all," Bodie says. "That was six years ago. Bury it, Lon."

"I might be willing to bury it, but *he* keeps bringing it up. *He* keeps retelling the story. He can't resist tormenting me. Told the whole tale again to everyone at his beloved Hawthorne family reunion two months ago. Remember? Your dad was so pissed at him. Grandma was mad too. She didn't talk to him for two weeks. He's never let the story die about the time you chickened out shooting your first deer, either. You were only twelve. He's supposed to be our grandfather, not a complete asshole."

"I am out of this one, Lon," Bodie says quietly, evenly. "And you should give up the idea too. It's got a bad feel to it."

When they arrive at their grandparents' house, everyone is seated around the dining room table eating.

"How many times do I have to say that Sunday dinner begins at six p.m. sharp?" John Hawthorne asks from the head of the table as Lonnie and Bodie take their customary seats across the table from each other.

"We had some late customers at the snack bar," Lonnie says. "Not like we could just kick them out."

Connie Gray pops up from her chair, circles around the table with the mashed potato bowl, delivers a mound onto their empty plates with an ice cream scooper.

"Lonnie, an information packet arrived from Drexel today," she says, searching for the smallest slice of ham for her daughter's plate.

John Hawthorne clears his throat, leans forward.

"Drexel as in Drexel University?" he asks. Around the table, everyone stiffens and bows toward plates. "That's a tall order, Miss Lonnie Gray. I don't have the impression you have the sort of grades necessary for an institution like Drexel, even with my legacy connection. What about some kind of technical school?"

"I am going to be a veterinarian," Lonnie speaks to Bodie.

Whenever Lonnie's grandfather laughs at the dinner table, he smacks the tabletop with his fist, erupting liquids from glasses. Water, milk, and cranberry juice flow onto placemats. The flames in the centerpiece tremble.

"That's utterly ridiculous and you know it. Be levelheaded, Lonnie. Be practical. My advice would—" John Hawthorne's laughter takes over and gets the best of him. He can't seem to get another word out.

"John, stop it," Lonnie's grandmother interjects, standing up from the table. "Lonnie, hurry to the kitchen and check the stove. I smell smoke."

Lonnie drops her fork onto her stoneware plate with a clang and a clatter, doesn't hesitate when her chair topples backward, and stomps out of the dining room.

"Get back here! Connie, retrieve that insolent daughter of yours. She's going to hear what I have to say to her whether she likes it or not."

"Leave her alone, Dad," Connie says. "Lonnie does have the grades. She can go anywhere she wants. Places better than Drexel. Leave her alone!"

When Bodie appears beside Lonnie in the kitchen, they head straight for the root cellar. The root cellar smells sweet, like rich, wet soil.

"Let's go get that trap and set it somewhere in the lower garden where he'll step on it right now," Lonnie manages to whisper, settling her back against a damp wall. "I hate him so much. He's such a son of a bitch!"

"He is." Bodie slides down the wall beside her. "He's the epitome of evil."

"I swear he thinks I am not intelligent enough to do anything I want to do because of the Shawnee part, because of Mom's part, your dad's part, Grandma's part. Why did he ever marry Grandma in the first place?"

"I don't know."

"I'll tell you why. So he can make all of us feel like complete pieces of shit every day of our lives. You should change your last name, Bodie. Your dad should too. Let's go and get that trap. Right. Fucking. Now."

"That's only going to get us into a lot of trouble, Lon. Besides, it's small, that trap. Won't do much more than bruise his ankle a little if he's wearing his sneaks and nothing at all if he's wearing boots. What's that going to accomplish? Forget it. Forget him. He is an asshole, and he always will be. You're gonna be a vet. I know you are. Who cares what he thinks of you or any of us."

"I'll hide his boots," Lonnie says.

"You don't want to do anything that could keep you from going to college. Think about it that way. Then he'd get the last laugh. He'd love that more than anything else."

"Shut up, Bodie," Lonnie says.

Accepting the whiskey bottle Bodie retrieves from their treasure pile, she tips it back, then cries as hard as she needs to.

—

Lonnie turns to her grandfather.

The opossum is running around in circles inside the cage trap, a tumbling, banging tornado. Down by a shed, the red wheelbarrow full of rainwater. Maybe they can put the opossum in that and wheel him to another part of the woods.

"Where should we take him?" Lonnie rasps.

In a blur of color and motion, Lonnie's grandfather raises his rifle. He sometimes carries it as a precaution when he walks as far as the lower garden. Lonnie has never seen the gun off his back. She's never seen it balanced on his shoulder, horizontal.

The trigger is pulled.

Gunshots are always a lot louder than you remember.

A crimson hole appears on the opossum's hind area, but he continues to spin. The air fills with an unholy sound, the wail of the wounded.

Lonnie cups her ears and screams.

More gunshots. Muffled this time.

When the world falls to silent, her grandfather steps forward, bends over to examine his work, and Lonnie's arms drop to her sides.

Some of the eyes inside the trap belong to babies. Three of them, clinging to the larger opossum's back. Lonnie watches as they melt down the sides of their mother's body, plop and curl around her in a limp halo.

When Lonnie and her grandfather return from the lower garden that day, a young Bodie launches off the tire swing and sprints to meet them.

Lonnie's head is down. She reaches out, grabs Bodie's hand.

"I'm sick," she wheezes.

The cousins peel away from their grandfather's trudging boots. They sit side by side on the creek bank below their grandparents' cabin and wait together for Lonnie to stop being sick.

—

The Sunday following the boy with the Sacajawea coins, thunderstorms hit hard. The new park ranger at Canyon Vista never closes the snack bar on stormy days. Only the lifeguards get to stay home.

"Cheer up, Miss Sunshine," Rick shouts to Lonnie. "At least we're getting paid for doing nothing,"

She ignores him, unwraps her third ice cream sandwich. Earlier, Rick dragged one of the picnic benches through the front screen door, placed it in front of the counter, and centered his spine on top. Sore from playing too much football, he explained, like she cared. He's been lying in the same position for hours.

Lonnie paces the kitchen's linoleum floor, keeps an eye on Rick through the pickup window. Hands folded over his heart, grinning like a fool. Utterly entranced by the spin of the ceiling fan.

Rick must know how to set a simple jaw trap. He probably sets traps with his dad. Lonnie could figure out how to set the trap herself, but she's never set a trap before, and she hates to take any chances.

Lonnie swings the kitchen door open, walks to stand over Rick.

"If I let you see my tits, will you do something secret for me and keep your mouth shut about it until your dying day?"

Rick sits up lightning-fast.

"Like what? Like, what do I have to do?"

"Just set a small jaw trap. I'm… I am… I want to help my grandpa out as a surprise."

Crusted mustard is stuck in the corners of Rick's mouth. He wrinkles his forehead.

"Why don't you just get Bodie to do it?"

"I am asking you. You have six seconds to decide before the offer is off the table forever."

Rick's eyes fall to Lonnie's chest, freeze, and glaze over like a Looney Tunes character who got hit over the head with an anvil. He reaches out to stroke her shiny hair, but Lonnie pulls back.

"Six, five, four…"

"Okay," he says, standing up. "Deal."

Rick follows Lonnie into the walk-in cooler. Stupid Rick. He didn't even ask how long she was going to let him look. She'll wait for him to blink. He'll miss everything. She points him to the other end of the cooler.

"Stay over there and turn your back to me," Lonnie orders. "I'll tell you when to turn around and look."

Lonnie tugs her T-shirt out of her shorts, pulls it up and over her head. Refrigerated air grips her shoulders. She shivers. She will just tip her bra up once. Really fast. She doesn't have to take it off. She should have left her T-shirt on too. Too late.

"Hurry up, Lonnie. I'm freezing over here."

Lonnie swallows.

Eight eyes.

A halo.

There has never been such a crybaby as little Miss Lonnie Gray.

What about some kind of technical school?

Keeping her fingers tight on her bra, Lonnie spins around.

Rick didn't stay on the other side of the walk-in. He is standing inches away, mesh shorts and the white flash of underwear around his ankles.

He reaches out, places his hands on the top of Lonnie's shoulders, and pushes down.

"I've heard you people are magic with this kind of stuff," he says. "How about showing me some of your ancient ways."

When Lonnie drops to her knees, Rick sighs deeply.

Waterfalls crash into Lonnie's ear canals again, but this time she doesn't scream or cry. She raises her jaw, swings her head to the side, and bites as deep as her teeth will let her into Rick's hairy thigh.

Soon she's outside the snack bar, running and spitting, poking her arms into the sweatshirt abandoned in the walk-in. It's not that far, less than six miles to the mobile home park. She knows the shortcut through the woods. Several times she glances over her shoulder, but Rick isn't there.

Lonnie heads straight to Bodie and knocks softly on his bedroom door. Bodie has seen this expression on Lonnie's face before. His eyes flicker recognition. He bites his lower lip, swings the door open.

"Don't ask," Lonnie says, folding into a beanbag chair across from an episode of *Everybody Loves Raymond* on Bodie's small, black-and-white TV. "I'll tell you later. Is *ER* on?"

Bodie is right. Bad thoughts tend to bring bad luck. Doing anything with that jaw trap is a rotten idea.

"Stop looking over at me. I'm okay," Lonnie says. "Can we switch to *ER*?"

"No, it's too depressing," Bodie answers. "Want some Doodles?"

"Do you even have some?"

"Not really."

"Shut up, Bodie."

Lonnie's hands tremble into the pockets of the sweatshirt.

"What happened?" Bodie asks.

"Nothing I couldn't handle. For real, no Doodles?"
"Not one curl."

—

Lonnie quit her job working at Canyon Vista Snack Bar, so Bodie has to drive farther to give her a ride home from work, but she's making good money waiting tables inside Dot's Diner in Montoursville. She buys Bodie a full tank of gas for his truck every week and more gas whenever he needs it.

Bodie and Lonnie are seated at their grandparents' dining room table. Another Sunday dinner. Outside, most of the trees have thrown their autumn leaves to the ground. They stand taller and lighter for it, black spines erect, limbs proudly exposed. Lonnie is busy burying little pieces of ham in her mashed potatoes.

"Did you decorate the diner for Halloween yet, Lon?" her mother asks from the other end of the long, oak table. "I have some extra skeleton lights you could borrow that we didn't put up at the Squirrel this year if you want."

"Sure. You know Dot. She loves Halloween."

"What are you going to be this Halloween, Arlo?" Lonnie asks her little cousin.

Arlo just turned seven. He's the youngest. Unlike Lonnie, Arlo loves ham. He's got a mouthful. No room for speech.

"Arlo is dressing as Sleeping Beauty," Bodie teases.

Arlo squirms and whines in his padded chair beside his big brother.

"Hey, Mom, where's Dad?" Connie Gray asks her mother, who has just returned from the kitchen with a basket of warm rolls. "I don't ever remember him being late for Sunday dinner."

"He'll be here soon, I'm sure," she answers. "He went to pull up the stakes in the lower garden. Getting ready for cold weather. You know how much there is to be done this time of year."

Pausing by the window, Lonnie's grandmother cocks her head to the side.

"Actually, I see him now," she says. "Something's wrong. He seems to be limping."

Lonnie's body stiffens.

Sometimes it is impossible to stop your mouth from exploding into a grin. Bodie set the jaw trap after all. He waited until the best time of year when leaves smother everything on the forest floor. Bodie is so clever about the laws of nature. The habits of men who lack pure instinct and good hearts are no match for him. He is Shawnee. He is superior. Lonnie finds Bodie's eyes across the table and climbs inside.

The Hocker House

The Hocker house was a source of gossip long before Jeff Moomah came around the corner and planted his Wiffle ball bat in the middle of the Ricters' cement patio like Charles Heston as Moses parting the Red Sea. Jeff was *scrawny*. My mother's word. *Skin and bones and nothing in the muscle department.* My dad's words. Jeff looked remarkably like the kid on the cover of *MAD* magazine. Same gap-toothed smile. Same giant ears set low on the sides of his head. I'd never seen Jeff in a suit and tie, though, like the magazine kid. Jeff dwelled in a predictable rotation of faded Phillies Baseball T-shirts year-round.

Hal Ricter, Jenny Brenner, and I were sitting at the picnic table sucking on rainbow-colored Fla-Vor-Ices, not talking about much of anything except how we always lost Super Balls after a day or two of ownership, and my mother's theory that our neighborhood's current mosquito infestation was our fault: frisbees collecting rainwater in backyards.

"Good thing you guys are sitting down," Jeff bellowed, one arm straight out in front of him, pressing that staff deep into the swirling sea. "Because I saw Mr. Hocker pushing a dead body in a wheelbarrow to the top of Maple Avenue last night."

"Jeff, what are you talking about now?" I groaned.

"Jeff," Hal echoed me. "Don't start. It's way too hot for your crap today. Nobody wants to hear it."

That summer of 1974 was a fireball. My mother couldn't slather enough Avon moisturizing products on her face. "Have you seen photographs of people who spend even small amounts of time in arid climates? Wrinkled raisins."

Is there such a thing as a smooth raisin?

The summer of '74, Jenny and I were twelve. Hal was eleven. Jeff was the oldest at thirteen. Jeff was notorious for making up stories. The silliest so far involved him falling out of the cherry tree in his front yard. He claimed his tumble had been intentional on account of ducking a BB that came flying out of nowhere. Our mothers got the real story from Mrs. Moomah. Jeff swiped his little cousin's BB gun and climbed the tree to try it out. Oh, the mighty recoil wielded by a little kid's Red Ryder BB Gun. We were still teasing Jeff about that one.

"What did the body look like?" Jenny's lips were blue from her raspberry Fla-Vor-Ice, but she was freaking out already. I could tell. Jenny was a scaredy-cat. Wouldn't even peek inside books about vampires or werewolves.

"He had it inside one of those lawn and leaf trash bags. Knees curled up to its chest. Like a big baby in a sack," Jeff said, grinning, silver braces phosphorescent with yellow rubber bands. Jeff's orthodontist gave him a new color of elastics every visit. Jeff was always fiddling with those elastics. He accidentally shot one through the air in his math class once, and it landed on Mrs. Barker's shoe tip. He liked to brag about that day. It was one of his few true stories.

"Okay, so wait a minute here," I challenged. "It was a black bag?"

"Duh," Jeff answered. "Aren't all lawn and leaf bags black?"

"It could have been anything," I said, returning to my Ice, which was quickly melting into nothing more than a plastic sleeve of neon-green sugar water. "Could have been yard trimmings, a dead raccoon he found in his drainage ditch. My dad found one in our drainage ditch not that long ago. Fox got him, or a giant hawk. Wasn't all there. For one thing, the whole head was missing."

"Gross," Jenny groaned. "Thanks for that."

"It was a human body," Jeff said. "I could see the shape clear as day."

"In the middle of the night, in the dark, inside a black bag, at the bottom of a wheelbarrow, you saw the shape of a *human* body as clear as day. Give us a break." I punctuated my plea with a giant roll of my eyeballs so expansive it was painful. "What time was it?"

"It was after midnight, but some lampposts were still on," Jeff said. "Why would Mr. Hocker be pushing something like lawn trimmings or a headless raccoon around in the middle of the night? That's nothing to hide."

"Cuz he's a weirdo and a hermit, and he doesn't want to see or talk to anybody," Hal said.

I laughed, seeing this whole thing as another lineup of me and Hal against Jeff, who was never going to be able to make up a good story to save his life.

"Should we call the police?" Jenny interjected, sniffy and quivery now. Jenny stayed out of all disagreements. She never picked a side. "Do you guys really think Mr. Hocker would actually kill somebody? I mean, he is a little weird I guess, but not evil or dangerous. Right?"

"Who knows," Jeff said. "Nobody knows much about that guy. Anything is possible. Maybe that's why his kids left here and never came back. Maybe he's a serial killer. Maybe he's got a torture chamber in his house. Maybe that's what the blood window was all about that one Halloween."

"Oh, my God!" Jenny gasped. "We should call the police right now."

"And tell them what?" Hal snapped. "Another one of Jeff's big fat fibs? Come on, Jeff. You're killing us here. You know it wasn't a *human* body. It had to be something else. I bet old man Hocker isn't even strong enough to push an *empty* wheelbarrow all the way from his house to the top of this street. Isn't he like a hundred and fifty years old? Are you sure it was him, or was it just someone who looked like him?"

"Okay, Hal, wowee, look at you," Jeff said. "Nice to meet you, Columbo."

"Shut up," Hal said.

"Kojak?" Jeff teased.

"Shut up!" Hal said, standing up.

Jeff was no physical match for Hal. Hal might have been about a foot shorter than Jeff, but his entire body reminded me of Popeye's blown-up forearms: muscled and bursting at the seams. He wore his older brother's shrunken hand-me-downs that would have been too tight for him new. Whenever Hal whizzed down Maple Avenue, struggling to stand up on his bike seat like a circus acrobat, my dad would say, "There goes G.I Joe. Kid's fearless. One of these days he's gonna sail right over the top of those handlebars and hit the pavement, *el splato.*"

"Make me shut up," Jeff challenged Hal.

"You really want me to? Because I will."

"Come on, guys," I interrupted. It was hot as blazes that day. "Who cares?"

"Okay, okay," Hal said, surrendering and stepping over to the grass to wipe his sticky, grapey hands. "Where did Mr. Hocker, our so-called suspect, end up with the bagged body in the barrow, our so-called victim?"

"I don't know. You think I was going to get out of bed and go chasing after him?" Jeff asked. Having tired of parting oceans, he was twirling the Wiffle ball bat majorette style. "He could have sliced my throat and jammed me inside that bag, too, for all I knew."

I swayed my eyes to Jenny. She looked white as a ghost.

"We should tell our parents at least," Jenny managed. Her Ice had slumped over. It was leaking steadily onto the top of the table.

Jenny's curly hair went wild when it was hot and humid. She was turning frizzy and hysterical on us at the same time. Adults seemed to think Jenny looked like Shirley Temple. I didn't agree. My mother had a porcelain Shirley Temple doll locked inside the china closet in our dining room. The only resemblance I could find was that Jenny had blonde hair. Jenny's eyes were green, not brown, and Jenny frowned more than she smiled. Also, Jenny lacked Shirley's trademark dimples.

"We can't tell anyone anything, Jenny, because there's nothing to tell," I said. "Jeff, you should shut up. You're lying. Just admit it."

"I am not."

"Are too," Hal said, plopping back down at the table. "Where did Mr. Hocker end up with this so-called body? You haven't answered my question. Did he and the dead body and the wheelbarrow just vanish into thin air?"

Jeff stopped twirling and began squashing a line of picnic ants marching across the cement blocks with the end of the bat. Jenny put her head down on top of the table. She was also prone to severe headaches.

"Stop killing the ants," I said. "Where did Mr. Hocker end up? Answer the question."

I wanted to turn the spigot on at the side of the Ricters' house and start running through their sprinkler. Sweat was dripping down my back in tingly rivulets. This ridiculous story and the itch were driving me nuts.

"I saw where his flashlight stopped and stayed, if that's what you mean," Jeff said. "I bet he was digging a grave."

"Where was he?" Hal asked, but quietly this time, like someone had plopped a metal bucket over the top of his head.

I looked over at Hal. He was pinching his dark eyebrows together like he did when he was beginning to worry about something. Jeff usually didn't stick to his guns this long. Was it possible that he was telling the truth?

It did seem strange that anyone would push a wheelbarrow to the top of Maple Avenue in the middle of the night, especially Mr. Hocker, if it had been Mr. Hocker. Mr. Hocker didn't leave his house very often. He walked to his mailbox, swept his front porch and sidewalk, drove in and out of the neighborhood in his shiny black Cadillac DeVille maybe twice a month. When his wife was alive, they sat in bright purple lawn chairs in their backyard when the weather was nice. We could see their shapes from our backyards. That ended when Mrs. Hocker died four years ago on Christmas morning.

"Why did you think it was Mr. Hocker?" Hal asked, reading my mind.

"He stopped to catch his breath right outside my house and our lamppost was still on and our lamppost has new lightbulbs. He stood there huffing and puffing, staring down into that barrow. It was him. No doubt. Cross my heart and hope to die."

"Sometimes I wish you would die," I mumbled.

"Beth!" Jenny scolded me, voice muffled. I rolled my eyes again, even though she couldn't enjoy the performance with her head glued to a table.

"Look, I fell asleep before I saw him coming back down the street, but he stopped up near the old horse stable. Was up there a long time. I have to leave. Stupid piano lesson, but we should all walk up there tonight before it gets dark. I'll show you where he was. I'm telling you the truth. There is a fresh grave up there."

"I don't think we should do that. It might be dangerous," Jenny whined. "We should tell our parents and call the police. This is bad, you guys. Really bad."

"Look, if Jeff is willing to put his money where his mouth is, I'll walk up there tonight," I offered. I'd had my fill of Jeff's ridiculous story and his smug smile. I stood up, leaned over, and snatched the bat out of his hands. "Stop killing ants! What did they ever do to you? I'm going home. I'm sweating to death. Meet at seven. Tonight. My yard."

"Fine," Jeff said. "I'll be there. It was my bright idea in the first place."

"I'll be there too," Hal said. "And shut up, Jeff. Just shut up. If this is another one of your wild goose chases, I swear to God, I will pound you into sand."

Jeff shrugged and kept right on grinning. He was so sure of himself; he was almost like another person. Very unnerving.

"I might not come," Jenny told us. "Don't wait for me."

"Jenny, don't tell anyone about this until we check this whole thing out tonight," Hal said.

"Fine."

Maple Avenue was a steep hill of identical, aluminum-sided split levels. My house and Jenny's house were in the middle of the street, side by side, directly across from the Moomah house and the Ricter house.

The only characteristics that set our houses apart were front porch decorations: an old school desk on mine, a stand-alone porch swing on the Brenners', a brass plant stand on the Rickers' and on the Moomah's, a fake wicker well where we used to find Easter eggs filled with jelly beans when we were little. The Hocker house was at the bottom of the street like a door to a dead end. The backyard bled into farm fields.

Over the years the Hocker family had less and less to do with neighborhood traditions. When the twins Doug and Denny hit their mid-teen years, the family stopped stringing Christmas lights and displaying flags on Memorial Day and July Fourth. On Halloween, the Hocker lamppost and porch light remained dark, and an orange traffic cone appeared at the bottom of their sidewalk to warn trick-or-treaters to stay away.

Doug and Denny Hocker got into more than their share of trouble in school. Mouthing off to teachers. Picking fights. Truancy. They and their "hoodlum friends," my mother's words, set off firecrackers and smoke bombs, aimed stones at squirrels with slingshots. And, of course, there was the legendary blood window incident the year before Doug and Denny left the neighborhood and our town for good.

Jenny and I were in the third grade the Halloween a curtain in the Hockers' bay window started to glow. Maybe it was "blood red," like some said later. I can't swear to that, but the window did look like a flame floating above the Hockers' front yard grass. Everyone stopped ringing doorbells to stare down the hill. I kept imagining glass shattering and an evil spirit sweeping out into the night air, a giant, black creature with wings and fangs and fireball eyes, whipping its tail, aiming for me and Jenny and Jeff, two black cats and a hobo, standing in the middle of Maple Avenue. Hal missed the whole thing at home in bed with strep throat. Kids began hollering back and forth about witches and evil curses. When Jenny heard "Satan!" she tore home.

"Think we should head in too?" I asked Jeff.

"Just because the Hocker brothers bought a red spotlight at Clemson's Hardware just to scare us? No way."

That's what Jeff had said, but his voice sounded like he'd been sucking on a helium party balloon. A few minutes later, the blood window vanished and the familiar tan shade of the Hockers' drapes returned to their bay window. Even so, Jeff and I decided we had plenty of candy and went home.

One year later, there was no blood window at the Hocker house on Halloween night, and no more twins either. By some miracle, Doug and Denny received diplomas from Masterman High. They headed out west to work on a cattle ranch owned by a cousin. As for the mysterious blood window, a few polite questions put to Mr. and Mrs. Hocker were met with them playing dumb. Eventually, the mystery was relegated to nothing more than a prank by demonic twin boys who never returned, not even when their mother died.

Feeling nervous about the seven o'clock expedition in search of a freshly dug grave, I decided to find out more information about Mr. Hocker during dinnertime. Family dinners were good for that sort of fishing expedition.

"You aren't using the car tonight, so why can't I?" Alex, my older brother, had become a broken record regarding the family station wagon. He and his girlfriend were high school juniors, but you'd think they were married given how much time they spent together.

"Why can't you and Pam find something else to do other than the drive-in movies?" Dad responded. It wasn't really a question.

"What's the matter with seeing a movie? That's what people my age do, *damn it.*"

"Watch your mouth or no car for a month."

"Okay, okay, we'll go to the library instead. You happy?"

"Giddy, Alex. Simply giddy."

"What's that supposed to mean? Can I have the car or not?"

Mom was stirring more fake sugar into her iced tea, letting Dad handle Alex's lip as usual.

"Mr. Hocker kept driving in and out of the neighborhood today," I interrupted. "He's so weird."

"Well, he's quiet," Dad said, smiling at me, no doubt thrilled for the change of subject. "Poor fella. Living all alone. Phyllis died, what's it been now, three or four years ago?"

"Wonder why the twins never visit," I continued.

"They live far away," Dad said, salting his plate heavily. My mother's food was seldom served with taste. "Those boys were a handful."

"Those boys were a pair of assholes," Alex said. "Enough salt there, Dad?"

"Watch your mouth," Dad said. "Last warning."

"They *were* assholes, though," Alex said. "They were always beating up the weak kids in their class. That Denny? I heard he was selling drugs in the parking lot behind the old lumber company."

"Terrible," Mom murmured.

"Doesn't Mr. Hocker have any friends?" I asked, scooping another helping of watery potatoes I didn't want. I looked directly at Dad, figuring he would know more about Mr. Hocker than anyone else at the table. It seemed like men on the street talked to the other men on the street about the other men on the street, and the women did the same thing about the women.

"Maybe he does, and we just don't know it?" Dad answered. It was a question.

"What did he do for a living when he was working?" I asked.

"He said he was in banking," Dad said. "Always left for work in that same black suit and tie."

"Why do you care so much about old man Hocker all of a sudden?" Alex asked.

If I could have kicked Alex hard enough under the table to cripple him temporarily, I would have.

"Remember the blood window that one Halloween?" I tried a different angle.

"I remember," Mom said. "A real mystery."

"No mystery at all," Alex said. "Apparently, either Denny or Doug or both of those morons set the house on fire."

"I never heard that," Mom said. "On purpose?"

"Who knows."

"Where were all the firetrucks?"

"I don't know. And who gives a shi...shimmer," Alex said. "Dad, what about the car?"

"I feel sorry for Mr. Hocker," Mom said. "I bet he's lonely."

"Do you like Mr. Hocker?" I asked Dad.

"Oh my god." Alex stood up and stomped to his bedroom.

"I don't really know him. I certainly have nothing against him."

"He's not very friendly, though, is he," Mom offered. "Neither was Phyllis. She was always a cold fish. And no one on the street was invited to her funeral as far as I know. I don't think there was a funeral held for Phyllis Hocker."

"Just private people, I guess," Dad said. "Now, what's for dessert?"

That evening, Jenny was a no-show, but Hal and Jeff were right on time. I was keeping an eye on the shape of Mom's head in the kitchen window over the sink. Soon, she would head to the basement. She was addicted to evening television, especially *Tony Orlando and Dawn* and *M.A.S.H.*

"My mom is still looking out here," I spoke quietly to the boys. "Let's play cards until she gets lost. By the way, did any of your parents get invited to Mrs. Hocker's funeral?"

"Don't think so," Jeff answered.

"Don't think so," Hal said. "But I've got some information you guys are *not* gonna believe."

We settled under the oak tree with a deck of Old Maid.

"I dropped Mr. Hocker's name at dinner and my mom started complaining about these Styrofoam boxes that keep coming to our house, 218, instead of Mr. Hocker's, 208," Hal began. "She's been walking them down the hill and leaving them on his front porch. She doesn't want to touch them, so she's been wearing mittens, and it's been way, way too hot for mittens."

"Why is she afraid to touch the boxes?" I asked.

Jeff said. "Look, it's gonna get dark before we know it. Who cares about boxes and your mom's sweaty hands. So, our mailman sucks. Who gives a rat's ass."

Hal's cards were shaking in his hands. He wasn't the person he usually was. He looked more like Jenny than Hal. Pale in the cheeks. Right kneecap tapping on the ground. Eyebrows knitted together. Jeff was off too. On a normal night, Jeff would have reminded Hal of how much his eyebrows resembled giant, wooly caterpillars.

"Funny you should say that," Hal said. "All the boxes say 'Dry Ice,' and guess what else?"

I wanted to guess something, but my tongue was a cotton ball, and my brain wasn't churning out thoughts as quickly as it usually did.

"The boxes also say: 'Pre-killed, Frozen *Mice*,'" Hal hissed.

Mom's head appeared in the kitchen window again, so I plucked a few cards from my hand and handed them to Jeff.

"These don't even match," Jeff stammered. "Are we really playing?"

"Of course we're not really playing," I snapped. "Mice? Pre-killed? Frozen? I mean, that's so creepy. What would Mr. Hocker be doing with dead, frozen mice?"

"Who killed the mice?" Jeff asked.

"Who cares who killed the mice!" Hal said, turning his eyes to me. "What do you think it means?"

I shrugged helplessly.

"Maybe he feeds people dead mice before he kills them?" Jeff made a stab at it.

"Makes no sense," I said, though I couldn't have done any better. Nothing was adding up.

Light appeared in the basement window wells. Mom was finally parked in front of the television set. The air felt cooler. I shivered and looked up to see if the moon was anywhere in sight.

"What should we do?" Jeff asked.

Hal looked at me.

"Figure out one thing at a time," I said, my brain starting its engines at last. "We should get going. It's going to be dark soon."

The expressions on their faces would have been funny, the same way they looked at the summit of the first giant hill of the roller coaster in our town's amusement park, except my heart was thumping too. Were pre-killed mice frozen in their own separate bags, or was it one block of ice with a tail or two poking out? I didn't want to think about the thawing process. I shivered again.

When neither Hal nor Jeff moved an inch, I retrieved the cards from their hands, gathered the rest from the grass, stood up, walked to the milk box on the back stoop, and stowed the deck inside. My knees felt weak, but I started toward the top of Maple Avenue. When I heard the boys following me, I drew in a deep breath.

The old horse stable at the top of Maple Avenue hadn't been used in years. The stable and apple orchard behind it were owned by someone who didn't live on the street. Nobody knew who that was, but it never mattered. Whoever it was didn't seem to care when the neighborhood invaded the property every fall to pick apples. Since no one sprayed the trees or tended to them, the apples were small and mostly full of worms, but sometimes you found a whole branch of good ones.

As we left Maple Avenue and crossed over Linden Avenue toward the stable, I looked up again for the moon. It wasn't there.

For once, Jeff remembered something important. A flashlight. He clicked it on when we reached the wooden fence around the stable. Same empty stalls, old piles of hay, dusty ground.

Up ahead, the orchard was turning pumpkin orange in the ebbing light. I scanned tree branches, craggy as the bones in an old witch's hands when their leaves were missing, but green life still hung to them now, leaves that nodded rhythmically in the breeze. The orchard looked welcoming and peaceful this way. My heart slowed.

"Where did he stop?" Hal whispered. "How far back did he go back?"

"I'm sure he went past the stable."

Jeff and his flashlight took the lead as we entered the orchard, a good size for a private orchard, eight of our yards put together. As we approached the first row of trees, an owl greeted us with a *hoo hoo hoooo*. We jumped, of course. The faint beam from Jeff's flashlight shot up a tree trunk, got lost in the sky. We watched as the flashlight arced away from us like a cast fishing line and plopped on the ground. We stood there, shoulder-to-shoulder, staring at a silver object in a thick bed of white-headed clover.

"You gonna get that, or what?" Hal asked.

I glanced over my shoulder, wishing a car or two would drive by on Linden, but the night felt emptied of everything except the three of us, an abandoned stable, an apple orchard rolling up a hill, and one very loud owl.

Like wild animals, untamed and hence safer in the natural world, we sensed movement together. Mr. Hocker was getting off his knees, standing up slowly, one hand on the crook of his back. He was to our right at the end of the first row of trees. Once straight, he sensed us, too, and turned toward us, shielding his eyes with a cupped hand. The ground around his feet was lumpy as if it had been freshly turned over.

The boys didn't hesitate. They turned and ran.

I wanted to run too, but my legs wouldn't move. Behind me, Hal yelled, "Beth! Run! Beth! Beth! Come on!"

I couldn't run, though. I couldn't move. I looked down at my sneakers, then back over at Mr. Hocker.

He moved his hand from over his eyes and waved once, a short, stiff gesture. I came to life, lunged for the flashlight. Gripping the cold object, I called across to Mr. Hocker.

"Hello?"

"Is that Beth? Beth Nelson? It's Mr. Hocker over here. Sorry if I scared you kids."

I looked over my shoulder again. Hal and Jeff were standing at the top of Maple Avenue, jumping up and down, waving wildly, but I had too much good training. Mr. Hocker was an adult. He was talking to me, and he had just apologized. I turned back, pointed the flashlight at Mr. Hocker like a loaded gun.

"Mr. Hocker?" It sounded like a scream.

"Really sorry about that, Beth," he called back in a hoarse voice, as if he'd been out here all day yelling at the top of his lungs. "I'm just putting my lizard to rest."

There was still enough sunlight, pale apricot now, slanting over the orchard to see that tears shimmered on Mr. Hocker's cheeks. He drew a handkerchief from his pocket. Blew his nose. Then he covered his eyes with it. Muted sobs. Shaking shoulders. I began stepping toward him.

There was a grave. A small one, about four feet long. Of course, I thought of a child, but I asked about a lizard.

"You had a pet lizard who died?" I stammered.

Mr. Hocker dropped his handkerchief from his eyes, blinked at me like he hadn't expected to see me up close. He smelled of pipe tobacco, cherry or maybe blueberry. A gold watch hung loose from his thin wrist like a woman's bracelet. I thought about turning and running, but then Mr. Hocker's swollen eyes shifted to something behind me. He had brown eyes, Mr. Hocker. Footsteps. Hal stepped up and stood beside me.

"Sorry there, my boy, a young Ricter. Am I right? I am sorry. I am just finishing putting my pet lizard to rest here, that's all," he said, blowing his nose again. "Sorry for the fright I caused you all."

I glanced over at Hal. I'd never seen Hal's eyes that big before.

"Your lizard?" Hal asked.

"Oh, well, yes, she was very old, and she passed the other day," he explained. "I'm really going to miss her."

Mr. Hocker bent over, reached for a round stone from a nearby pile. Behind him, the wheelbarrow. Empty. He was making a frame of stones around the grave. The stones weren't ones you can find yourself. They were all the same size and perfectly smooth. Landscaping stones.

When I remember it now, it was like being in a trance, but not a scary, haunted one. Hal and I just seemed to know what to do. We walked around the freshly dug dirt, grabbed some stones, walked back around, got down on our knees, and started decorating the grave from the other side. Hal had the idea of making it a double line of stones, so I followed suit. Mr. Hocker, tears falling like crazy, looked over at what we were doing and did the same thing.

When the task was done, we stood up. The stones added a lot. I walked a few feet away, picked some yellow dandelions, pinched their damp stems together, and placed the bright bouquet on top of the grave. It looked too small, but it was getting late.

"Thanks, kids," Mr. Hocker said, tossing a few leftover stones into the empty field beside the orchard.

"What was her name?" I asked.

"Well, my sons called her something else when they first got her, but Mrs. Hocker was the one who always fed her and made sure she was warm enough. She called her Pearl. We should all be heading back. Getting dark."

When Mr. Hocker started toward the wheelbarrow, Hal hurried over and grabbed the handles. Mr. Hocker didn't object.

I led the way out of the orchard, Mr. Hocker next, blowing his nose, and Hal in the rear. After the stable, we got out of line and walked side by side. Ahead of us, centered as a child's drawing over the exact middle of Maple Avenue, the moon, a grayish white, delicate crescent in a darkening sky. When the owl called out this time, it sounded like a song, a lullaby.

"Do lizards make good pets?" Hal asked as we were crossed over Linden.

"Pearl sure did. She was peaceful. She came right over to you, let you hold her," Mr. Hocker answered. "They are not easy to keep. I'll warn you. They need to be kept warm all the time, need a basking light and a special diet. She was a monitor lizard, a savannah monitor."

"Hey," Hal began, "you want us to keep her grave up? Like no weeds and stuff?"

"Yes," I said, "and we could add real flowers. Maybe other things."

Hal and I glanced at Mr. Hocker marching between us. More tears, but also a quick smile. Up close, Mr. Hocker looked a lot like Norman Rockwell.

"That'd be nice of you kids, really nice," he said. "Anything you'd want to put up there for Pearl, why, that would be much appreciated."

When we got to Hal's house, Mr. Hocker stopped.

"I can take it from here," he said to Hal.

"Are you sure?" Hal asked. "I don't mind walking the wheelbarrow down."

"Thanks, but it's pretty easy going downhill."

"What if the person who has the orchard gets mad at you about Pearl being up there?" I asked.

"Well, then I'd have to be mad at myself," Mr. Hocker answered with a gruff chuckle. "Night, kids. Thanks again. Maybe I'll see you up at the orchard again soon."

Hal and I watched to be sure Mr. Hocker made it to his driveway. When he did, he turned and waved. We waved back, swallowing and blinking fast.

How easily the blood window flew away and hid on the far side of the moon that night. Now behind the shape of the bay window floating above the Hockers' front yard, all I could see was Mr. Hocker with no Pearl to feed. No Pearl to keep warm. No Pearl to hold in his arms.

I could sense Jeff's eyes on us from his bedroom window, but I didn't look up. For one moment of that brutally hot summer, this was a story for only me and Hal Ricter to know. The moon reached down and gently shoved us apart. I turned one way, and Hal turned the other.

Scar

It's an old story. Good girl lusts after bad boy. But this girl only wants a taste of the wolf in the woods, one lick even.

Ash is a perfect name for him because God knows he is good at burning things up, including hope in the chambers of his mother's heart and the family auto repair shop. What this girl doesn't know is that in three years' time, this boy will stroll into the lobby of the bank in their New Hampshire hometown of Longbred and set the cold barrel of a sawed-off shotgun to the manager's tender temple. She doesn't know he's going to turn out to be that bad of a boy.

Lansing Marone knows what everyone else knows about Ash Canton the evening she borrows her father's car and sets out to find him. He's a loner, mostly hangs out with his older brother hunting or fishing, a high school dropout who sent Canton's Auto Repair *Family Owned and Operated Since 1927* up in smoke when he crawled through a window one night, leaned back in an office chair, fell asleep, and dropped his cigarette. He managed to escape unharmed with a goldfish in a bowl, something his father and grandfather always kept on the office desk. Now Ash installs aboveground swimming pools. He is also renowned for coming out on the winning side of a lot of bar fights at the Crystal Cove, where they have proudly served minors since 1967.

Ash lives by himself in a trailer in the woods behind the Clairemont Dairy Queen. That seems like it would be a perfect kind of life to Lansing. High school out of the way. No more standing at her locker pretending to hunt for a book because her one close friend, Janet, can't always be around when Lansing needs her. No more eavesdropping on girl talk about the best way to cover up hickeys with a mixture of pancake makeup and vinegar paste. And a place of her own free of her father's trademark conversation-starters from behind his morning newspaper asking Lansing what she has planned for *her* day like the calendar day has been reserved just for her, and she better think of something earth-shattering to do with it. No more childhood bedroom, no more stuffed Pink Panther whose plastic eyeballs mock Lansing. That fat cat knows as well as she does just how uninspired she really is.

It's not that Lansing doesn't want to inspire the world in some way like Dian Fossey, who has been all over the news lately for single-handedly saving the endangered mountain gorillas of Rwanda. It's just that Lansing is smart enough to know that a copycat life can't be the answer. You can't swipe someone else's passion and jam it down your own esophagus. Lansing is doing all she can to discover her purpose. Her name will appear on the high honor roll list again this spring. She will attend college next fall, Yale University to boot, class of 1983. She never throws gum wrappers out of car windows. She's never been in a room with snowy lines of coke on a glass coffee table, never rolled a couple of Quaaludes around inside her palm and tossed them back like candy, never sucked herself silly high with an ice bong. A drag of a cigarette here and there, the ability to drain several cans of cheap beer from time to time. That's about it.

Lansing Marone certainly has no intention of surrendering her good-girl status on this night, either. The problem is, she's been missing Ash Canton. He used to be in her life before he vanished from high school around Christmas two years ago. They weren't friends. She never addressed a single word toward those smirking lips of his, but when they passed in hallways, when her eyes met his dark brown eyes surrounded by that tangle of shoulder-length, greasy-looking, black hair, she became a wild animal inside. Ash nodded at her first, sniffing her out, and then she would nod back.

As of two p.m. this afternoon, Lansing embarked upon a different journey of longing to see Ash Canton again with the persona of a slightly different wild animal. White foam should begin bubbling from the sides of her mouth any minute now. Bored, Lansing had walked to People's Drugstore to browse for a new flavor of roller ball lip gloss. In the next aisle, two girls from her senior class were discussing condoms and Lansing's senior prom date from the previous weekend. That had been Lansing's first date with Tim Benson. She'd be willing to go out with him again, even though his breath smelled like rubber tires, and he mostly said, "You bet." Tim Benson was a big step up, a popular, star athlete, not like her usual dates: Bob Duncan about a month ago, head of the chess club, and Frank Sellers before that, former head of the chess club.

"Tim loves these ribbed ones," Shelly Brill was saying. "Shit, maybe I should get us the pleasure pack. This one includes Ribbed, Bare Skin, and Trojan Horse."

"How was it after the prom? Didn't you see Tim last weekend?" This was Rita DeLiberty. Equally as popular and chased by boys as Shelly Brill.

"Amazing, although he was so pissed off by the time he finally got to my house. He had to drive Lansing Marone to her aunt's house in Trumball because she was babysitting her little cousin early the next morning. How lame is that?"

"I can't believe his mom made him ask Lansing Marone."

"His mom and her dad work together, I guess. Tim didn't have a choice. He said it was worse than being stuck with a fifth grader. She kept talking about dumb shit like her cat and her violin lessons. What in the hell is a pegbox?"

"Our cafeteria lady, that one with the mustache? She's got more sex appeal than Lansing Marone," Rita said.

The sound of their laughter heading in the direction of the registers sent Lansing scurrying in the opposite way. She ducked behind a display of Charmin bathroom tissue, cold arrows landing and halving her gut.

It isn't the best evening to pay Ash Canton a surprise visit. Thick fog has settled over the county and curled herself up for a long nap. Lansing drives past the handful of businesses along Longbred's Main Street, turns left at the only traffic light. Clairemont is a village with a lake for fishing and boating ten miles west of Longbred. There is nothing between these two dots of civilization except farms and fence lines hugging the contours of rolling countryside.

Dairy Queen is closed by the time Lansing arrives in Clairemont. Dumb luck allows her to locate the shape of the store's unlit sign against a rapidly darkening sky. She hits the brakes, spins the wheel, cuts the top ten hit blaring from the radio. She's going in under a cloak of silence. Anyway, if she hears Donna Summer singing about how hard it was to bake that cake melting in the rain at MacArthur Park one more time, Lansing is sure to slip into a coma.

Lansing's headlights illuminate the rust-red picnic tables behind the ice cream stand. She remembers her father's broad shoulders and her younger self sitting across from him there, gobbling butterscotch sundaes, bellyaching about the skimpy squirts of whipped cream. Her father wouldn't like her being here. He'd be worried. She's worried too. Lansing rests a palm across her pounding chest, thinks of one year when Ash was in her homeroom. He never put his hand over the top of his heart, never recited The Pledge of Allegiance. Just stood up, didn't pretend, and got away with it.

And there was that day when Mr. Cunningham asked if anyone had watched the presidential debates the night before. Lansing's arm shot into the air like a rocket ship. She tried retrieving it as quickly as she could when no one else raised a hand, but Nick Bernelli happened to be sitting beside her. "Only our dear nerd Lansing. No surprise there!"

Nick's boom of a voice left the whole class in stitches. When the bell rang to end the class, Ash stood up, walked slowly to the front of the room, where Nick sat at his desk, hauled off, and kicked Nick's ankle hard. Nick was missing from the starting lineup of the basketball team after that for a few weeks, limped to his classes and to the table of his friends in the cafeteria, and Ash got suspended.

Lansing isn't going to stay very long anyway. She just wants to see where Ash lives, that's all. Maybe she won't knock. Maybe she will.

The road behind the Dairy Queen, paved at first, soon turns to gravel, then dirt, then ruts and mud. Dense pines draw in close to the sides of her father's car the deeper Lansing gets into the woods. Their branch tips scrape against the car doors like the long, stiff fingers of a forest witch. What will she tell her father if there are scratches on the paint? How will she explain the mud splattered on the whitewall tires?

Lansing counts to ten, twenty, fifty. Why set a trailer this far away from a main road? Once you can no longer see out to civilization, what's the point of drilling deeper? Lansing is smiling, though. Heart jumping up and down. She should have done this a long time ago.

Vibrating on the passenger seat, her little cousin's library book: *Snow White and the Seven Dwarves*. Last weekend Lansing read the book several times to Cameron. Lansing has such admiration for the huntsman in the story. He was so clever, bringing the queen a pig's heart to fool her. If the evil queen wanted an innocent girl to die in some secluded glade, she should have killed her herself.

Lansing moves her foot to the brake, stops the car, rolls the window down, sticks her head out. There's not enough room to make a three-point turn. She'll get stuck for sure. She glances in the rearview. Nothing but pitch, and it is too far to back up. She sighs.

Too bad she did this. Too bad she isn't at home in the basement thumbing through TV Guide watching an episode of *M.A.S.H.*

Lansing performs a celebratory fingertip drum roll on the top of the wheel when she finally spots something ahead. A weak oval of yellow light that turns out to be a small window beside the door of an equally diminutive, silver trailer stitched tightly into the spines of the tree trunks standing behind. She takes a quick snapshot of the scene for her memory before snuffing the headlights: pickup truck parked to the right of the trailer, garbage can, silver too, four wooden steps, and the shape of a pointy-hatted garden gnome on the landing next to the front door.

Lansing rolls to a stop, cuts the engine, peers up through the windshield, feeling more like a deep-sea diver who has come upon a submarine at the bottom of the ocean than a high school senior at the end of a dead end. The night is even more gloomy inside the woods. Overhead, a clouded moon is making one part of the sky a tad brighter. If she heads back now, it will be like she never came at all.

Lansing shivers even though she's wearing warm clothes: jeans, her tightest T-shirt, gray hooded sweatshirt unzipped halfway. Parts under the car's hood tinkle, cooling down. Lansing flips the visor down. It's too dark to see her facial features in the vanity mirror. The mirror used to have working lights but that was years ago when the car was new. She studies the contours of her silhouette in the mirror, thinks about the scary movies she and Janet scramble to see as soon as they are released by Hollywood.

Someone hiding in the back seat pops up, perches a chin on the driver's right shoulder, hisses: *Lansing...* Lansing whips around. In the back seat, only the slim outline of her father's umbrella. When Lansing looks back over at the trailer, Ash's shadow walks past the gold window.

Maybe she will tell Ash she is lost or make up a story about some strange car following her. She was desperate to lose the car, so she turned down the first road she came upon. It all sounds asinine, and even though she one hundred percent knows better, Lansing wraps her fingers around the door handle and turns.

Outside, she shivers again. Instead of the expected crickets or peep frogs, the faint notes of music are playing inside the trailer.

No sense in carrying her purse with her all the way to the trailer door. She should leave it behind. But what if someone comes along, even all the way out here, and steals it? It has her driver's license, library card, photo identification for the community pool, two twenties, and that new lip gloss.

She hesitates, lets the purse slip from her fingers, and drops onto the driver's seat. She presses the car door shut, barely an audible click, and walks quickly to the trailer steps.

On the landing, she places her ear against the door. She may not knock.

No Donna Summer. Here it's Black Sabbath, that song titled "Symptom of the Universe," something about love that never dies and a mother moon and some sort of womb. Lansing's mother has been dead for almost her entire life, another old story. Drug addict.

Beneath window light, the gnome is frowning instead of smiling like most garden gnomes. Hands planted on his hips. Head cocked to one side. He seems permanently peeved. Lansing imagines him scrambling down the steps, scaling up the garbage can, diving in for scraps of leftover breakfast toast or frozen pizza, biting the ankles of trick-or-treaters and other invaders who dare venture this way. Lansing counts to ten, twenty, fifty. Knocks on the door.

"What the fuck. You expecting someone?"

A female voice. Lansing stiffens, catches her breath. She makes a decision. She turns away. To go back. To go home.

There is a creaking. Behind her, someone opens the trailer door.

Brightness floods the ocean floor. Weeds and moss flare fluorescent green. Lansing has no choice except to face Ash. He'll recognize her, hopefully. Lansing turns around.

"Who are you?" a girl asks.

The girl is from one of the "tougher" high schools, as Lansing's father describes them. Lansing has seen her around once or twice. She's badass, which means she's got killer good looks. Pixie haircut dyed matte black; cut off jean shorts; red halter top; pierced belly button with a fake (probably) diamond stud; black fingernails, chipped; no face makeup except for white lipstick; slender nose; huge, round eyes—a Japanese cartoon figure come to life. The cigarette dangling from the girl's mouth the white crayon that drew her snarl into place.

"Who the fuck are you?"

"I am, I'm..." Lansing manages, voice garbled as if she is underwater, and her voice box is back on the boat.

"Who?" the girl demands again, opening her hand, slamming her palm on the outside of the trailer door.

That wasn't the smartest move on her part. Bet that hurt. She should have made a fist.

Behind the girl, a lumpy, navy-blue couch, plastic milk crate cluttered with amber beer bottles, heaped-up ashtray, wall poster depicting one of those flaming red sunsets over an ocean that never happened, a near-dead spider plant in a macramé sling, leaves brown and curled as mummy fingers.

Lansing has nothing to offer this girl except her name. She doesn't mind giving that away to anyone. Her mother must have been completely in love with herself when she chose her own name for her only baby.

"I'm Lansing."

Lansing delivers this introduction with a pissed-off tone she didn't consciously intend and immediately doesn't care. She drove all the way out here, and this girl isn't going to destroy her adventure in the first five minutes.

"Lansing? Lansing? Oh, for Christ's sake. Now, that's just perfect. Just perfect. That is some name you got there; little miss tender pussy. Hey, Ashie! Your middle school spelling bee champion virgin is here."

The girl arches her slender neck backwards, looks to the side where there might be a kitchen area or maybe a bed or both. Hard to guess. This is a one-room trailer.

"Ash? Get over here. You got something to tell me? You're a real pervert, Ash Canton."

Returning her attention to Lansing, the girl plucks the cigarette from her teeth, taps the ashes onto Lansing's sneakers. Slow and steady she moves her eyes up then down Lansing's figure.

"What are you doing here, little Miss Lansing Michigan?"

The girl must think that makes her seem intelligent, knowing there is a place named Lansing in the state of Michigan.

Ash's tall frame appears behind the girl. He's wearing jeans with a belt and no shirt. Lansing doesn't look up at his eyes right away as she planned to do when she saw him again. Her gaze is locked on his bony chest, so "vampirey," so sickly pale. Very entrancing. Lansing imagines running her fingertips slowly from Ash's prominent Adam's apple down to his stomach, which, her heart pinches to note, is a bit furry.

"Oh, my, my, just look at that. She's blushing up real cute for you."

The girl drags hard on her cigarette, juts her neck forward, the ugly movement of a barnyard rooster, and blows smoke into Lansing's eyes. Lansing doesn't flinch. Instead, she inhales deeply and blows back.

"Lansing Marone," Ash says evenly, like he says her name every day, like he isn't surprised, like he's been expecting her.

Lansing smells the booze on them, and the cooler air drifting from the trailer carries the sweet scent of pot and something else. Burned baked beans? Lansing's stomach flips like a griddle cake.

"What's going on?" Ash's deep voice asks.

Ash doesn't sound mad. He sounds conversational. Lansing drops her eyes from his belly button, returns them to the gnome standing beside her. Those glittering, unblinking eyes. That arrogant expression.

Such a control freak. So convinced Lansing doesn't know what she's going to do next. I am going to look up at Ash Canton's face, you arrogant little turd. Lansing lifts her foot, intending to give the ogre a nudge with her toe, but he's not solid concrete like the garden gnomes Lansing's aunt collects. He's hollow. Lansing sends the gnome somersaulting backwards into darkness, where he rolls underneath the trailer and stops dead.

"You bitch!" the cartoon character scolds.

The girl doesn't sound angry either. She sounds more amused, maybe a tad shocked. Or is that admiration? Maybe the two of them could be friends, unlikely friends but very close all the same. This magnificent dragoness could come visit Lansing at Yale. Wouldn't that create a sensation? They could kick some ass together.

When the girl lunges forward and shoves Lansing, Lansing is caught off guard. She stumbles backwards down the steps. Finds solid ground on the ocean floor.

Up on the landing, the girl sniffs her palms, snorts.

"Jesus Christ. Snowy Bleach."

The girl jumps the steps now, touching down just shy of Lansing. In the dim halo of light, Lansing can see she is majorly fucked up. Her pupils are gigantic, and she is swaying herself seasick. She might fall into Lansing's arms, assuming Lansing would open her arms to catch her, which she won't.

"Stupid toddler queen," the girl hisses into the bridge of Lansing's nose, a spray of her spit landing on Lansing's fruity-scented bottom lip.

Lansing gets in one good punch, square in the girl's stomach, before the girl tackles her. The back of Lansing's head hits hard. Lansing doesn't throw a second punch. She saw the flash of silver inside the girl's hand just before they both hit the ground. It's hard to be stealthy with a knife.

Everything happened so fast. The ground, surprisingly solid under Lansing's back, the sensation of a piece of sharp ice swiping across the middle of her neck, the weight of the girl disappears as Lansing's neck catches on fire under murky, rocky waves, the sky clouds nudging the sky away.

Ash turns out to be a savior of sorts. He makes the girl howl like the wounded animal she deserves to be. Tosses her inside the trailer as if she is as light as a twig. Then his long arms pierce darkness for Lansing. Grabbing her around her waist, he pulls her up and out of the pounding surf. Lansing wants him to kiss her, to scoop her up into his scrawny arms, carry her into the woods and devour her there. But he doesn't. He grabs something from the bed of his truck instead. Flicking on a flashlight, he steadies a blinding beam on Lansing's throat, leans in, dabs with a soft cloth, leans in again, and then orders her to hold the cloth in place. The fabric smells of gasoline.

"Not much more than a scratch. Only a penknife. You're okay. Go home, Lansing. Go home and don't ever come back here," Ash whispers into her ear like they are about to tell each other all their deep, dark secrets.

Lansing opens her mouth and closes it, decides not to apologize. Ash's arm humped around her shoulders feels almost forgiving, even understanding, but as he walks her to her car, opens the door like a perfect gentleman, Lansing knows it is pity.

Ash Canton jogs behind Lansing as she weaves her way out of the woods.

He taps the trunk twice with his knuckles just before she turns onto the main road.

Lansing rolls down the car window halfway back to Longbred, tosses Ash's T-shirt. She'll stop at Janet's house, borrow the hose, spray the tires.

Her neck feels sticky.

A trembling examination confirms the cut isn't deep. It will leave a scar, though, a white choker witness.

—

Three years later, when Lansing hears about the attempted armed robbery at the Longbred National Bank, she is standing in a phone booth, the lobby of her dorm, an honors student at Yale in Political Science. As usual, her father is running through all the news that's "fit to print."

"Why would he do something like that?" Lansing asks. "He must have known he'd be caught."

"Nobody knows why. He isn't talking. That boy's always been troubled. Too bad."

Lansing rests her fingertips on the satin thread looping the middle of her neck. Her heart squeezes, wrings itself dry in her chest. Her eyes brim.

"Are you there, Lansing?" Her father's voice echoes from the other half of the world. Lansing hangs up.

She imagines it as a sunny day. She is sitting in a car. Windows rolled down. Her hair billows in a warm breeze. When the prison gate parts, Ash Canton is finally a free man.

He strides toward her car, folds his long legs into the space beside her, leans across, kisses—no, bites—her neck, taps his knuckles on the dashboard twice, and Lansing floors it.

She is irresistible to the wolf in the woods. Her life begins.

Just About There

The name of the teen wellness retreat in upstate Pennsylvania has a name that's hyena hoot-worthy: *Just About There.*

"Are you shittin' me with this place, Mom? That's the quintessential parental lie. That's what you and Dad always said every car trip."

Jana is reclining in the back seat of her mother's brand-new, jet-black Escalade, staring out at a cloudy, platinum sky. She's hoping for a UFO. A greenish-gray disc like a birth control pill case materializing in Earth's atmosphere just long enough to give her hope.

Her mother sighs, shifts in the driver's seat to the left of Jana's head. Jana likes it when there's no way her mother can swivel her bepearled neck around and glare at her.

"Hope you aren't paying much," Jana snorts, delivering a few punches to the back of the driver's seat.

Over the years, therapists have complimented Jana on not becoming violent toward people, meaning her mother. *You've done an admirable job of constructing myriad ways to deal with your frustrations on your own.*

Jana did punch a boatload of holes in her bedroom. Drywall makes for a soft skull. She doesn't do that anymore. Not since her father hightailed it to the West Coast. Now that she never sees him, she's able to pity him less. She's even getting used to her mother's current midlife crisis: a law firm associate thirty years younger. Poor guy. It must be hard to say no to the managing partner. Still, sometimes Jana misses going batshit in her bedroom, stinging the hell out of her knuckles, the sound of her mother pleading in the hallway.

"What's in a name?" her mother says. "Just a two-night stay. To reenergize your efforts, as Dr. Clark says."

"Dr. Clark is an asshole," Jana almost answers, but then her mother will counter, and this will spin into another argument. Jana already has a headache. As far as Dr. Clark, Jana spends her time inside that office lying, so who's getting the last laugh now? The only upside about Dr. Clark's is the whirring sound machine Jana gets to kick over just before she empties the candy bowl into the bottom of her backpack on her way out.

These teen retreat places are all the same. None of them "work." There's always a way to get stuff, a cafeteria dishwasher dude, some tattooed, former street gang member wearing a spiderweb hair net. Or the maintenance guy with no teeth and a habit of his own.

Just About There amounts to a smattering of log cabins encircling a weed-ridden courtyard of Adirondack chairs with crumpled, decorator throw cushions: black bear cubs all in a row, rainbow trout, a couple of deer heads with don't-shotgun-me eyes. A firepit, volleyball net, and cornhole game complete the dull scene.

Steam from the chimney of a larger stone building set behind the cabins stamp it as the dining hall. A wilderness retreat with at least one substantial building crafted from creek stones. Nothing new there. Free material dredged from nearby native waterways. Ovals of various sizes smooth as eggs. Flowing water does that. Pours around and over you, files down sharp ends, the angles you could hurt someone with but not mean to.

Two surprises: no fencing around *Just About There,* only the open, dark-treed woods and a cute, long-haired boy lounging on the front steps of the other stone structure. A silver watch hangs loose around his wrist. The sign above his head: *Counselors' Residence.* The boy stands up slowly, stretches. He's tall.

"Damn," Jana whispers as her mother hands her the backpack from the trunk.

"Behave," her mother hisses, slamming the lid. Without another word or any physical gesture of farewell, the woman slides behind the wheel and loops back toward civilization by way of the horseshoe drive.

String bean boy hesitates, then steps toward Jana.

"Jana Conway? Welcome. I am Eli Mason," he announces formally, floating up a hand. "Nice to meet you."

A nail-biter. One thing they have in common. That's promising. His skin is icy.

"Everyone is having lunch. Would you like some food?"

"Does it suck?" Jana asks.

"Not too bad. Camp food. Hamburgers, hotdogs. Chips will be stale. Everything up here is damp."

"I thought you were going to say everything up her is a dump," Jana jokes, but Eli's expression is stalled on serious.

"Any candy?" she asks.

"Nope," he answers in his monotone. "You like candy then, I guess."

Eli's eyes are black. Not dark brown. Black on black. Like the pupils spread out and took over. And another thing. The guy barely ever blinks.

"You don't like candy?"

"Everyone likes candy," Eli responds and turns in the direction of the dining hall.

He smells nice. A combination of campfire smoke, decent weed, and maybe lavender fabric softener. He's wearing tattered jeans, skeevy-looking black Converse sneakers, and a faded Dodgers T-shirt. Close up the face on his watch is a rain cloud trapped inside a snow globe. Opaque, completely unreadable.

"Seriously, how is this place?" Jana asks, trying to match Eli's long strides. "Same dumb theory about the outdoors leading to self-discovery?"

She approves of Eli's vibe. That shoulder length, ebony hair, pin straight. That skin bone pale. He could pass for Satan's sexy younger brother.

"It's bearable," Eli answers, highlighted by a sigh. He stops, turns toward Jana, tips a chiseled chin in her direction, offers her a fading hint of his smile. She watches as his dark eyes drop quickly from her pale green ones to her freckled nose, blonde braids, worn-out jeans like his, and finally, her equally shot-to-hell sneakers.

"I was just thinking, I was wondering, thinking…" Eli stammers, raking long, thin fingers through his hair. His pale cheeks have swapped to crimson. "I guess we should drop your bag at your cabin, but Dr. Kemble didn't say which one."

Shy then. Even cuter. And Jana has never seen a guy with glittering anthracite eyes. What luck. Eli in the sky with diamonds.

"It's fine," she tells him. "This backpack's light."

Eli drops his hand.

"Good," he intones, lips barely breaking.

In the dining hall, Jana opts for a hotdog and chips. Eli mounds his paper plate with coleslaw, plops an olive on top like a maraschino cherry on an ice cream sundae, and they head for an open table.

Two probable eating-disordered girls sitting at one table glance up at Jana. Smile-less, mirror reflections of each other. At another table, a girl with a sheared head—probably did it herself judging by the number of red nicks—and overkill on the nose rings sits across from a dumbass football player guy wearing a numbered jersey, *#23, The Tunkhannock Titans.* The titan looks over, nods. Not a talkative group.

Soon the screen door slams, another boy enters, heaps up two plates, and hurries over to Eli and Jana's table. Seriously overweight, ankles thick and fluid-filled. He introduces himself to Jana with a formal bow and plops down beside Eli. Learning not to overeat must be a steep uphill battle for Lawrence Van Oden: eight dogs, a walloping serving of beans, slaw, and olives. A credit to his discriminating palate, no stale chips.

"I know, I know," Lawrence says, eyeing Jana from across the table, taking a giant bite of hotdog. "I look like a teenage version of Homer Simpson."

A few amused murmurs from around the room. It is true. Something about Lawrence's oversized forehead, the way his glasses magnify his eyes, bulgy and froglike, a wide mouth so much like Homer's: the type of mouth that seems custom-made for nothing but big grins. As Lawrence chews, he winks mischievously at Jana. He is wearing a mustard-yellow T-shirt, the same color as Homer Simpson's cartoon skin, and some exceedingly well-pressed khaki cargo shorts.

"What has the proverbial cat dragged in?" Lawrence mumbles good-naturedly once he's staved off starvation.

"You think you have enough pockets in those shorts?" Jana counters, mocking Lawrence's repetitive winking. "Let me guess. One has your Cub Scout knife in it. And you do look like Homer, except you have hair."

"How'd you like being greeted by our resident specter?" Lawrence asks.

"Specter?" Jana echoes.

"Eli here is our own resident ghost. He looks exactly like one of *Just About There*'s infamous bubble people. Astonishingly so, I might add." Lawrence elbows Eli, who has yet to pick up his fork.

Eli sits statuesque, apparently transfixed by the progress a carpenter ant is making across the middle of the table.

"Bubble people?" Jana asks.

Lawrence raises a thick index finger like he means to scold her. "You'll find out all about them later tonight. It's better to meet the bubble people in person. However, just to wet your whistle, one of the bubble people happens to be Isaiah Hecht, born on August 17, 1857, dead and buried in these very woods behind us on August 23, 1874, and arisen, I maintain, this very summer, the summer of 1999. The only difference is that Isaiah has changed his name to Eli, and now he goes around wearing even crappier clothes."

With that, Lawrence gives Eli a hollow thump on his back.

"Okay, Lawrence," Eli says kindly, coming back to life. "As you can see, Lawrence is plagued with an overactive imagination."

The food isn't half bad. Jana's faced worse. When her hotdog is gone, Lawrence plops one of his onto her empty plate.

"Help a rotund guy out?" he asks. "There's a reason they call me 'gut boy' back home."

It's hard not to laugh along with Lawrence. She suspects Lawrence may be the epitome of a "good egg," her father's term for harmless souls who try to make life easier for other people even when they can't find a way to stop deep-sixing their own.

"Your plate's a tit, Eli," comes a sudden boom of deep, male vocal cords from behind Jana's shoulders.

Number 23 and the shaved-head girl have made their way over. Not a bad joke. Eli's mound of coleslaw does resemble a breast.

"Jana, meet Forest," Lawrence says. "Yep. This is Forest, who is indeed in rehab inside a forest. And this is Sally."

"Hey," Jana says, turning around to look up at them.

"Where you from?" Forest bellows.

There's nothing not huge about Forest. Boulder head. Tree trunk shoulders. Superman chest. Even his teeth are mammoth. Like the chompers on a Clydesdale.

"Philadelphia area," Jana says. "You?"

"Ever hear of Tunkhannock?" Forest roars.

"Stop shouting, Forest," Sally snaps.

"No, but I've heard of the titans," Jana says.

"Really? The Tunkhannock Titans?"

Sally rolls her eyes. Next to Forrest, anyone would look small, but Sally almost disappears. She's very thin and about half his height.

"No, *the* titans," Jana says.

"But we are *the* titans," Forest insists, forehead crunching. "Anyway, here for the weekend, then?"

"Just the two-night option," Jana answers.

"Enough of this shit," Sally says. "Come on, Jana, I'm supposed to show you where you will be sleeping."

Lawrence is busy polishing off Eli's untouched plate.

"Titans isn't the greatest name for a football team, is it?" Eli says to Jana. "Considering they all ended up in a dungeon in the underworld."

"All rotting in Tartarus." Jana nods.

Some knowledge of Greek mythology. Something else she and Eli have in common.

By the look of the inside of Sally's cabin, Sally has been at *Just About There* for some time. In addition to her bed, which is all Jana has on her side, Sally has a small refrigerator, an ancient boom box, a small desk with a reading lamp, and piles of books and magazines, all relating to astronomy: *Sky and Telescope, Time for the Stars, The Milky Way's Fiery Center.* In front of the window between the beds, a silver-and-black telescope on a squat tripod. A purple satin pillow rests on the floor for the comfort of the stargazer.

Jana tosses her backpack onto her bed. Steps toward the telescope.

"Don't touch the scope," Sally says.

Jana stops, turns to face her.

"Look, this is how I do this. I do not care about your life. Why you are here, any of it. I don't want to get to know you. I'm not interested if you want to get to know me. But you can have anything you want in the fridge. My big brother brings me drinks and other stuff. Help yourself."

"Fair enough," Jana says. "Can I just look through the telescope when it's dark and the stars are out? I won't touch it."

"Maybe." Sally is on her bed, back turned toward Jana, scribbling in a notebook. "Technically the stars are always out. It's just that during the day, the sun's light is so bright that we can't see the other celestial objects."

"Right," Jana says. "Can I open the front window? It's stuffy in here."

"It's stuck. You can't get the stink out anyway. All these cabins reek."

Jana opens the refrigerator, takes a can of Sprite to her bed, opens her backpack, and pulls out the book her father sent for her sixteenth birthday. Her heart squeezes, picturing him in a bookstore somewhere in San Diego.

Reading is not Dad's thing. Jana never saw him read. Never heard him try. She misses hanging out at his auto repair, gliding underneath cars, her back on one of those little boards with wheels on the bottom, handing tools back and forth like they were surgeons putting a person back together.

"Hey, Sally?"

"Fuck," Sally says. She seems easily agitated. "What?"

"Do you believe in UFOs?"

Sally leans back on an elbow to study Jana over her shoulder, bones poking her shirt upward. Sally looks boss with that shaved head of hers and such a pretty face. An emaciated version of Sinead O'Connor. Somewhat of a coincidence, considering the book Jana's father sent is set in Ireland: *Angela's Ashes*. Jana knows what the book is about. Essentially, starvation. Some people would see the dark circles under Sally's eyes as a sign of acute hunger. It is malnutrition of another variety. Sally is a class-one junkie. Jana doesn't need to see what her arms look like under the long sleeves of her sweatshirt. It's cooler weather up here in the mountains, but not that cool.

"I do," Sally answers emphatically.

Her eyes race across the title of Jana's book.

"Most definitely I do. Now. Shut the fuck up, Jana."

It's dark outside when Sally shakes Jana awake.

"Pizza?" Sally plops a paper plate with a slice on Jana's bed.

"How long have I been out?"

"Long enough. Dr. Kemble said to let you sleep. Want to see the moon? It's full tonight. I have it focused. Don't touch anything."

Jana settles on the stargazing cushion. As soon as she positions her eye in front of the lens, something cold pours into her stomach. The brightness is breathtaking. That part is there but magnified; the moon looks like a black-and-white photo of the Earth. Dark areas mimicking the continental shapes. The vast white space between, so similar to the earth's oceans. Jana was hoping the moon would be different somehow.

Two knocks. The cabin door swings open onto a middle-aged woman with wavy, waist-length gray hair parted in the middle. No makeup, deep laugh lines, brown eyes, silver hoop earrings, red Looney Tunes T-shirt, black shorts, and muddy Birkenstocks.

"Get a new delivery from Woodstock Time Warp Incorporated?" Sally asks. "Nice spoon ring."

"This ring an original, Sally, but thank you," the woman, Dr. Kemble, answers. "I bought it on Coney Island in 1969."

There was a younger image of Dr. Kemble in *Just About There's* brochure. University of Pennsylvania School of Psychiatry. Specialty: Teen and Young Adult Therapy.

"See anything good up there?" Dr. Kemble asks Jana.

"The moon."

"Is that good or bad?"

"It's an object," Jana replies.

"Right," Dr. Kemble says. "We're easygoing around here, Jana.

Welcome aboard. Mandatory group session at ten a.m. tomorrow in the courtyard."

Dr. Kemble is a former flower child. A holdover from some faded psychedelic era. Hippies were all about peace. And drugs. The good doctor takes her time examining the offerings in Sally's mini fridge, selects a bottle of Yoo-hoo, and leaves.

"She doesn't seem horrendous," Jana says, but Sally doesn't respond. She is busy sorting through a stack of sky charts, head down, mumbling to herself.

Outside in the courtyard, Eli and Lawrence are seated side by side, staring into the fire pit. Forest is on his back on the ground behind their chairs. Familiar music from somewhere, the current hit "Scar Tissue" from the Red Hot Chili Peppers. Lyrics about an addict shooting up under some bridge with nothing but dirty pigeons for company. How fitting. Jana is squeamish when it comes to needles. That has always held her back from flying as high as she wants to.

"Jana," Lawrence greets her. "Finally, amongst us. We've been awaiting your presence. Up for it, Jana? The infamous bubble people?"

"Maybe later," Jana says.

"No probs," Lawrence says cheerfully, but Jana senses his disappointment. He's changed into a pair of navy basketball shorts.

Jana slumps into an Adirondack across the fire from Eli and Lawrence.

"This fire is too hot," Jana complains.

"There's a water bottle under your chair," Lawrence says.

"No, thanks," Jana says.

"Not optional," he says, a gentle smile appearing on his full, flushed face.

Jana reaches under for the bottle, opens it, and tips back. Gin and Sprite. Pretty weak, but better than nothing. She gulps some more.

"Thanks, Lawrence," she says. "Where's the annoying music coming from?"

"Deanna and Diane's cabin," Lawrence answers. "You're out of luck if you don't like the Peppers."

Jana steals a slit-eyed peek at Eli. Yellow and orange ribbons snap inside those haunting eyes of his. He's not blinking as usual. She waits. Waits. Nothing. Eli's sockets, windows. His brain, on fire. Jana shakes her head. Takes another swig from the water bottle. Then chugs it. Maybe Lawrence is right. Maybe Eli is a spook.

"Hey Lawrence," Jana says. "Can I have another? I can pay you."

"Coming right up," Lawrence says, reaching under his chair. "They're on the house."

Forest snatches the bottle from Lawrence before easing his body into the chair on the other side of Jana. The frame creaks its objection. He hands Jana the bottle.

"You gonna be a senior?" Forest asks Jana.

"Yep."

"Me too."

"Look up, Jana," Lawrence interrupts.

Jana remembers night canopies like this one from vacationing with her dad in the Pocono Mountains. Night skies crammed full of bubbling stars. When Jana tilts her chin back down, Eli is watching her. The black pools of his eyes, the empty space between stars.

"It's now or never for the bubble people," Lawrence announces, standing up. "Let's go, Jana. Not optional."

Forest and Lawrence lead the way down a makeshift road behind the dining hall, two troughs dug deep by tractor tires.

"It's not that far," Eli tells her, stepping up to walk beside Jana.

Thanks to Lawrence, Jana is enjoying a pleasant buzz.

"The bubble people. Who are they?" she asks Eli.

"Dead people in the cemetery back here. Pretty cool."

"Been stuck up in these mountains too long, Eli, or what," she teases.

"Maybe."

Good ole Eli. Humorless.

Soon, the group turns to enter a mowed, open space with a scattering of headstones. Lawrence offers Jana his flashlight.

"It's a family burial plot," Lawrence explains. "The Hecht family. They used to own this land. You'll see them, portraits of them, inside glass."

The grave markers are thin stone slabs covered with green moss and gray lichen. They lean backward, a row of crooked, caved-in teeth. The front stones have small half-orbs of glass centered at the top. When Jana shines light into the first orb, it illuminates the face of a pale, serious-lipped woman, hair pulled severely back. As Jana moves the light back and forth across her features, the woman begins to appear more and more alive, nearly as present as the three flesh-and-blood people standing behind Jana. It's the woman's eyes. They glitter as if wet with fresh tears.

"I can't believe it," Jana manages.

"I know, right?" Lawrence says, fanning his arms excitedly. "Lifelike. Even though they're just tintypes under blown glass. They all died in the late 1800s around the same time. Plague. That's Sarah. Her husband Jonah is next to her. Then daughter Franny. And, drumroll, son Isaiah."

Jana steps from stone to stone, examining the amazing bubble people. They are dressed in similar black garb with high, white collars. They share the same narrow faces, unsmiling, thin lips, angular noses, and dark, wet eyes that seem to track Jana's movements. Eli is right. They are cool.

"Go ahead," Forest says, chuckling. "Check out Isaiah."

"Yes," Lawrence chimes in. "Do it."

Jana almost doesn't have to. She can see it already. Eli Mason looks so much like a member of the Hecht family. She wants to rush to Eli's defense. *What's the big deal? People resemble one another all the time.* But when her beam travels over the portrait of Isaiah Hecht, frozen in time, as in life, it is Eli. Just exactly. Same hair. Same chin. Same mouth. Same nose. Same darkness in the eyes. There aren't any eyes like Eli's eyes. Jana whips around to face the others, helpless to close her mouth. That's what they were waiting for. Laughter whoops and echoes through a once-silent wood. Even Eli's shoulders are shaking.

"Holy fuck," she manages. "You look just like him."

"Yes," a shrugging Eli admits, kicks at a tuft of ferns. "Maybe similar ancestry."

"Or maybe you *are* him." Lawrence just can't help himself. "Eli? Or is it *Isaiah*? Huh, buddy? You can tell us. We can keep a secret, can't we, folks?"

As the others lounge at the edge of the burial plot, draining more water bottles, Jana illuminates the engraved names of the Hecht family, traces the rough, grooved letters of their names. In his portrait, Jonah Hecht means business. He looks determined to conquer the world. There is a deep scar over his right eye. Sarah is exhausted. Franny seems frightened. Her eyes are flared wide. A small locket rests around her milky-white neck. Two dark braids have been pinned on the top of her head, and she clasps a daisy against her chest.

This time, when Jana passes a beam over Isaiah's portrait, the lips appear to move. When she directs the light back over his features, he seems to be trying to say something to her. And his expression. Jana has seen this fading hint of a smile before. It is Eli. Sad Eli. She shakes her head. Unbelievable.

"Gotta go," Lawrence says. "Let's get a move on."

"Our tour guide has spoken," Forest adds.

On the walk back, Jana and Eli fall behind, pass a joint between them.

"Does it freak you out?" she asks.

"Kind of," Eli answers. "What are the odds? But there he is. You like Greek mythology?"

Eli sounds less serious than he did earlier. Jana's stomach flips.

"I like stories about places that aren't here, that's all," she says.

Eli reaches into the pocket of his jeans. Hands Jana a Charms Blow Pop.

"I love these. Thanks. Where'd you get it?"

"You're welcome, candy girl."

"Unusual watch," Jana ventures.

Eli inhales deeply, holds his breath, answers through his exhale.

"My dead grandfather's."

Jana looks over at his face in the moonlight.

"I don't want to pry."

"It's fine. He was teaching me to drive. I took a turn too fast, hit a guardrail. And, well, as you might guess… I killed him."

"Oh my god. So sorry."

"It was an accident," Eli says.

"You can't punish yourself for things that were accidental," Jana says, kicking herself for saying something as worthless as Dr. Clark would have said under the circumstances.

"I'm working on it. Nice car your mom was driving this morning."

"She's horrendous." Jana's words shoot through her teeth more vehemently than she intended.

"Not prying either," Eli rushes to say.

"All she's ever done is dump all over my dad. Finally, he couldn't take it anymore. Started drinking, lost his job. Then he moved far away, and I don't blame him. That's my story anyway."

Jana had said more than she meant to. She feels pathetic and crummy for feeling sorry for herself. At least she didn't kill anyone.

"Life is crappy," Eli says, pinching the orange end of the joint, tossing it into the trees.

The next morning everyone except Dr. Kemble is on time for the group session. Lawrence is a pea soup green, teenaged, hungover Homer Simpson, slumped and miserable in his chair. The shrill, clean cry of a hawk boomerangs through the quiet morning.

"Sorry I'm late, folks," Dr. Kemble says, dragging a chair over to the circle.

"You're always late," Sally says.

"Does that bother you, Sally?"

"And you always ask me that," Sally says.

"Let's go around the circle with names first."

Sally closes her eyes. She was snoring by the time Jana got back to the cabin last night. Jana considered giving the moon another chance, but she held off in case she might bump the telescope in the dark room. The telescope seems like more than a telescope to Sally.

"Who wants to begin this morning?" Dr. Kemble asks. "Anything is fair game. No judgment here."

Most times, in group sessions, no one says much of anything. That's the good part. Everything voluntary and no volunteers makes for a peaceful hour.

"I'll start then," Dr. Kemble says. "I had a rough night rest-wise. Had an anxiety attack. Nothing new there, as some of you know. I finally fell asleep at five a.m. only to wake up an hour later with a spider in my mouth."

"A real spider?" Diana asks.

Diana is wearing an ankle-length black knit dress. She has short lilac hair and pink cat-eye eyeglasses almost as big as her pinched-in face.

"Yes, I believe it was real," Dr. Kemble responds. "I don't think the spider was a dream if that is what you are asking, Diana."

"I dream about pulling stuff out of my mouth all the time," Diana offers.

"I didn't know that," Dr. Kemble says.

"Usually toffee or something like pasta or licorice, something I keep pulling and pulling. Like those clown top hats with the scarves all tied together."

"You make up so much crap," Sally says without opening her eyes. Her arms are folded across her chest as if she means to crush it.

. "Sally, you know that kind of comment is never acceptable here," Dr. Kemble says.

"I never dream," Lawrence says. "But I drool like crazy. I mean, a river."

"God," Forest groans.

Jana won't mention that when she falls asleep, she sometimes dreams she is sharpening one of her mother's stainless steel kitchen knives.

"Jana made her acquaintance with the bubble people last night," Lawrence says.

"What did you think of our beloved Hecht family?" Dr. Kemble asks.

Jana shrugs in response. There's a pleasant breeze tapping against her temples. More silence.

"Forest," Dr. Kemble says. "We ran out of time yesterday when you were talking about football and college. Want to continue that now?"

"Not really," Forest says. "Nothing to say. I got to play."

"You probably do have to play," Dr. Kemble agrees.

"Got no choice," Forest says, cracking his knuckles, something he does often.

"He has a damn choice." Eli's emotionless voice.

"Not if I want to get into a halfway decent school," Forest says. "One that will ignore all my DUIs."

"Just play the first season and quit," Lawrence suggests.

"Not a bad idea," Dr. Kemble says. "As long as you can stay enrolled if you quit."

"I'll check into it," Forest says.

"Anyone else have any thoughts for Forest?" Dr. Kemble asks. Eli frowns but doesn't offer anything more, and Dr. Kemble ends the group session.

That afternoon, Jana decides to read through her 12:30 private therapy session with Dr. Kemble that her mother paid extra for. Surprisingly, there is no knock on the cabin door. She skips lunch too. Frank McCourt's book is so hopeless it's hard to put it down. At three o'clock, she finds Forest, Lawrence, and Eli at the firepit. Saturday's optional fresh air activity: a hike to nearby Bushkill Falls.

"Don't the other girls ever do stuff with you losers?" Jana asks.

"Never," Lawrence says. Another change of clothes. Jeans and hiking boots. "Have any boots, Jana? There's a land mine of rattlers on the path into the falls."

"Do I look like I would have remembered to pack fang-proof boots?"

Lawrence says, "Wait here. I'll be right back. I'll duct tape your ankles, so you don't get killed."

"Forget it," Jana says. "I'll take my chances."

The way to Bushkill Falls is a narrow footpath.

"Doesn't Dr. Kemble worry about us just taking off?" Jana asks. "We could get mauled by a giant bear."

"We think maybe she's got surveillance cameras all over these woods," Lawrence says.

"Or she's grossly negligent," Eli suggests.

"Is she the only therapist here?" Jana asks. "I thought there was some man too."

"That's Dr. Grayson," Lawrence answers. "He's not as cool as Dr. Kemble."

The late afternoon sun is pulling a punch, dragging moisture from fat, green life, draping layers of heavy humidity onto Jana's back like a wool blanket.

"How much farther?"

"Hear it?" Lawrence asks. "We're getting close."

"Anyone have real camping gear?" Jana asks. "Like a canteen with potable water?"

"You can drink the creek water. Tastes like dirt, but it won't kill you," Forrest says.

An arc in the path brings the group parallel with a fast-tumbling creek at the bottom of a gorge on their right, a sheer drop of about twelve feet. Not a good place to lose your footing. To their left, the forest bank is a right-angled wall of black and gray stone dotted with small bouquets of yellow and purple wildflowers. Up ahead, the waiting waterfall plummets and roars.

Bushkill Falls is bigger and better than Jana expected. The way it leaps from the ledge. The satisfying crash and splash onto the flat surface below. The spray of icy pinpricks that stab Jana's cheeks and forehead.

"It gets really slippery from here on out!" Eli shouts to Jana. "Take small steps!"

Eli seems to be looking out for her. Maybe he's flirting with her.

The only way to get from the footpath to the creek below is to lay on your back and slide down the bank like a raindrop on a windowpane. Jana watches Eli free fall until his feet find ground. She hesitates, then imitates him. When she lands, Eli takes her hand and leads her around the side of the waterfall and behind it.

Jana has been near waterfalls before, but never behind one to discover a secret, sacred cave, such an exhilarating place. She reaches out, cups some water. Bushkill Falls is a metallic, deliciously cold drink. After a few minutes, Jana shouts to the others, "It's freezing back here!"

The boys are shaking too. Eli more than the rest, lips as blue as the fake corpses on autopsy tables in movies and television detective shows.

"We're going under!" Lawrence yells over to Jana, his eyes wide with excitement. "But we have to do it at the same time, or we'll all get dragged in!"

"What?" Jana looks desperately from Lawrence to Forest, to Eli, back to Lawrence, all grinning like a row of carved Halloween pumpkins. "What do you mean we're going under?"

"It's worth it!" Lawrence yells, giving Jana an exuberant thumbs up. "Trust us!"

"I don't trust you!"

"Yes, you do!"

"Me and Forest on the ends!" Eli shouts.

They form a line of Eli, Jana, Lawrence, and Forest and join hands.

Eli bends down to Jana's ear: "Whatever you do, don't let go!"

"What the hell are we doing?" Jana screams back.

"On the count of five!" Lawrence yells. "One, two, three, four, FIVE!"

As the boys step forward, Jana does, too, a blind mouse with a flipping heart. The force of the water is incredible. When her knees buckle, Eli and Lawrence grip her hands harder and lift her up. Jana tilts her head back. It's not possible to open her eyes so she opens her mouth instead. She chokes at first, then she laughs. Everyone is laughing. Hyenas all. Forest launches a long, deep wolf howl: *AHHWHOOOO*.

That night, pizza at the firepit is the repeat dinner plan. Sally has lugged her telescope outside in the courtyard and assembled a taller tripod there. She is ignoring everyone except the celestials. Recording observations in a notebook.

Dr. Kemble appears and sits down near Deanna and Diana. Deanna manages half a slice of pizza. Diana scrapes the cheese and sauce off her slice. Then she spends half an hour slicing the soggy dough into tiny pieces, which she eventually chucks into the fire.

Forest and Eli show incredible patience teaching Lawrence how to grip, hurl, and catch a football. He sends the ball straight into the firepit once, launching miniature, fiery missiles. Some of the flying sparks take aim at Jana's paperback. She beats the book on the ground. *Either that or Angela will turn to ashes,* she thinks, smiling to herself.

"I missed seeing you this afternoon," Dr. Kemble says, taking a seat across from Jana.

"Yeah, I wasn't into it," Jana says unapologetically.

"That's fine. I get it. Has it been good to be away? In a very different environment?"

"Look, I don't need another therapist."

"I bet," Dr. Kemble says. "I read the paperwork you filled out to come here."

"I had to write something. I wrote what my therapist told me to write."

"Everyone does. I have some advice for you if you want it. Totally up to you."

"You have a real knack for instilling confidence in your patients," Jana says. "You can keep your advice. I've heard it all already."

Dr. Kemble is wearing essentially the same clothes as yesterday, though her T-shirt is plain and navy. She takes a sip from a thermos, looks skyward. Jana follows her gaze toward the tops of the trees cutting in from the forest edges. It occurs to Jana that Dr. Kemble's thermos might be similar to the water bottles Lawrence prepares. Maybe that's why nothing seems to piss her off or worry her much.

"I am only a fellow person, Jana. Not anything more." With that, Dr. Kemble leans forward, preparing to push herself up and out of her chair. Jana opens her mouth.

"Actually, I'll hear you out."

Dr. Kemble eases back down. In the firelight, Dr. Kemble looks younger. It's easy to imagine her as the teenager she might have been. Removing her smock top at some rock concert. Hurling her bra toward the stage. Sitting bare-breasted on the shoulders of a shirtless, sweaty guy. Flicking a silver lighter. Seeker of a decent buzz, but not at any cost, not unlike Jana.

"When you get back home, Jana, get your ass into the college placement office at your school and grab as many college pamphlets as you can. Sign up for as many college visits as they'll let you. Spend the next twelve months planning every detail of your move to a different town—a different state, preferably. Hell, a different country and continent if you can make that happen. Just get the hell out of where you are now. Go live. Understand?"

Jana swallows. Nods.

"Night then. Very nice meeting you."

Jana watches Dr. Kemble's shape retreating toward the Counselors' Residence. Maybe Jana should become a therapist. Get paid big bucks for totally useless advice: "Go live."

Eventually, it is Jana, Lawrence, and Eli left outside watching the fire die.

"How long will you guys be here?" Jana asks them.

"I'm going home next week," Lawrence answers, sounding more like Eli tonight.

"Unsure on my departure date," Eli says and stands up. "I'm calling it a night. Nice meeting you, Jana. Take care."

Jana doesn't answer. She detests that saying. *Take care.* People say it absentmindedly. They say it just for something to say. They say it when they don't care. She doesn't shift her gaze from the firepit coals. Eli hesitates, then turns to go.

"What did you expect?" Lawrence asks as Eli disappears inside his cabin.

"Nothing," Jana says. "What do you mean?"

"Bull. Every girl who comes up here likes Eli. Nothing ever happens. So don't take it personally. Nobody gets so much as a goodbye high-five from him. Join the legions of the rejected who came before you."

"I'm heading in, too," Jana says bitterly.

"One second," Lawrence says, winking those patented Lawrence winks again. "Sorry. I've been here all summer with the guy. First off, Eli is majorly depressed. I mean… Really bad. Stayed in bed more than a week once. Had to go somewhere else and come back another time. I don't think he can handle much more than swinging his legs over the side of the bed every morning. This weekend? The best I've seen him. The guy actually smiled, laughed a couple of times, but he's depressed, just so you know."

"Right," Jana says, softening. "Because of his grandfather?"

"He told you about that?" Lawrence asks, raising his eyebrows.

"Yeah."

"Maybe he is into you after all," Lawrence says, chuckling.

"Funny, Lawrence. Just hilarious."

Lawrence hands Jana another water bottle. She reaches for it.

"Sure you don't want some bucks?"

"No. On me," Lawrence answers. "It might be his grandfather. I don't know what to say about Eli. The guy is so down in the dumps. He'd be better off six feet under with the bones of Isaiah Hecht if he can't find a way out of where he is now."

Lawrence is pawing at the back of his neck, light blue eyes red and watery. If there was ever a fellow person worthy of knowing, it would be Lawrence Van Oden.

Jana says, "Dr. Kemble seems pretty good, actually."

"She's had all summer and nothing much has changed with Eli," Lawrence says. "Anyway, let's change the subject."

"What will you take in college?" Jana asks.

"I'm going to become a filmmaker," Lawrence says. "Maybe I'll make a movie about this place someday."

Jana groans. "God no. Please don't. Not another cheap knockoff of *The Breakfast Club*. Worst movie ever. I can see it now. Forest the athlete. Sally the brainy scientist. You're some stereotypical fat kid. Tweedle Dee and Tweedle Dum are starving to death. I'm the criminal who can light a match on the bottom of my shoe. I guess that leaves Eli to be the princess. In your movie, he's two characters. A prince and the Ally Sheedy headcase."

"Okay, Jana, just forget it." Lawrence's mouth has settled into the first frown she's seen on his face.

"Sorry," she mumbles, digging her fingernails painfully into her palms.

Lawrence hoists himself out of his chair. Adjusts his shirt back over his round belly.

"It's okay," Lawrence says. "Don't worry about it."

"I'm an asshole," Jana says. "Sorry. I think you'd make a great filmmaker."

Lawrence hands Jana an index card folded in half. "I'm bushed, but it's been real. That's my address. I give it to everyone who comes up here so that I'll get a boatload of Christmas cards this year."

Jana can picture Lawrence trudging hopefully to the mailbox through a blizzard. Lawrence is laughing now.

"What's so funny?" Jana asks. The blood is sticky and itchy inside her palms.

"Think about it," he says, gulping. "The idea is righteous."

"What idea?"

"An updated version of *The Breakfast Club*," he says.

Lawrence places his hands on his hips. Puffs his chest out like a comic book superhero. "Come on, Jana. Us at the waterfall? Can't you see it? How fuckin' hokey was that? I'll be filthy rich. It's genius."

Walking back to her cabin, Jana tries to remember the last time she laughed until she cried. Wiping her cheeks, something tight and ugly inside of her uncoils a fraction or two.

In the morning, Jana is waiting for her mother on the steps of the Counselors' Residence. Her mother is always punctual. She arrives at 9:30 a.m. on the dot.

When Jana turns around for a last glimpse of *Just About There* through the rearview window of the Escalade, Eli is standing at the edge of the dense woods looking even more like Isaiah Hecht than ever in a dark shirt. His watch face flashes once, catching a ray of early morning sunlight. Jana lifts her hand to wave, but it is too late. Eli has already disappeared into the darkness.

Near the end of January, Jana receives a holiday card from Lawrence Van Oden. She recognizes Lawrence's address in the upper left corner of the envelope: 409 Long Street, Ricketts Glenn. She sent him a card in early December. The Simpsons, of course, seated around a bedraggled, horribly decorated tree. Homer draining a can of Duff beer.

Lawrence's penmanship surprises her. Very loopy. Inside the envelope, she finds a neatly folded copy of the obituary of Lawrence Van Oden II and a note in what must be his mother's handwriting: *Jana, thank you for being one of my son's special friends.* In the mail that same day, an acceptance letter for Jana from the University of Toronto. Canada should be far enough. She places the obituary in the same envelope as the acceptance letter, zips her backpack open, and drops them inside.

ABOUT THE AUTHOR

VIRGINIA WATTS is the author of poetry and stories found in *CRAFT,* *The Florida Review, Reed Magazine, Pithead Chapel, Permafrost Magazine,* and *Broadkill Review* among others. Her poetry chapbooks are available from Moonstone Press. She has been nominated four times for a Pushcart Prize and Best of the Net.

More at virginiawatts.com

Printed in the USA
CPSIA information can be obtained
at www.ICGtesting.com
LVHW041122271223
767471LV00001B/65